Text Classics

T0363332

MARTIN À BECKETT BOYD was born in Switzerland in 1893 into a family that was to achieve fame in the Australian arts. His brothers Merric and Penleigh, as well as Merric's sons Arthur, Guy and David, were all to become renowned artists, while Penleigh's son Robin became an influential architect, widely known for his book *The Australian Ugliness*.

After leaving school, Martin Boyd enrolled in a seminary, but he abandoned this vocation and began to train as an architect. With the outbreak of World War I, he sailed for England where he served in the Royal East Kent Regiment and the Royal Flying Corps.

Boyd eventually settled in England after the war. His first novel, *Love Gods*, was published in 1925, followed by *The Montforts* three years later.

After the international success of *Lucinda Brayford* in 1946 Boyd decided to return to Australia, but by 1951 he was back in London. In the coming decade he was to write the Langton Quartet: *The Cardboard Crown*, *A Difficult Young Man*, *Outbreak of Love* and *When Blackbirds Sing*. In 1957 he went to Rome, where he lived and continued to write until his death in 1972.

CHRIS WOMERSLEY lives in Melbourne. He is the author of the acclaimed novels *The Low Road*, which won a Ned Kelly Award, and *Bereft*, which won the ABIA Award for literary fiction and the Indie Award for fiction. His third novel, *Cairo*, will be published in late 2013.

ALSO BY MARTIN BOYD

Fiction
Scandal of Spring
The Lemon Farm
The Picnic
Night of the Party
Nuns in Jeopardy
Lucinda Brayford
Such Pleasure
The Cardboard Crown
A Difficult Young Man
When Blackbirds Sing
The Tea-Time of Love: The Clarification of Miss Stilby

Under the pseudonym 'Martin Mills'
Love Gods
Brangane: A Memoir
The Montforts

Under the pseudonym 'Walter Beckett'
Dearest Idol

Non-fiction
Much Else in Italy: A Subjective Travel Book
Why They Walk Out: An Essay in Seven Parts
Autobiography
A Single Flame
Day of My Delight: An Anglo-Australian Memoir

Outbreak of Love
Martin Boyd

Text Publishing Melbourne Australia

textclassics.com.au
textpublishing.com.au

The Text Publishing Company
Swann House
22 William Street
Melbourne Victoria 3000
Australia

First published in the United Kingdom by John Murray 1957
This edition published by The Text Publishing Company 2013

Cover design by WH Chong
Page design by Text
Typeset by Midland Typesetters

Printed in Australia by Griffin Press, an Accredited ISO AS/NZS 14001:2004
Environmental Management System printer

Primary print ISBN: 9781922147073
Ebook ISBN: 9781922148155
Author: Boyd, Martin, 1893–1972.
Title: Outbreak of love / by Martin Boyd; introduced by Chris Womersley.
Series: Text classics.
Dewey Number: A823.2

CONTENTS

Undercover Operations
by Chris Womersley

IN 1913 the first volume of Marcel Proust's *À la recherche du temps perdu* was published, the Geiger counter was invented and Albert Camus was born in Algeria. Nationalist movements simmered across Eastern Europe, resulting in sporadic outbreaks of violence. Meanwhile, in Melbourne, the complicated saga of the Langtons, and their myriad familial and amorous entanglements, continued to unfold. In *Outbreak of Love*, the third volume of Martin Boyd's famed quartet, the Langtons, ever determined to maintain their social status, find it increasingly difficult to set themselves above the concerns of ordinary folk and are dragged into the fast-moving tide of world events.

In the preceding volume, *A Difficult Young Man*, the narrator Guy Langton observes with laconic precision that 'the repeated patterns of heredity' are one of the defining aspects of his life. Indeed, the actions that propel the plot of *Outbreak of Love* have their antecedents in the adventures of Alice and Austin Langton in the late nineteenth century, recounted in the series' opening salvo, *The Cardboard Crown*, and continue with Guy's brother Dominic (the titular Difficult Young Man of the second volume) running away with another man's betrothed, 'the greatest social fiasco Melbourne had ever known'.

The Langton Quartet is an indispensable glimpse of the social and political mores of upper-middle-class Melburnians in the years leading to World War I. The characters are conflicted about their origins, where they belong and against which yardstick they are to measure themselves. And such ambivalence extends to the novel itself. The quartet was published between 1952 and 1962. While the work bears the unmistakeable hallmarks of modernism, Guy Langton is sceptical of the worth of the artistic movement that defined the twentieth century. 'At the risk of making this party as tiresomely elusive as Kafka's castle...' he begins one chapter.

Elsewhere, Le Corbusier's maxim that houses are machines for living is treated with derision. In yet another scene, a discussion of the painter Brian's latest work, Cynthia Langton urges the artist to experiment a little more. 'It was surprising,' Guy notes sardonically of this exchange, 'how soon in that remote place she had caught the atmosphere that was to corrode the soul of her generation.'

The place names are familiar (Collins Street, Fitzroy Gardens, Brighton) but the world of the Anglo-Australian upper-middle classes, and the complications that arise from their love affairs and quests for social advancement, today feel remote. Despite this, many of the observations that Martin Boyd gave his characters remain as wise and amusing a century later. And while it is a mistake to assume the words of fictional characters always reflect the thoughts of their creators, some of these seem irresistibly the result of Boyd's battle for recognition in Australia. (His 1946 novel, *Lucinda Brayford*, had sold handsomely overseas, but received scant attention at home.) 'A single success is a mischievous thing,' Russell Lockwood warns, but 'without repetition, it's worse than failure.'

Another of the recurring themes in the Langton novels is Anglo-Australians' suspicion of their inherent social inferiority to the old world of Great Britain and Europe. As noted in *A Difficult Young Man*, the Langtons, emblematic of their class, suffer the 'family disease of always wanting to be somewhere else' and have inadvertently inflicted upon Guy the dilemma of not knowing where his true home might be.

Guy forgives the behaviours of certain characters by explaining that they had 'no basic reality. They spent their time trying to fit their lives to a pattern which existed on the other side of the world, the original of which most of them had never seen.' It is no accident that A. A. Phillips' essay 'The Cultural Cringe', in which he named and explicated this colonial inferiority complex, was published in 1950, two years before the first Langton novel appeared.

Published in 1957—two years after the preceding Langton volume, *A Difficult Young Man*—*Outbreak of Love* more or less adheres to the slightly awkward narrative model established by its predecessors. The story is told by Guy Langton, and once again it centres on key members of his large family. How Guy manages to access and record the intimate moments of his relatives is never explained, but we take the veracity of the account for granted.

Guy is articled to a Melbourne architect and lives with his unmarried Aunt Mildred, rather than with his parents at the ramshackle family estate at Westhill, some distance from the city. Mildred has an unhealthy, possessive relationship with young Guy. 'Like most unmarried ladies,' Guy notes with the pomposity of youth, 'she sought compensation in excessive loyalty to her family as a whole.'

Mildred's loyalty assumes a vaguely sinister complexion when threatened by Guy's potential relationships with girls, most notably with his caustic twin cousins, Sylvia and Anthea. 'Now you're not to speak to the twins,' she warns Guy as they set out to a reception given for his Uncle Wolfie to perform his latest preludes, a party which—with its coy subterfuges, extramarital attractions and social anxieties—sounds the opening motifs for all that follows.

Like Nick Jenkins in Anthony Powell's twelve-volume epic *A Dance to the Music of Time* (to which the Langton Quartet has been favourably compared), Guy Langton is content to remain in the shadows, revealing himself only to the extent that his observations of others mark him by default. In many ways he is a perfect guide: observant, droll, wise enough to understand and to forgive. The portrait he paints of his family and their milieu is clear-eyed, witty and always affectionate. 'We can only satirise those things which part of us admires,' Aunt Mildred observes with an uncharacteristic bolt of insight.

Although Guy's romantic interest in his cousin Cynthia Langton is obvious, *Outbreak of Love* concerns not his own amorous adventures but mainly those of his Aunt Diana who, aged forty and for twenty-three years married to the lazy and boorish German émigré musician Wolfie von Flugel, falls for another man's charms. Russell Lockwood, also forty, is an Australian recently returned from many years abroad. He is on the lookout for someone 'of his own appreciations', and the two begin a hesitant flirtation.

Diana thought about Russell. She talked with him more easily than with anyone she knew, although she had only seen him three times since his return. She found talking to him extremely refreshing to her mind, after a married life deprived almost entirely of mental, if not emotional, contact. She had long given up trying to reach intellectual understanding with Wolfie. In one way she understood him perfectly, as one understands a charming Labrador, which whimpers at the door to go out, or cheerfully sweeps a coffee cup on to the floor with its tail, or complacently eats up all the butter left on a low tea table.

The situation Diana finds herself in—and the decisions she must make as a result—is similar to that in which her mother, Alice, found herself a generation earlier. In this manner the family disease makes itself apparent and articulates precisely the dominant theme of the quartet: where do one's loyalties really reside? Operating within such social strictures, love—as the title suggests—is akin to an undercover operation behind enemy lines or an illness that must be managed.

Diana and Russell conduct their delicate romance with care. There are discreet assignations and elaborate plans that are invariably frustrated. Love continues to break out in inconvenient places: Diana and Wolfie's daughter Josie becomes engaged, and the prospective wedding further disrupts the secret lovers' hopes for the future; Guy's affection for Cynthia grows, causing friction with Mildred.

Meanwhile, a world away in Sarajevo, Archduke Franz Ferdinand is assassinated and the Great War—that blood-soaked cataclysm which eradicated any vestigial beliefs in the superiority of European 'civilisation'—darkens the horizon. By the close of this sharp-witted historical drama Australia is at war with Germany, setting the scene for the quartet's final instalment, and Diana is forced to declare her romantic allegiances—for better or for worse.

Outbreak of Love

CHAPTER ONE

Our minds are like those maps at the entrance to the Metro
stations in Paris. They are full of unilluminated directions.
But when we know where we want to go and press the right
button, the route is illuminated before us in electric clarity.
We may go through life with no light ever shining along
the unused tracts of our minds; or something, the influence
of our parents or our friends, our environment or our own
stupidity may cause us to press the wrong button, so that
instead of reaching stations of which the names glow with
history and devotion, Sèvres Babylone, Cluny, Strasbourg
St Denis, we arrive only at Monge. The right button is more
often pressed by some accident than by our own choice, as
when a line of poetry or a glimpse through a doorway may
show us where we long to go.

Adolescents, whose tracts are most sensitive to illumination, are always pressing buttons, but they do not

necessarily take the train. For one thing they can seldom afford the fare. When I was about eighteen I had one of these accidental illuminations. I was walking with my parents through a museum in Rome, when we came upon a sculptured group of a faun, who with a cheerful grin was grabbing a nymph round the waist. The nymph, struggling to free herself, had a handful of the faun's curls. Although this suggested that she had not lost her head, she had in fact lost it in the passage of the centuries, and remained only a lovely brainless body.

My parents glanced at the group and walked on. When they had turned a corner I hurried back to give it a closer inspection. It was even more candid than I had imagined, and the paganism, the innocent animalism that is in all of us, awoke with joy. The nymph had pressed the right button, and the resulting incandescence in my mind, although it faded, was never entirely extinguished, but would often glimmer, and from time to time shine with intoxicating radiance.

It was a few years later than this, that two or three people, a generation older than myself, experienced a similar illumination of the forgotten tracts of their minds. For them it was not pure joy, but almost painful, the searing light along the unused wires. It happened at a party in Melbourne towards the end of 1913. To understand why this happened we had better glance at the events which led up to this party, before we attend it.

My aunt Diana was now forty years old. She had married at seventeen Wolfie von Flugel, a musician, and she had spent twenty-three of her forty years in his moral and

4

financial support. She did this because she loved him, but she excused herself by saying that he was an unrecognized genius. She had to support him, but she did all kinds of extra things for him, which he could easily have done for himself. On a morning a month or so before the party, she warned him at breakfast that if he ate some very hard toast he would probably break a tooth. He ate it and broke the tooth. He was very upset and said he must have it mended as soon as possible. Diana had to take his plate into the dentist in Collins Street the same afternoon. He could not take it himself as it would be embarrassing if he met a friend while he was without it. She supposed that the friends he was afraid of meeting were his young lady pupils.

Russell Lockwood was walking up Collins Street to the Melbourne Club, as Diana was coming down from the dentist's. He also was forty years of age. She had known him as a boy, as their parents had been neighbours in St Kilda, but for the last twenty years he had been in Europe, and had only returned to Melbourne a week earlier. He had come back partly out of curiosity, to see how much his imagination had distorted his memory of his native land, and partly because, although his European life had been as successful as he had hoped, at times he felt that it was too floating, and he longed for the comfort of old association. He was not exactly ambitious, but he did like people and things of the best quality, perhaps things rather more than people, and he was a little anxious about the quantity of quality obtainable in Melbourne. He was soon thought to be very smart and all the rich hostesses tried to lure him to their houses, though he would far rather have gone to the simplest cottage if he could have found there someone with his own appreciations. He was on the lookout for people of this kind. He would like them if possible to be in the fashionable world, as that made for greater pleasure and freedom, but it was not his first consideration, as people thought.

When he walked in the streets he glanced at the people he passed, looking for familiar faces, and also to see if the general ethos of the place was likely to be sympathetic to him. He saw Diana coming towards him and his attention was arrested, not so much by her looks, although at times she could look beautiful with her well-cut features and graceful bearing, as by her expression, which was patient and ironical, as she was thinking how absurd, and yet faintly amusing it was that she even had to take Wolfie's tooth to the dentist. She did not look rich or smart, but her shoes were good, and she had some fine pearls round her neck, and he thought: "That woman is somebody," by which he did not mean someone who had money and went to the right houses, but someone who from childhood had been accustomed to certain ways of thinking and who knew the different modes of life, and above all, whose awareness was similar to his own. This impression was immediately followed by a vague feeling of familiarity, and as quickly by recognition. When he reached her he stopped, and she glanced at him.

"Diana Langton?" he said.

"Yes," she replied, a little dazed, as she was still thinking of Wolfie. Then she exclaimed: "But it's Russell Lockwood."

6

"You remember me?"

"Of course I do. But I thought you were in Italy or somewhere."

"I came back a few weeks ago. I'm so glad that you remember me."

"I'd be very foolish if I didn't. But I'm not Diana Langton. I'm married—von Flugel. Don't you remember Wolfie?"

"Yes, I knew you most as Langton. How is Mr von Flugel?"

"He's very well, but he's broken a tooth."

"Oh, I'm sorry," said Russell, and they laughed. "Look," he went on after a pause, "are you doing anything now? This very minute I mean."

"Only going home."

"Why don't you come and have tea with me?"

"I will. That would be lovely. Where?"

"I'm at Menzies."

"Oh, I'm not smart enough."

"That's absurd."

"There's a new little place in the Centreway. It's all yellow poppies. Couldn't we go there?"

They settled themselves on a sofa against the wall in the tea-room which was quiet and empty, as it was not yet widely known.

"I expect you've come back trailing clouds of civilization," said Diana.

"It seems very civilized here—more so than when I left. There are some beautiful new houses."

"Have you seen Elsie Radcliffe's?"

"That is one I was thinking of."

"I don't suppose you will stay here long, all the same."

"I hope to. It's very lonely in Europe by oneself."

"There are plenty of people there, aren't there?"

"Oh, millions, but I don't know them."

"I believe I heard that you knew everybody."

"Yes, but they don't know me. I mean we met and talked and all that, and I even became friendly with one or two, but they still didn't know me, because they had no conception of the way I had grown up, and when they learned I was Australian they always were surprised and said: 'I should never have thought so,' intending a frightful insult to my country as a compliment to me."

"Yes. I long to go to Europe again, all the same," said Diana. "We may be able to now that the children are grown up."

"How many children have you?"

"Three. Harry, who has left school and gone on to a station in Queensland. Daisy, who married one of the Bynghams and lives in incredible artistic discomfort in a cottage at Frankston, and Josie, who's just eighteen. She's my last hope of survival. I mean survival for at least one of my family. I would like you to meet her."

"I'd very much like to. But I hope you're not off to Europe too soon."

"Oh, no!" Diana laughed. This talk of going to Europe had been cropping up between herself and Wolfie for years past. They only half believed it would happen. Russell had enough money to move about the world as he chose, and imagined that others had the same freedom, as a rich

8

man talking to a new but penniless acquaintance who has expressed his admiration for the paintings of Tiepolo may ask: "Have you many in your collection?"

"We should have to make a good many adjustments first," said Diana. "Things are very different from when you were here last, at least for us. We were in Europe when the boom burst. If Mama had not transferred some money to the Bank of Australasia only a few days before the banks closed their doors, we should all have been starving in the south of France. When we came back we were dreadfully poor and we had the children to educate. The idea of travelling anywhere was fantastic. All we could do was to go to Tasmania for the holidays, and Mama paid for that. Since she died we have been better off, and now that the children are more or less settled, except Josie, we may think of enjoying ourselves, and I don't mind squandering a little money on Josie. It will be a pleasure. One gets awfully tired of forking out as a duty."

"I was very sorry when I heard about Mrs Langton," said Russell. "She was a wonderful woman. I owe a great deal to her. She was really responsible for my love of Italy. She loved it herself. I remember sitting with her in the garden on an autumn day while she described autumn in the Campagna, and the wonderful golden sense of timeless antiquity one has when looking from the Capitoline hill across the city on a late summer evening. She told me about the stone-pines and the fountains and the colour of the Alban Hills. So as soon as I was free I went there. I owe a great deal to your family."

"That makes me feel rather responsible. I hope you don't regret it."

9

"Not for a minute. I'm eternally grateful."

"But you've come back again."

"Yes, but I'm glad I went away. I'm like a cow that has plenty of cud to chew."

Diana laughed. "I hope it will last a long time," she said. "Then you won't go rushing off for more."

"There seems to be a good deal of clover in Melbourne."

"Yes, there is, of one sort."

"Well, I shan't let it grow under my feet."

They talked about different people they had known and what had happened to them. When she rose to leave he said: "May I call?" Diana, after a slight hesitation said: "Yes, do. But we live at Brighton, you know. It's rather far."

"I have a motor car. At least I shall have it next week."

"Oh, then that will be easy. Good-bye, and thank you for the tea. I enjoyed it very much, and I'm so glad you've come back."

"This has been much the nicest meeting since I arrived," he said. "I'm looking for the Melbourne I knew. The Langtons were the major part of it."

"Have you met the Edward Langtons?"

"I'm dining there this evening."

"With the twins?"

"I suppose so."

"The sparks will fly."

He smiled and she repeated her good-bye.

During the half-hour train journey to Brighton, she thought over this meeting, and the smile remained faintly on her lips. She remembered more about Russell as she had known him—the boy from next door who was rather like a cat about the place. He had attached himself to their family while remaining oddly detached. He preferred their fireside to his own, and appeared to be in a constant simmer of delight at their conversation, occasionally himself producing a quiet *mot*, which was received with slightly surprised appreciation. He had his meals indifferently in their house or his own, and it was usual for the parlour-maid, when asking how many there would be for luncheon, to add: "Will Master Russell be staying?" They all liked him, but they all thought him rather an odd boy, especially when he would come to tea alone with Mama. It was only now, twenty-three years later, that she learned what they had been talking about—the fountains of Rome.

Although they were the same age, she had regarded him as a younger brother, and she had been married when he was still a schoolboy, and doubtless she had thought herself incomparably more sophisticated than this quiet adolescent. It was curious to think that he had not only caught up to her in age, but had apparently far surpassed her in knowledge of the world.

She was very glad to have met him and she hoped that she would see him again soon. They had talked easily together, and had been amused with each other. Some accord or understanding, formed unconsciously in their childhood, must have survived. He was very lively and simple and pleasant, with all his grand European associations. She hoped very much that she would see him fairly often, but she expected that the Toorak ladies would lap him up.

11

She walked from the station to her house on the sea front. She could have come out by the new electric tram which ran along the esplanade, but it meant changing at St Kilda, and she had a prejudice against electric trams. As she opened her gate she saw a liner steaming down the bay. It was a frequent sight but it never failed to stir a nostalgia for Europe, a wish to be on board. She stood a moment to watch it, and today because of her conversation with Russell Lockwood, this feeling was stronger than ever. Then she turned through the sandy garden, on this side further impoverished by sea winds and a pine tree, into the house.

They had bought this house when her mother died, and they were still under the illusion that a solid lump of capital was a widow's cruse. It was only one storey, surrounded by a veranda trimmed with iron lace, but it was much too big, especially now when only Josie was at home. After living for so long in small cottages, they had imagined that size was the first necessity for comfort. After seven years of treatment by schoolchildren the whole place needed reconditioning, but she put it off because of the expense. Large lofty rooms opened off a wide passage, running down the middle of the house, and ending in a huge useless lobby. One of these was Wolfie's music-room, and from it came tentative chords, followed by a loud discordant bang. She went in and found him sitting on the piano stool with a tea-tray on the floor beside him. He rolled his eyes at her.

"I waited for my tea," he said reproachfully. "I ate it alone."

"I'm sorry," said Diana. She explained that she met Russell and had tea with him. Wolfie did not seem interested.

12

"When will my tooth be ready?" he asked.

"On Saturday morning."

"But I must have it tomorrow. I told you it was essentially necessary."

"He said it wouldn't be set or something."

Wolfie, whenever he was disturbed by emotion, pleasurable or otherwise, appeared to quiver.

"Then all my plans are dissolved," he exclaimed passionately. "It is most necessary that I go to Melbourne tomorrow. How can I go with a black gap between my teeth? You have ruined my tomorrow."

"I'm not the dentist," said Diana. "Anyhow it doesn't show."

"It shows when I laugh."

"Then don't laugh."

"I must laugh if I enjoy myself."

"You can smile. Surely you can control yourself for a day?"

"I do not wish to control myself," said Wolfie with dignity.

"Then you'd better ring up the dentist and tell him so. How is the prelude going?"

"It will not go. The bud will not blossom in my mind. Today all is against me. Very well, I submit myself to this fate."

He played three savage chords on the piano and banged down the lid.

"You've been in all day. You'd better go for a walk along the beach. It may loosen your buds," said Diana, and went to take off her hat. Wolfie was at the telephone.

She heard him say: "If I may laugh, I shall not bite." She gathered his tooth would be ready tomorrow, but that he must treat it gently.

He did not go for a walk, but returned to the music-room, where noises from the piano began again. She went in to ask him what the dentist had said. He nodded his head impatiently in reply to her question and, irritated, she repeated it more sharply.

Wolfie flung out his arms and said: "It is no good, it will have to wait."

"Won't it be ready tomorrow?"

"Yes, yes. But my prelude. I nearly had the phrase I seek, but you enter and speak to me, and all music is fled."

Diana picked up the tea-tray from the floor and took it to the kitchen. There were two servants, one Helga, a German girl from Harkaway, who doted on Wolfie, and the other Bessie, very fat, who was perpetually indignant at his selfish untidiness. Diana had to do many small jobs like taking out the tea-tray, as the house was so big that otherwise the two women would be overworked, and also to act as a buffer between Wolfie and Bessie, who would have complained if asked to stoop to lift a tray from the floor.

Diana went from the kitchen out into the garden, which she alone kept in order. They could only afford wages to two people, and she thought it better to have indoor servants and to do the garden herself. She had long ago given up trying to persuade Wolfie to help her. On the few occasions he had done so, he had sighed and panted, and after a quarter of an hour had said: "Now let us rest and enjoy it."

She took the clippers and began to tidy the hedge between the croquet lawn and the vegetables. Wolfie was outrageous, she thought, but she had accepted that long ago. In fact it was one of the reasons why she loved him. All her relatives had either their consciences or their sense of humour overdeveloped. Wolfie had neither conscience nor humour or it might be truer to say no wit. She had been brought up in an atmosphere of witty over-cerebration, and he was like "the hush after a sweet sound". He also made her feel that she owned some amusing and exotic animal. All the same there were times when she would have welcomed a more rational response. This afternoon was one of them. She had taken a good deal of trouble to do something which he should have done for himself, and he had only blamed her for the result. She wondered why he was so anxious to be able to laugh tomorrow. She imagined that he was going to meet some girl, possibly one of his pupils, and take her to tea or a concert. She no longer questioned him about his engagements, as she found that his answers were dictated solely by what he thought she would like to believe. She accepted, with everything else, his mild infatuations and regarded them much as a mother who, with slight irritation, tolerates the calf love of a schoolboy son. She did not think them serious, though there had twice been trouble with parents, and there was that dreadful day when he had kissed Anthea, one of the Edward Langtons' twins, at a Sunday tea-party in Uncle Arthur's garden. It was only, as Wolfie explained, that he loved youth. All the same she thought it just a little too outrageous to send her into Melbourne to get his plate mended, so that he could take a girl out to tea.

15

Then she thought she was now upset because he said she had interrupted his composition. At one time he said that he could not compose unless she was near him, but that was only as long as she retained her first youth. He said youth was necessary to his music, and she accepted the schoolgirls because of that, and because she really believed that he was a great composer. Those three savage chords he had played had given her a slight shiver of pleasure. They came to him in sudden inspiration from his anger. The trouble was that he had genius, but not great talent. Unless some spirit flowed into him he could not create. He could not sit down at any time and compose a competent piece of music. When he tried it was dreadful. The buds did not blossom. Then she began to feel amused with him. "Oh well," she thought, "he's like that. I've always known it, and it's silly to start hurt feelings at this stage. And after all if I hadn't gone to Melbourne, I should not have met Russell, and that was pleasant."

She went on clip-clip-clipping at the hedge. The cut cypress was pleasantly aromatic in the evening air, and she felt peaceful and contented, as so often when gardening.

CHAPTER TWO

On the following afternoon Wolfie dressed himself with unusual care, and immediately after tea he left for Melbourne, so that he would not be too late for the dentist. When he had retrieved his tooth he walked down Collins Street to a new block of flats, and rang the bell of one occupied by a Mrs Montaubyn. She opened the door herself, dragged him inside, and enveloping him in soft lace and scented feathers, kissed him long and moistly on the mouth. Wolfie melted in bliss.

"Well, you old Dingo," she exclaimed as she released him, "for once you're not late." She called him by this name as it was more Australian than Wolfie, and it was her very own.

"It is because I had to collect my tooth from the dentist," said Wolfie, "who is nearby."

"So you think more of your dentist than of me," retorted Mrs Montaubyn. "You don't keep him waiting."

"That is foolish. I do not love my dentist," explained Wolfie. "But I had to obtain my tooth or I could not have come to you."

"You are a scream, Dingo," she cried in her rather throaty powerful voice. "I don't love you for your tooth." She shook with silent laughter, like some confection of which the basis is jelly, carried by an unsteady waiter. When the laughter ceased she gave out a long gust of air, like an expiring balloon.

"You would not have admired my laughter," said Wolfie seriously, which drew a fresh gust from Mrs Montaubyn, who was in what has been called "the tea-time of life", which suggests another comparison.

A friend may give us in London, in January, some tulips in a pot. At first they stand, breathing of the countryside and the wholesome earth. Then in the heated room they begin to droop a little, at the same time opening their petals. One afternoon, carelessly, thinking they are about finished, we pour on them the remains of the highly scented China tea, and soon the stems which were limp stand stiffly erect, but with serpentine twists, the result of their wilting. The petals open wider until they are as flat as passionflowers. Livid white streaks appear in the red. The edges become brown but still the petals expand themselves rigidly in their final ecstatic sacrifice, and these innocent flowers, corrupted by the artificial life of cities, no longer breathe of grass walks and the potting shed, but suggest a group of dancers in an Asiatic ballet, the warriors and

18

the young girls of Poltava, or the exotic singing merchants of Sadko.

Mrs Montaubyn was like the tulips when the tea first begins to seep through to their roots. With her the stimulus was a legacy. She too was of German parentage, though she did not know it, and she had been a barmaid in Sydney. There she had married the wild but chivalrous son of a clergyman, a man of aristocratic origins but weak lungs, who had come to Australia for his health, and had soon been appointed a Canon of St Andrew's Cathedral. After about a year during which Dick Montaubyn had found it impossible to live with her without the daily mortification of his sensibility, he went to the South African War, where he was killed. His father, barely convalescent from a serious illness, was overcome with grief, had a relapse and died. His will, made some years earlier, left all he had, a comfortable fortune, in trust for his wife, and after her death uncondi-tionally to his son. The elder Mrs Montaubyn would give nothing to her daughter-in-law, whom she regarded as the source of all their misfortunes, and the latter went back to her work at the pub. Two years ago the canon's widow had died and Mrs Montaubyn the barmaid came into the estate. She moved to Melbourne where, her past being unknown, she thought that she would have more opportunity of going "into society" to which she felt her money and her grand name entitled her. However she was only welcomed by the younger bohemians, who called her "good old Glad" and on whom, now and then, she bestowed money and her favours. Wolfie was the only person whom she had so far met with the faintest connection with people "in society"

19

and he showed no inclination to introduce her to them, which sometimes gave her a sense of unjust treatment. At present this was dormant, but having been ignored by her husband's family had made her alert to any hint of a slight.

"Will we have a little love first, or will we go straight out to tea?" she asked, putting an arm affectionately round his shoulder. Although they were going to have oysters, a roast duckling each, and various accessories, which could then be had in a French restaurant for about three shillings, she always called her evening meal "tea" which was one of the reasons for her husband's flight to the war, but Wolfie was not sensitive to these idioms, though a false note of music caused him anguish.

"Let us go to tea first," he said. "I am not happy tonight."

"What's up?" she asked with a touch of hostility. "Wouldn't a little love make you happy?"

"After tea, yes. But not now."

She looked at him as if uncertain whether to take offence, then she said: "You're a comic old love-child. I suppose I'll just have to put up with you."

He was touched by the beautiful expression "love-child", not realizing that it was her euphemism for a much coarser word. He gave her an emotional glance of gratitude.

"Anyhow, what's given you the hip?" she asked.

"My wife does not inspire my music."

"Never mind, dear, I'll do my best."

"That is why I have come to you," he said simply.

She was not sure that she liked this explanation. She was quite sure that she did not like his anxiety, when they were in the street, lest they should be seen by anyone who knew him, especially by one of Diana's numerous relatives. Mrs Montaubyn would be more difficult to explain than the simple girls with whom they sometimes saw him, and who, he was able truthfully to say, were his pupils. His frequent appearance with them in teashops was one of the things which, whether they approved it or not, the family had come to accept. He was more at ease and sighed and smiled at her as if she shared his relief, when at last they were seated in the restaurant. For the first half of the meal they were entirely preoccupied with their food.

"Mine is a nice duckling," said Wolfie. "Let me give you this piece." He cut off a leg and put it on her plate. She gave him a wing in exchange, saying:

"I have to think of my figure, Dingo."

"It is good for a woman to be soft and fat," he said, looking at her with tender appreciation. Then she saw his expression change into one of dismay. He sat frozen with apprehension as two men came towards the table. They were Steven and George, Diana's brothers, who sometimes came here for a foreign meal. They saw Wolfie and crossed over to say good-evening. Wolfie rose and bowed formally. He tried to stand so that he would conceal Mrs Montaubyn, a difficult thing to do, and as he did not introduce them, they passed on. He would have been astonished and even morally indignant if he could have heard their conversation.

"Thank goodness Wolfie's at last got someone of his own age," said George, who was cynical about marriage.

"I hope Diana doesn't have to pay for her," said Steven crossly. "It's the limit."

21

"I believe he pays for his own pleasures, but she looks rather expensive. Anyhow, it's safer than schoolgirls."

"It's squalid."

"Wolfie is squalid," said George, "but I quite like him."

They sat where they could not see Wolfie unless they turned their heads, and in a few minutes forgot him. Wolfie did not know this, and for the rest of the meal his manner to Mrs Montaubyn was respectful but aloof, as if she were someone with whom he was only slightly acquainted. He had been careless about displaying his attachment to his pupils, as they were technically innocent, and in the security of his good conscience he did not know that they were more shocking to the public than half a dozen discreet Mrs Montaubyns.

"Who are the swells?" she asked, detecting in Steven and George the same intonation as her late husband's.

Wolfie could never resist an opportunity of adding to his own importance. As Mrs Montaubyn had classified Steven and George as swells, he had to announce that they were his wife's brothers.

"Why didn't you introduce me?"

"It is bad already. Now trouble may come upon me."

"What can those two sticks do?"

"They can tell my wife and I am ruined."

Mrs Montaubyn's cheeks reddened, but controlling herself she asked: "What's wrong with having tea with a friend?"

"That is so," said Wolfie thoughtfully. "Perhaps we look modest."

"You bet we do," said Mrs Montaubyn, and she shook silently, and then emitted the long gasp of air.

But Wolfie's manner remained aloof, and he fidgeted to leave the restaurant and return to the flat. Mrs Montaubyn's bedroom had a rich appearance of pink satin, given not only by the curtains and the bedcover, but by pink satin bows tied on the dressing-table and on the looking-glass. Here Wolfie recovered his peace of mind.

"Now let us forget all worldliness and malice," he said, and Mrs Montaubyn was only too glad to fall in with his change of mood. She took off her hat and feather boa, and flung herself back on the bed, much as some wanton peasant girl amongst her forebears might have flung herself beneath the haystacks of Garmisch-Partenkirchen.

Wolfie undid her hair, and the tumbling masses of hyacinthine gold, or perhaps brass, spread over the pillow and enveloped her shoulders. He buried his face in it for some moments. Then, lifting his shining eyes, he said: "You are my dear German childhood. You smell of the hedge-roses." He believed that the strong scent she used had this delicate fragrance, as the only fastidious thing about Wolfie was his ears. He lifted her hair in handfuls and let it fall again, and while he did so he sang to her softly, a song of his own composition. When he had finished, Mrs Montaubyn, touched by an only dim understanding of his charm, his childlike love of play, which, freed from his normal pomposity, he carried up to the most intimate moments of lovemaking, said: "You are a scream, Dingo," and she pulled his head down on to her bosom.

The ritual continued. He unveiled the splendid mysteries which to him were the vineyards of the Rhine and the apple orchards of Bavaria. They awoke in him intimations of a greater antique glory, the breasts of Ceres and the tumbling grapes in a Sicilian winepress, all the fruitfulness of the earth.

If an observer could have been freed alike from sensual stimulus and the repugnances of the flesh, Wolfie and Mrs Montaubyn might have been beautiful to watch, like two large roses, blown into gentle contact by the afternoon breeze, for the spirit which moved them was, after all, that from which springs most of the beauty that we know. Even those who were unable to view them *sub specie aeternitatis*, would have found in them the composition of a magnificent Rubens, with perhaps a hint of Fragonard in the way the light gleamed, against a background of rosy shadows, on the voluptuous centre of the bed.

Just as Mrs Montaubyn was subsiding into sleep, Wolfie exclaimed: "Ach, if I do not hurry I shall miss the eleven-thirty-three."

"Don't be an old fusspot, Dingo," she said drowsily. "You can make up some story. Stay for once."

"I cannot deceive my wife," said Wolfie, meaning that Diana was not easily hoodwinked. Mrs Montaubyn thought the reference to his wife, at this moment, in very bad taste. She also noticed, as Wolfie began to dress, that he had not taken off his socks.

Every class of society has its own refinements. A Victorian girl might burst into tears if a man offered her

24

bread on the point of a knife. Anthea and Cynthia, the twins whom we shall meet presently, used to quote: "No lady helps a man on with his coat, struggle as he may," and they would stand convulsed with laughter while some shy guest groped for the arm of his overcoat. A lady novelist has pointed out that a section of the landed gentry can tolerate any amount of butchery and adultery, but not the word "mantelpiece". Mrs Montaubyn's most cherished convention was: "No gentleman enters a lady's bed with his socks on." Wolfie had violated this. He embraced her hurriedly and rushed for the train.

When he had gone she lay brooding on his treatment of her. He had mentioned his wife three times during the evening, and twice with the implication that she was more important than herself. He had hurried her through the streets, and had failed to introduce her to his brothers-in-law. She liked old Dingo, and she had good times with him, but she was not going to put up with his being ashamed of her. She had money, and very fashionable clothes, and if he introduced her to his friends he would see she could be refined. On top of all this he showed clearly his lack of respect by his failure to remove his socks. She was sure that he would have taken them off if she had been a lady. This, more than any of the other indications of his attitude, stuck in her mind. Lying abandoned in her rich bed, her cheeks flushed with love, drink and anger, she tried to think of some way of getting even with Wolfie, without breaking with him. The best way to do this would be to penetrate independently the circle of his friends, but she did not know how to set about it.

25

Wolfie caught the train with two minutes to spare. Unaware of the fuse he had lit in Mrs Montaubyn's resentful bosom, he thought of her with dreamy affection. As he leaned back against the green leather cushions, the noble contours of her body were vivid in his mind. He once more associated her with his native hills, the orchards and the vineyards, and he smelled the hedge-roses in her hair. As he did so his fingers tapped on his knees and he began to hum. The train started, and as he was alone in the carriage he sang. The rhythm of the train acted as a metronome. Suddenly his eyes lighted with joy. "Dum-ti-dum, dum-ti-dum," he sang. "Dum-ti-dum dum dum." He took an envelope from his pocket and began to scribble notes on the back of it. He had found the missing phrase for his prelude. The buds had blossomed in his brain.

There was some dead wood in the banksia rose which climbed along the veranda. Apart from this it wanted thinning as it darkened Diana's bedroom. The next morning was bright and still, and the branches would not blow in her face, so she decided to tackle it now, then all the spring growth could go into the young wood which she would leave. She cut the dead shoots close to the roots. Wearing thick leather gloves, she tugged at them, and the whole branch came away, disentangling itself and damaging those which remained. She enjoyed pulling them out, and thought one ought to do the same sort of thing with one's own life, though that too would damage the still living parts of one's being. Josie was up at Westhill for the week-end, and she felt rather alone. Wolfie was in the music-room, from which came bursts of melody, followed by periods of silence which in turn were broken by loud chords and difficult strummings. She could tell from long experience of these sounds, that the prelude was going ahead satisfactorily. The sea was still and shimmering in the morning light, a ship was steaming down the bay, and everything was very beautiful. She thought of Russell Lockwood and wondered when he would call.

Suddenly Wolfie appeared at the window. "Come," he cried excitedly. "Come. I have finished. It is magnificent."

She went into the music-room and sat, still wearing her thick gloves, while Wolfie played his prelude. It seemed to her to contain more lyrical motifs and richer harmonies than anything he had written for a long time. When he had finished he beamed at her with self-satisfaction.

"It's lovely, Wolfie," she said, "it's really lovely. Oh, I am glad!" and she kissed him with affectionate pride.

CHAPTER THREE

Wolfie had completed his prelude on Saturday morning. On Monday Josie returned from Westhill, and on Tuesday Diana was lunching with both of them on the veranda. They generally had luncheon out of doors on the fine days of spring and autumn, and even on days of winter sunlight. In the summer it was too hot and the flies were troublesome.

Wolfie's elation at his creative achievement had lasted until Sunday evening, when it had been succeeded by depression at the thought that few people would hear his prelude. He could play it, like his other compositions, to a small group at the Conservatorium, but he wanted to be heard by a wider public.

"I want to play it before ladies with diamonds," he said.

They discussed during luncheon how this could be brought about. Josie was the only one of the three children who took an intelligent interest in the general welfare of the family. Daisy before her marriage lived in clouds of self-centred romanticism, and in spite of burdens heavy enough to bring her down to earth, still did. Harry's contribution, before he left for the sheep station, had been to mow the lawn and grumble because his family were unconventional. But Josie seemed to want her parents to be happy. She encouraged Diana in any activity which brought colour or fun to their home. She alone was appreciative of all the artistry her mother had used to make the details of their lives charming and their parties original and amusing, as when Diana had constructed a marionette theatre, and with the governess had acted *Little Red Riding Hood, The Three Bears* and *The Snow Queen*. Diana often thought that Josie, though the youngest, had done most to help keep the house together. She now sat at the edge of the veranda with the sunlight in her hair, and looking very young and full of hope she said:

"Couldn't we have a big party here, and ask all the diamond ladies for Daddy to play to?"

"It is too far out," said Diana, "and there's not a big enough room. All the rooms are too big and too high, but the drawing-room's just the same size as Harry's bedroom. And I don't think we know enough diamond ladies—only Elsie and Maysie, and Sophie, who wouldn't come, and anyhow she wears garnets."

"Why not hire the Auditorium, and have a concert?"

"We might not sell the tickets," said Wolfie, determined to be gloomy. "We should lose money and I would be humbled. People will not come largely to pianos alone."

29

"Well," said Josie, "why not sell this house, and build quite a little house in South Yarra, but with one absolutely enormous music-room?"

"We could not leave our fine house for a little house," said Wolfie, shocked. "To look not at the noble expanse of sea but the opposite neighbour."

Diana thought this might be a good idea, and yet she was a little hurt that Josie could so lightly suggest selling the house which they had entered with so much pride and hope. She was perhaps more reluctant to sell it, because it had not quite fulfilled her hopes, and to do so would be admitting a failure. And yet it would be better for all of them to have a little house, white and clean and modern and easily run, with a room big enough for Wolfie to give small concerts in. It would be delightful. It would also be better for Josie. She could give dances for her, and she would meet more young people. She did not want her to be wasted in a marriage like Daisy's, but when she tried to think of the marriage she would like her to make, her mind was a blank. She supposed that she would like her to marry a young man of their own sort, sensitive, belonging to one of the families which had lived near them at St Kilda when she was a girl— the Lockwoods, the Bynghams, the Cranes. But the younger generation of these families had little money. Daisy had married one of them and had begun a life of hardship. The rich people were the squatters. Many of these were what she had been taught to call gentlemen, but they did not appear to think of anything but horses, like their opposite numbers in England. Several of them were the grandsons of Scottish crofters, and although they were good, useful people who had developed the country, and had been able to afford expensive educations, she could not see Josie, who had been brought up, in spite of certain deficiencies, amongst people whose lives were devoted to artistic creation, to pleasure, and to the almost over-exercise of a sharp and simmering wit, living happily with a sprig of Calvinism.

They dawdled on over the luncheon table, but nothing was settled. Josie went to change for tennis at a neighbour's house. Wolfie went into Melbourne, giving a detailed explanation of the lessons he had to give, which only had the effect of convincing Diana that when he did not give these explanations his rendezvous was dubious. Thinking of this she was a little dispirited when he had gone, and felt disinclined to continue working in the garden, which she had attacked with vigour for the last few days. She pulled out a deck-chair, fetched the morning papers and settled down on the veranda to read, but she could not give her attention to the paper.

Perhaps Josie was right and they should sell the house. It did seem that she had come to the end of a phase in her life. Until now, she thought, she had been learning a lesson. The time had arrived for her to live by it. When she was young she had been impatient and selfish, grabbing at the things she had wanted, one of which was Wolfie. At last, when it appeared that she would never have them, she had thought: "Well then, let me at least see that someone else has what he wants." Whereas more evil natures would say: "If I can't have it, I'll see that no one else has." From then on she devoted herself to trying to prevent the frustration

31

of those nearest to her. By frequent self-denials she could satisfy the children, give Daisy a bedroom carpet, Josie a new party dress, or make a slight raid on capital to send Harry to an expensive school. And this had effected a change in her character, which was not yet fully recognized by her relatives, who continued to regard her as clever, but spoilt, as if anyone could be spoilt living with Wolfie. Even so, she would have strained all her resources to their limit to bring Wolfie recognition, but it was beyond her capacity.

Her reverie was interrupted by the sound of a motor car stopping at the gate. It looked very large and new, as much as she could see of it, and she thought that it must be Russell's. She went through the French window into her room, and tidied her hair. She was wondering if she had time to change her dress, when she heard Elsie Radcliffe in the hall, calling out: "Is anyone at home?"

Diana laughed at herself, and went to greet her.

"I saw a huge motor car and didn't know whose it was," she said.

"Yes. It's my new toy," said Elsie. "Jack gave it to me for my birthday. I've brought it to show you."

They walked back through the sandy garden to the road. The toy was a new Rolls-Royce, grey and silver against the blue sea. Elsie asked Diana if she would come for a drive.

"You look as if you need to go out," she said. "What have you been doing? Slaving in that garden while Wolfie sat on the veranda feeling tired for you?"

Elsie Crane was Diana's oldest and most faithful, almost tenacious friend. She, like Russell Lockwood, had lived nearby in St Kilda when they were children. She had admired Diana from the beginning, feeling that she had graces which must guarantee her a brilliant future, and that it was a privilege for herself, the good-natured, dumpy little girl to know her. But it was Elsie who had the brilliant future, as far as one was possible for an Australian girl in her own country. She had married Jack Radcliffe, one of the richest squatters, who was also very popular, had been to Cambridge and had good connections at home. She was perpetually indignant at Diana's hardships, and did all she could, without the appearance of patronage or of interference, to mitigate them. The word "hardship" applied to Diana's life is of course only comparative, and used with reference to the standards of her relatives and friends at the time. Above the level of insecurity and want, which alone it is permissible to describe as poverty, hardship consists of not being able to live comfortably on the level of one's associates.

While Diana went in to put on a hat, Elsie stood looking at the garden, and seeing the clipped hedge and the pruned banksia and evidence of even harder work in the flower beds, she knew that Diana had done all of it and she simmered with indignation, and wished she could do something to help her to lead a life more like her own. She said to herself: "Wolfie isn't a man. He's a sucking-pig."

When she came out Diana again admired the car.

"It's so pretty," she said. "All sparkling. Does it go very fast?"

"It can do sixty miles an hour, madam," said the chauffeur proudly.

"Goodness, I hope it won't."

"You wouldn't know it's doing sixty. She's so smooth."

They set out along the coast road. The air was bright and the little waves danced on the sea. Diana was enjoying the air and the smooth speed, when she was startled by a question from Elsie: "Do you remember Russell Lockwood, the shy lanky boy who lived near us in Alma Road?"

"Yes, I do. He's back from Europe. I've seen him," she said.

"Oh. He didn't tell me."

"When did you see him?"

"I've seen him twice. He dined with us last night. He's very much in evidence. He's quite changed—very much a man of the world."

"I didn't think him like that. He was very friendly."

"Yes, he is, but Jack doesn't like him. At least he doesn't dislike him, but he says he can't live up to him."

"Good gracious!" exclaimed Diana. "If Jack can't live up to him, who on earth can?"

"I don't know," said Elsie. "I suppose we'll just have to admire him from a distance."

After this Diana did not enjoy the drive so much, and when they came back to her house for tea, she had a slightly less cheerful air than when they set out, partly due to Elsie's comments on Russell, but also to her preoccupations when Wolfie and Josie had gone their separate ways, leaving her, as she had thought, alone for the afternoon.

"Something's worrying you. What is it?" asked Elsie.

"Nothing, really. Wolfie has just finished some preludes and I think they're very good. His best thing since the symphony."

"Why does that worry you?"

"It's so hard for him to get recognition." She told Elsie of their discussion at luncheon, and of the idea of having a private concert at home, and of the disadvantages.

In the evening Elsie rang her up.

"I've been talking it over with Jack," she said. "Why not hold the concert here? The house is big enough, and the ballroom will hold quite a crowd."

"That would be very nice," said Diana, though realizing that it was not likely to help Wolfie's ultimate success. Then she thought that at least it would be unusual, and would be talked about. "In fact it would be lovely, but it's too much for you to do."

"No it isn't," said Elsie. "The house is asking for a party."

They talked it over for ten minutes on the telephone, and then Elsie said that she would come down again the next afternoon to discuss the arrangements.

Elsie's house had been built only a year earlier, designed by a young man who had a genius for the circumstances of entertainment. It had escaped from the Italianate influence of the boom mansions, and from the terra-cotta gargoyles and sham half-timber of the "Queen Anne" which followed them. It was cool and white and simple, with a cloister and panelling in Australian woods. A little arcaded gallery led to a flight of steps into the drawing-room, and beyond that was a ballroom with a domed ceiling.

Elsie came down several times to talk over the details. They fixed a date in the week after Cup Week, as then the big functions would be over, but people would not yet have gone away. A Lady Pringle, the wife of a professor at the University, who admired Wolfie's music, agreed to make a brief introductory speech before each of the preludes. They decided to make it a party as well as a concert, and Elsie arranged to have a sit-down supper in a marquee. "We want it *talked* about," she said. It became known that this party was to be something special, and invitations to it were more welcomed than those to dine at Government House. A woman who had avoided Diana for five years crossed the street to speak to her and to ask after the children. "They've grown up," said Diana.

When they were going through the tentative list of names Elsie had drawn up, she said: "We must have Russell Lockwood." Diana had an impulse to say: "No, don't ask him," but restrained it, not wishing to show any interest as to whether he came or not.

He had not called at Brighton, and when Elsie came down to talk about the party, she still half expected that the motor car might be his. She was annoyed with herself for being hurt, or for giving any thought to him. Since he was the cat about the place twenty years ago, she had only seen him for three-quarters of an hour. Yet she could not help wondering why he did not call. She heard from Elsie how much he was sought after, and from Arthur that he was often at the Edward Langtons', the house where the Flugels were not received since Wolfie had kissed Anthea in the garden. The twins had been taken to Europe for a year for Anthea to recover from her terrible experience, and they had only returned a month before Russell. Abroad they had acquired even richer layers of culture, and she imagined that their house would provide a very congenial atmosphere for him. She thought it likely that there he would have heard disparaging references to Wolfie, and perhaps slighting ones to herself, or worse, a damning silence if their names were mentioned.

She was right about this. The twins, although their mother had taken the greatest pains to imbue them with the notions of English gentlewomen, combined with the rapier wit of *le grand siècle,* the wit sometimes, especially Anthea's, rudely erupted from the polished surface of their minds. When Russell mentioned that he had met Diana, she said: "Oh, you've stepped off on the wrong foot." She went on to give a lively, wildly exaggerated and mostly untrue account of the Flugels' *ménage,* describing them as living in domestic chaos and on the brink of ruin. Having met Diana he found this hard to believe, but when he made other inquiries he was not reassured, generally being told something to Wolfie's discredit. Melbourne had changed in twenty years and he felt himself a little at sea. He did not want to become involved with a disreputable group. The Edward Langtons' was the most amusing and cultivated house he had been to so far. He did not feel very sure of himself in the unknown territory of his native land, and he did not like to ignore their opinion.

All the same he was uneasy that he had not called, and he excused himself by Diana's hesitation when he had suggested it. He was not very clear about the situation. He felt that there *was* a situation.

He was astonished when he received a card from Mrs Radcliffe for an evening party at which Wolfie

37

was to play. Even the twins thought the Radcliffes' the most impressive house in Melbourne, and its doors the most desirable to enter. Then he heard the twins themselves were going, and he thought how stupid he had been with all his experience not to realize that people in society will tear every shred off a relative's back, and greet him affectionately next morning. He wished that he had called on Diana, but if he did so now, it would look as if he went as a result of the invitation, and he thought he had better wait to see her until this party, towards which we are proceeding, and at which, it seems, there was an illumination of the tracts of different minds.

CHAPTER FOUR

At the risk of making this party as tiresomely elusive as Kafka's castle, we might glance at some of the guests shortly before they set out. The twins came in to dinner in their newest evening dresses and Cousin Sophie, their mother, in what for her was a ball dress. Edward Langton, their father, the son of a High Court judge, was himself a K.C. He belonged to a part of the family which was regarded and actually called by our branch the Enemy, largely because of their success and their censorious respectability. The hostility was more the concern of the older generation, but my elder brother Dominic having snatched his first cousin, the bride of another man, from the altar steps, had again split the family in two, while Wolfie's having kissed Anthea in the garden made the breach complete. Because of this I had hardly seen the twins until their recent return from Europe, which apparently had broadened their minds so that they decided to know us again.

Edward's marriage to Sophie had greatly strengthened the enemy forces. She was an Englishwoman with a background, by Australian standards, of immense moral, intellectual and social power. She belonged to one of those high-minded Victorian Liberal families who voiced the best part of the conscience of England, and who kept Tory brigandage in check by the classic nobility of their protests, which today, when they are most needed, are no longer heard. At home she had moved in the highest circles, and had attended meetings in the drawing-rooms of those great Whig peeresses who found themselves in strange alliance with middle-class Radicals, Baptists and ironmongers and who, when their meetings were over, exclaimed: "I hope to goodness the things we're working for don't happen in our lifetime." Cousin Sophie had met Edward when she was out on a visit to the Governor-General, and had made in her own eyes a morganatic marriage. Although she was not prepared to admit any diminution of her social position, she was more concerned with culture than society, and her greatest pleasure was to give small dinner-parties to people from the University at which she capped quotations with Mr Hemstock, a lecturer in English.

Cousin Edward, seeing that his wife and daughters were exposing more of their arms and bosoms than when they spent the evening at home, asked with that politeness but little interest which he took in women's affairs—an interest so slight that Cousin Sophie had hoped he would not question them:

40

"Are you going to a dance?"

"No," she replied. "We're going to a party at the Radcliffes'."

"Am I supposed to be going?" He sounded depressed at the idea.

"No. It's music, so I refused for you."

"What music?" asked Edward, not that he cared, but to fill in the time until he was given his soup. The twins made faces at Cousin Sophie not to be detailed in her explanation, but she would not contemplate the slightest deception of her husband, with whom she lived in mutual trust.

The twins had bullied her into accepting the invitation. She had imparted to them her own strong-minded assurance of manner, and she found that they were beginning to use it against her, further armed with Langton wit. Sophie liked wit, preferably recalled from the past, to give a delicate academic savour to conversation, not as a sudden jab in the ribs. She was almost in tears at the vigour of the twins' attack, when she said that it would be out of the question to accept the invitation.

"If we go on not knowing people, we'll end up by no one knowing us," said Anthea. "Mr Lockwood's tired of us already because we know more poetry than people."

"Nonsense," said Sophie, but rather than provoke the twins to repudiate the standards by which she had brought them up, she accepted, and hoped that Edward would be dining at his club on that evening. But he was not, and now with the relief of no longer being able to conceal her weakness from her husband, she said:

"Mr von Flugel is playing some of his preludes."

41

Anthea made a gesture of despair. Edward marshalled the considerations in his mind, and when the servants were out of the room he said:

"D'you think it wise to take the girls to this party, Sophie?"

"Lady Pringle is going to give talks."

"And who could be immoral with Lady Pringle in the room?" asked Anthea. The twins had not been sent to school, as in Sophie's youth, girls of her class were educated at home. The result of this was that instead of having more refinement Anthea blurted out things of which she did not understand the implication, while Cynthia, more thoughtful and aloof, was apt to question the foundations of society.

"Anthea!" said Sophie sternly. "The Wendales and some of the Government House people are going," she went on to explain.

"H'm," said Edward doubtfully. "All the same I can't understand Jack Radcliffe having Flugel in his house."

"Elsie is a great friend of Diana von Flugel's," said Sophie. She could not very well call her husband's first cousin Mrs von Flugel, so whenever she had to refer to her she minimized the relationship by adding her surname. The Enemy were always afraid, not without reason, that we might do something to disgrace them, as both our respectability and our fortunes had an Alpine pattern, like the temperature chart of a man with Mediterranean fever, from which intellectually we suffered. Diana had to endure attacks from her own side, as Maysie her sister, though not one of the Enemy, always spoke of her as if she had not enough to eat and from time to time she sent

42

her any particularly ugly pieces of furniture which she no longer required in her own house, and which actually were rather useful in some of the large empty rooms at Brighton.

The discussion between Sophie and Edward went on through the whole of dinner, and at last she said plaintively: "I really think I can go anywhere." She was unwilling to modify her belief, held for the last twenty years, that any house she entered, by that fact alone became respectable. "We can't possibly back out now without appearing rude and ridiculous." She added with an unusual touch of modesty, "People are already too inclined to think us rude."

This was the first disagreement on a matter of this kind that Sophie and Edward had ever had, and it upset both of them. They would have been more perturbed if they had known that it was, indirectly, one of the disruptive results of Wolfie's visit to Mrs Montaubyn.

Highly respected as Sophie and Edward were, others more exalted were also arguing about who should go to the party, but not from the same angle. There is a popular misconception that the aristocracy are not class-conscious. Anyone who finds himself labelled "lord" or "honourable" at birth, who lives in a house full of treasures with possibly three or four lodges, each at the end of a two-mile drive, while the vast mass of the population are called "Mr" and live in villas or cottages, and who is not conscious of these differences, must have singularly weak powers of observation. The occupants of Government House at this time had normal observation, and they were very class-conscious. This was aggravated by their having become a kind of synthetic royalty. As they were all related, and as, except Lady Eileen Cave, the Governor-General's wife, they spent their time in physical rather than intellectual activity, they often bickered about their respective importance. But their class-consciousness, far from making them insolent to others, made them extremely gracious and amiable, as they thought they must do everything in their power to bridge over the appalling chasm between themselves and those in less favoured circumstances.

Sir Roland Cave, the Governor-General, was a rich Dorset landowner who had gone into Parliament. When he realized that he had little hope of obtaining Cabinet rank, he accepted his present appointment. He had chosen his staff entirely from his relatives, partly from a natural instinct of nepotism, and partly so that he would feel at home. He had also brought out from his enormous Palladian "seat", magnificent paintings by English and Italian masters, Vandyke and Gainsborough, Bronzino and Titian, Gobelin tapestries, gold plate, state carriages and footmen, so that Government House was quite homelike. On the evening of Elsie Radcliffe's party, this *gemütlich* feeling was heightened by the friendly bickering going on in Lady Eileen's sitting-room, where the members of the household were having coffee after dinner.

Lord Wendale, the Military Secretary, was Lady Eileen's brother. Freddie Thorpe, one of the aides-de-camp, was Sir Roland's nephew. John Wyckham, the other aide-de-camp, was Lady Wendale's nephew. Miss Rockingham, who was staying with them for some months as a kind of unofficial lady-in-waiting, was Lady Eileen's oldest friend. Even Lord Francis Derham, the Chamberlain, a permanent official not chosen by Sir Roland, was a second cousin of Miss Rockingham's. They were now discussing whether Freddie Thorpe should or should not be forced to go to the party.

"I don't like classical music," he protested.

"It won't be all music, and there's sure to be a good supper at the Radcliffes'," said Dolly Wendale.

"Why can't John go?"

"He hasn't been asked."

"That doesn't matter. They're keen to get any of us."

"I shouldn't think that Mrs Radcliffe was terribly keen on you, Freddie," said Lady Eileen, looking up from her petit-point, and breaking a thread in her teeth.

"All the rich girls will be there," said Patrick Wendale. Everyone knew that Freddie had come out in search of an heiress, and that he was badly in need of one. John Wyckham, although he had no such intention, also came in for a good deal of chaff about fortune-hunting, which he did not mind much, as he thought the idea of marrying for money so horrible that the chaff had no meaning. He was the only son of another Dorset landowner but with a more modest property than Sir Roland's. He had gone into the army at his father's suggestion to occupy himself until he inherited, though he would have preferred something more congenial to his alert and curious mind. He had the ordinary fair, good-looking "guardee" type of face, but more sensitive, with a shy and attractive smile. When Sir Roland offered him the appointment as aide-de-camp, he accepted eagerly, as he wanted to see different people and places, though his fellow subalterns called it "poodle-faking".

45

"Which ones?" asked Freddie.

"The Langton twins for certain."

"They're not vulgar, but they've got no money."

"None of the people here are more vulgar than any of you," said Sir Roland, brutally including the whole company, who irritated him by treating this country, in which he held the highest position, as if it were half a joke. There was an awkward silence, as when a group of people all become ashamed of themselves at once.

"Actually," said Lord Francis, "Judge Lanfranc told me the other day that Edward Langton has £10,000 a year."

"Has he, by Jove?" said Freddie.

Dolly Wendale, aware of the dangerous eyes Sir Roland was directing at Freddie, said: "The twins are always taken to any display of culture. Lady Pringle is going to give talks on the meaning of the music, so you may be able to follow it, Freddie."

"Do you mean that professor's wife with pince-nez?"

"I believe she does wear pince-nez."

"Great Scott!"

"I rather like culture," said John.

"Or d'you mean you like the twins?"

"Well, they are rather stimulating."

"Intellectually, or emotionally?"

"Or financially?" The voice of Miss Rockingham, a muted foghorn from which in later life she removed the silencer, sounded its warning note. During the conversation she had been smoking, with great deliberation, a cigarette fixed in a holder six inches long. She had far more money than any of the girls they talked about and she wanted to be

46

married. She was prepared, like Cousin Sophie, a guest at Government House twenty years earlier, to make a morganatic marriage. She was even prepared to marry Freddie Thorpe, finding, something in the same way as Diana with Wolfie, a rest for her complexity in his simple animal stupidity, though Wolfie was a moral giant compared with Freddie. It was true that she was five years older than he, but she had a beautiful figure and moved with unusual grace, and she thought that this combined with her income would make the difference negligible. With a contempt for those proprieties which a bourgeoise would allow to interfere with her pleasures, she was prepared to buy him as she would buy a fine horse. But he appeared hardly to be aware of her presence, and when Patrick Wendale said to him: "Why don't you marry Marcia?" although he had never been to Rome, nor seen the headless nymph, nor willingly looked at any other statue in his life except when he attended the unveiling of a bronze general on horseback, he said: "She might be all right if one could knock off her head."

For Miss Rockingham, with her tremendous assets, was handicapped by a very long face, and did look surprisingly like a horse. This added to her grandeur, but not to her feminine charm. She was believed in Melbourne, with justification, to be grander than anyone at Government House. She was known to be on intimate terms with the Queen of Spain, with whom as a girl she had climbed trees in Windsor Great Park, and she was called "dearest Marcia" in five different languages by the royal family of Europe.

"You could have one each," she went on, pressing the thorn into her breast, "the clever one for John and the jolly one for Freddie. If you brought them to live here it would be most stimulating—such war, such wit."

"Is one of them jolly?" asked Freddie.

"They're both very nice girls," said Sir Roland. He would have expressed his dislike of the conversation more forcibly, but even he was affected by the deference which Marcia Rockingham commanded.

"I'll ring up Mrs Radcliffe," said Dolly putting down her coffee-cup on a satinwood table from Dorset, "and ask her if John may come instead of Freddie. I'll say that he's particularly fond of music. You are, aren't you?"

"I like tunes from Gilbert and Sullivan," said John.

"That's good enough."

In a few minutes she returned, looking guilty and amused. "I'm awfully sorry, I've messed it up," she said. "Mrs Radcliffe thought I meant could John come as well, and she said of course, and then it was impossible to say that Freddie didn't want to come."

"You could have made something up," said Freddie sulkily.

"I know it's awful, but I can't be rude to people."

"We're not here to insult the populace," said Sir Roland.

"I don't think Mrs Radcliffe would like being called the populace," said Lady Eileen, threading a needle.

"I'm sure the twins wouldn't," said Dolly. "Well, we'd better go and shed our glory on them."

"Only reflected glory, dear, from us," Lady Eileen reminded her. She and Sir Roland were not allowed by the protocol to attend parties in private houses.

"Dammit, I am a peeress," said Dolly Wendale.

"You have to curtsy to my wife, Dolly," said Sir Roland with friendly malice.

"I shan't when I get home."

"I rather like curtsying," said Miss Rockingham.

"You're so used to it, Marcia, and you have such beautiful movements."

"You make me sound like a horse." Miss Rockingham stared at Dolly with her heavy-lidded eyes, and puffed calmly at her cigarette. There was a moment of astonishment. Did Marcia know that they said she was like a horse, and was she deliberately trying to embarrass them? It was the sort of thing she would do. Before the moment was prolonged into recognition of her intention, Lady Eileen said:

"You might give lessons to some of the people here, Marcia."

After a little more chaff, those who were going to the party moved towards the door.

"You can make some excuse for me," said Freddie.

Sir Roland turned on him. "You can either go to the party or go back to England by the next boat," he said curtly.

"Yes, sir," said Freddie, subdued, and he followed the others.

Lord Francis went off to attend to something connected with his office, and Sir Roland sat alone with his wife. After a minute or two of silence in which he calmed down, and they had that kind of telepathic conversation, possible between the married, on the scene that had just passed, Lady Eileen said:

"You know Freddie isn't really a gentleman."

"That's rather rough," said Sir Roland, who did not much like Freddie, but who disliked more such an extreme criticism of his sister's child. "He behaved very well when I told him to go to the party or to go home."

"Yes, but only like a trained animal. If he'd been born in a cottage he wouldn't be different from any other village boy. If John had been born in a cottage and you saw him playing with the other village boys, you'd notice him immediately. There's nothing inherently fine in Freddie. Most of his gentlemanliness is due to the fact that he's been taught the right things, where to get his guns and boots in St James's and to stand up when a woman comes into the room. It's all material things and antics. Because he has those guns and boots he believes that he is a superior being, and that some decent Australian girl, probably not nearly as common as himself, will be lucky to be allowed to buy his polo ponies for the rest of her life. Half the young men we know are like that. You see their smug trained-animal faces in London ballrooms."

"That's Socialism, Eileen," said Sir Roland crossly, though he liked listening to his wife's ideas, even when, as an Irishwoman, she had digs at the master race.

"On the contrary, it's the opposite extreme to Socialism. It's a dislike of oafs amongst the people of our sort. It's the Teutonic English who are like that. They are dreadful unless they are modified by Celtic or Latin blood."

"Am I Teutonic?" asked Sir Roland. "I haven't any Celtic or Latin blood as far as I know, thank God."

"You were a little Teutonic just now, when you suggested that we were all vulgar, simply because Freddie annoyed you. That kind of inexact punishment is very Teutonic. So it was to threaten him with dismissal before the rest of us. Teutons have no conception of what other people feel. Their bad manners result from lack of imagination— perhaps their courage too."

Lady Eileen's remarks could have been applied, with varying emphasis, not only to Freddie, but to Anthea, to Wolfie, to Cousin Sophie, and above all, to Mrs Montaubyn.

At the same time that the discussion was going on in Lady Eileen's sitting-room, my aunt Mildy and myself were also preparing to leave for the party. I lived with Mildy as my parents were now living up at Westhill, and I was articled to an architect in Melbourne, having twice failed in English Composition in the entrance examination to the Univeristy. Mildy was very excited about the party for various reasons all connected with her state of life. Like most unmarried ladies she sought compensation in excessive loyalty to her family as a whole, and she saw this grand party given for one of our group as a smashing victory over the Enemy, who since the return of the twins appeared to her more menacing, not so much because of their parentage, as because they were young and pretty girls of about my own age, and so belonged to a vast army threatening her happiness. I was the first male who had ever lived in her house, the first person with whom she had ever been particularly associated. She loved to hear people speak of "Mildred and Guy" and one of her greatest pleasures was for us to arrive together at some party, and if it was a formal one for our two names to be announced in the same breath. This would certainly happen tonight, and as Elsie Radcliffe's butler had a very loud voice, she anticipated with delight the moment when "Miss Langton and Mr Guy Langton" would be bellowed through the charming rooms.

She was ready early, and as usual on any festive occasion, swathed in clouds of blue chiffon to emphasize the colour of her eyes.

"We mustn't be late," she said. "We want to make a good impression." She always used means to produce the opposite effect from the one she wished. She always paid her bills immediately, saying: "Then, if ever I were short of money the tradesmen would not press me." Whereas it was obvious that as she had been so regular they would at once suspect something wrong. When she said "press me" she gave a little giggle. It was also obvious that by arriving late at a party one made far more impression than by hanging about waiting in empty rooms. This consistent inverted reasoning of Mildy's may also have been due to her condition, as when she acted instinctively, without exercising her brain, she often showed sense and dignity.

As we waited for the car she had ordered, both of us rather pleased at our appearance, she was suddenly overcome by elation. In the manner, as she thought, of a coy and wilful mistress, but which unfortunately was only that of a schoolmistress, she said:

"Now you're not to speak to the twins."

I was outraged. I still had an attitude towards her of affectionate gratitude for all the comforts with which she surrounded me, and could not be openly rude. Her voice held a tremor at her own rashness, and when I did

52

not answer she realized that she had again started off on the wrong foot, which was to put her out of step for the whole evening.

When our cab drew up at the Radcliffes' door, Steven and Laura, my parents, had just alighted from the car ahead of us, and we all went in together, so that when we were announced Mildy and I were only part of the excess of Langtons. As we walked on into the drawing-room, I said: "Doesn't Aunt Diana look marvellous?"

"My sister always looks a lady," Mildy replied primly, confusing my adolescent impulse towards the glorious and superlative, with her dreary standards.

"Who said she didn't?" I muttered, and turned to speak to my father.

Diana did look striking. Her mother had left her several rolls of beautiful materials, which she had bought when on her European travels—in Paris, Lyons and Genoa. Now and then when Diana had wanted a dress for some special function, she had brought out one of these rolls, and had it made up. There were only three left and she had used one of these for this evening. It was of gold and crimson brocade, and she had discussed with Josie whether it was not too magnificent. Finally she had said: "If I can't wear it now I'll never wear it," and she had it made to her own design. It gave her a slightly renaissance appearance, but with her dark hair, into which she had twisted her pearls, she could carry it off, and when Bessie, before she set out exclaimed with a different intonation from Mildy's: "Lor', mum, you do look a lady when you're dressed up!" she knew that it was a success.

53

When Russell Lockwood came into the little gallery which led to Elsie's drawing-room, and saw Diana, with Wolfie and the Radcliffes, standing at the top of the low flight of steps, he received a slight shock. He had not expected her to be receiving the guests, and he had certainly not expected her look of beauty and immense distinction, so that he could hardly believe that she was the same woman whom he had met in Collins Street.

Diana saw his start of surprise and she was amused and pleased by it. It gave her a sense of restored self-possession, and wiped out the slight hurt she had felt at his failure to call, so that when he shook hands she was able to say with pleasant indifference:

"How d'you do? D'you still like Melbourne?"

In spite of her easy tone, they were both aware of the fact that he had not called, and for once his perfect composure was a little disturbed. This showed in a certain delicacy of his walk as he passed on.

Arthur Langton, our great-uncle, was standing at the side of the room, and we had gathered round him for the sake of his conversation which was either ribald or sentimental. I repeated that Aunt Diana looked marvellous.

"Yes," he said, "is she meant to be Beatrice d'Este or somebody? There is that precious ass Russell Lockwood bowing over her hand as if she were. He walks as if he were carrying his heart in an alabaster vase and is afraid of dropping it."

Arthur, aware of the defects of his own generation, spent much of his time conveying that they were a race of heroes and ravishing beauties who could not be

54

reproduced nowadays, so that if one of a younger generation did achieve anything, if only as Diana this evening, in beauty and distinction of appearance, he had to pretend that it was slightly ridiculous. It had been said by some victim of his wit that he had begun life as a conscious hypocrite and was ending it as an unconscious one. He now certainly gave an exhibition of humbug of which he appeared quite unconscious. Russell came over to our group and said:

"Do you remember me, Mr Langton? I'm Russell Lockwood."

"Of course I remember you, my dear boy," said Arthur warmly. "Your mother was one of my greatest friends." Yet it was possible that he was sincere in his greeting, and only trying to amuse us when he ridiculed Russell's delicate gait. He may also have done this to repudiate the aberrations of his own youth when he had adopted most of the affectations of the aesthetic movement. It is easy at seventy to pretend that one was a robust and athletic young man, as no one remembers or cares enough to question the pretence.

Our attention was drawn away from Russell by a burst of what my father called "high-powered English voices", those of Cousin Sophie and the twins. They saw Russell and came over to us. Cousin Sophie, partly as a result of the moral struggle she had been through to get here, but more because of the shock of having to shake hands with Wolfie, which like Russell she had not foreseen, did not give out her usual emanation of erudition and social strength, but had almost an air of apology as if she had condoned immorality.

The twins surrounded Arthur with cries of affection, and then turned to me.

"Why, it's the runaway curate!" they exclaimed, calling me this name for reasons which have been explained elsewhere. "We never see you about. You're very elusive."

I smiled at them shyly.

"Can't you say something?" demanded Anthea.

"I don't know what to say except how d'you do," I protested.

"You should say I've been longing to meet you."

"Well, I did want to."

"Did want to? Oh how feeble! You should have been desperate. You live with your aunt don't you?"

I admitted this, feeling it was rather disgraceful.

"Why d'you live with your aunt?"

"I have to live somewhere, don't I?"

"You could live with us."

"You haven't asked me to."

"We'll see what you're like first. He's not nearly as sophisticated as we thought, is he?" Anthea asked Cynthia.

"Only his clothes. I suppose because they're English," said Cynthia.

"As a matter of fact I got this suit in Melbourne," I said. "It's my first tails."

"You shouldn't tell us that. You keep giving yourself away."

"What else can I do with myself?" I asked. This amused them very much.

"You ought to put a high price on yourself. People take you at your own valuation."

"Do they take you at yours?" I was beginning to rally. They did not like this at all.

"Now you've been gauche," said Cynthia.

"We shan't ask you to live with us," said Anthea. "But we'll ask you to dine. Mother, ask the runaway curate to dine."

Cousin Sophie was saying to Russell: "It was so strange meeting Father Talbot in Rome. I'd known him years ago at Dublin Castle, when he was in the Lancers." Her conversation was freely sprinkled with references of this kind. It was the sort of thing Russell listened to with attentive interest. Overhearing it I imagined that I was at last in brilliant circles, and that the twins' adolescent badinage was the kind of wit that sparkled across the dinner tables of European embassies.

"Would you come to supper on Sunday night?" asked Cousin Sophie, giving me a moment of attention.

"Oh thank you. I'd love to," I said eagerly.

"Then you can come to my tea-party first," said Arthur.

"Oh thank you. I'd love to," I said again, eagerly.

My mother asked me if I were coming up to Westhill for the weekend.

"I can't," I replied. "I've been asked to the twins."

"That will be amusing," she said, but she looked a little disappointed. "Perhaps you would like to come?" she suggested to Mildy.

"If Guy is going to be out all day, I may as well go away," said Mildy plaintively.

"You'd better come up on Friday," said my father. "Which train will you catch?"

"Oh!" Mildy turned on him her reproachful blue eyes. She did not want to go away, and had only threatened to do

57

so to "tease" me. No one knew this, and no one knew what she meant by these reproachful stares. He thought that she was being too sweet and feminine to cope with such manly things as time-tables, though the three daily trains had been the same since their childhood.

"We'll meet the afternoon train," he said firmly. Mildy looked very sad.

The party from Government House came in. The room was now fairly full and people turned to watch them. Arthur said:

"If you took a plaster cast of Lady Wendale's face it would be very pretty. As it is, it isn't sufficiently convex."

"The concave countess in fact," said Anthea.

Russell looked rather startled.

Cousin Sophie being English, and having mutual friends with the vice-regal staff, was on more intimate terms with them than most Melbourne people. Lady Wendale caught sight of her and with Miss Rockingham and the two aides-de-camp, John Wyckham looking diffidently amiable, and Freddie Thorpe like a resentful bull, also joined our group, of which the original central attraction was Arthur. Miss Rockingham's proud and sagging eyes which showed that every year she was spiritually refreshed by the kiss of the Queen of Spain, glanced with gracious expectation round the room, lighting with satisfaction on Russell.

My parents who, from some obscure and involved psychological motives, always avoided the society of English people in Australia, moved away. Mildy for the simple reason that she thought they would despise her, and anxious to detach me from the twins, said: "Come on Guy, let us find a seat." I pretended not to hear her, and torn between her desire for my company and her terror of the great, she went into the ballroom and sat by her repellent friend Miss Bath, whom Arthur called "the wrong end of the magnet".

Freddie Thorpe gave an appraising glance at the twins, and immediately fixed his attention on Anthea.

"You like music?" he asked.

"Yes. Do you?" she replied.

"No. Hate it. Don't mind a band." Anthea, because of the blue lapels and gold buttons on his coat, and his direct, masculine and rather brutal blue eyes, thought this very amusing.

"Why have you come?" she asked.

"Had to. Don't mind now I've met you."

"You liven things up a bit yourself."

"D'you mean that?" he asked, looking at her with a sharp and potent glance.

"I couldn't possibly tell you," said Anthea.

He did not know what she meant, and he hoped to God, a vain hope, that she was not going to be clever. But she was a good-looker, nice legs, and her voice was all right. With a decent allowance now, and £5,000 a year in the future, she would not be a bad investment for his manhood.

Miss Rockingham in her muted foghorn voice asked Russell how long he had been out.

"About two months," he said, "but I was brought up in Australia."

59

"I didn't know," said Miss Rockingham, being too well bred to give the usual exclamation of surprise and say: "I'd never have thought so."

"Are you returning soon to England?" she asked.

"I don't think so. I shall probably stay a year at least."

"I have come for a year."

"I'm glad," he said. There was a comfortable feeling between them that they would meet fairly often. He liked people with her knowledge of the great world, and she thought that he looked intelligent.

Josie was staying with some school friends and had not come with her parents. She was almost the last to arrive, and was alone. Elsie's butler, who had known her since she was a baby, and was proud to see her for the first time in a grown-up evening dress, and moved by the delightful smile she gave him, and also because she was Diana's daughter, announced in a particularly loud and impressive voice:

"Miss Josephine von Flugel."

This sudden bellow brought an immediate silence, and everyone turned to see what had caused it. They were amused at the contrast between the pompous circumstance of her entry, and this young girl standing in a clear space near the door, looking faintly surprised and smiling to find herself there. It was as if a thunderclap had passed and a crocus had sprouted from the ground. Though it may have been said too often, it is true that young girls do look like flowers, if they have any looks at all. Their petal skins and the delicate tendrils of their hair have an affinity with the beautiful growths of the natural world, so that whoever embraces a young girl seems to hold the

60

whole realm of nature in his arms. Everybody smiled, but John Wyckham gaped at her almost in astonishment. His lips were parted and his eyes smiling in a sort of wonder, and I thought he must have met her before and for some reason be surprised at finding her here this evening.

She stood a moment in the open space, and then seeing Uncle Arthur, she came over to him and the babel broke out again. Miss Rockingham shed on her one of those smiles of pure benevolence and love which the young receive in this first bloom, while there is still something childlike remaining in physical maturity, and which are scattered on them like blessings as they enter a room, or walk along a city street; until that bloom fades and they are aware that something has gone from their lives, a brightness has left the air, but they do not know what it is.

When Josie had greeted Uncle Arthur, and rather diffidently Cousin Sophie and the twins, as she had a vague feeling that they were the Enemy and had been unkind to Wolfie, Miss Rockingham spoke to her.

"You are the daughter of the composer," she said.

"Yes, I am," said Josie, a little surprised, as she had never before heard Wolfie called "the composer".

"We are looking forward very much to hearing your father's music."

"Thank you," said Josie, and Miss Rockingham laughed, which brought an extraordinary transformation to her face. Her sagging eyes crinkled up into a rich and twinkling mirth, which gave the impression of a capacity for immense enjoyment. She saw John looking at Josie with impatient admiration, and having like Diana a noble

61

nature, which found some compensation in bringing to others the pleasures she could not have herself, she said: "May I introduce Captain Wyckham? Miss von Flugel," and she left them together.

By now all the guests had arrived, and the Radcliffes with Diana and Wolfie moved from the door and came over to join us. They talked for a few minutes and then Elsie Radcliffe said to Wolfie: "I suppose it's time to begin."

We straggled towards the ballroom, where most of the guests were already seated on rows of hired chairs. Miss Rockingham was beside Dolly Wendale and she said with a note of approval and the slightest hint of surprise: "That woman's a lady."

"Oh yes," said Dolly, thinking she meant Cousin Sophie. "She knows a lot of our people at home."

"Yes, but I mean the other one, Mrs von Flugel."

Russell happened to be close behind them and he overheard this endorsement of his own opinion, as he felt that Miss Rockingham by the word "lady" meant something beyond mere upper-class *savoir faire*. He loved the highest when he saw it, and in her own *métier* Miss Rockingham was the highest, and he expected the highest to have all the graces, and to be possessed of some degree of creative imagination. Miss Rockingham had this gift, though she applied it solely to her own personality. Diana obviously had it, and when the former said that she was a lady she meant that she had a wide instinctive knowledge of what social life should be. He was disgusted with himself that he had not trusted his own initial judgment, but had allowed himself to be influenced by the airy gossip of the twins.

There was no one whose endorsement of his appreciation of Diana he would value more than Miss Rockingham's.

"Let us cling to the noble and wealthy," said Anthea, as we followed in their wake.

We were unable to cling for long, as Mrs Radcliffe took the Government House party to some seats she had reserved for them in the front row, although as Lady Eileen had pointed out, except when in attendance on herself and Sir Roland, they had no vice-regal status. But this was the kind of mistake Australians were apt to make.

Although we were separated from the noble and wealthy, I was determined not to be separated from the twins. Mildy had kept a seat for me between herself and Miss Bath, and she was patting it and trying to catch my eye, but feeling guilty and unkind, I pretended not to see her. Nobody knew why Miss Bath was invited to parties. She was neither entertaining nor ornamental. Her face was expressionless, except for a touch of impassive greed. Her skin was mud-coloured, her eyes darker mud-coloured and her dress of very good quality mud-coloured silk. Her necklace was of polished New Zealand greenstone. She also had been one of the neighbours in Alma Road, and people like Elsie had become used to her.

Arthur was put in the front row between Lady Wendale and Miss Rockingham, which he did not enjoy. Although in the family he posed as the authority on everything European, with recent arrivals from Europe, which he had not seen since his twenties, he was shy and oddly deferential, feeling that the world had grown beyond the knowledge which he affected. Though he was fifty years older than myself he had just as ardent a longing to be with the twins, who to their disgust found there was no room for them in the front row, though Josie was there beside John Wyckham, to them a reversal of natural order. I sat with them on three hard chairs against the wall.

"Now that Captain Wyckham's gone off with a milkmaid, we'll have to fall back on you," said Anthea.

"You can fall as hard as you like," I replied enthusiastically.

"The intention is good but the expression unfortunate," said Cynthia, with whom one felt that one was the subject of a perpetual book review.

"Hush!" said Anthea.

Wolfie had seated himself at the piano and, with a quaint affectation of being unselfconscious, was rolling his eyes at the ceiling. Elsie Radcliffe was standing, facing the audience, and had begun to speak.

"Lady Pringle has very kindly offered to give a little talk before each of the preludes," she said, "to explain to those of us who are not very musical what we should listen for. Mr von Flugel is too modest to do this himself." This was quite untrue, but Diana was afraid that Wolfie's peculiar idiom might turn his explanation into a comic entertainment. There was a little polite laughter and applause and Lady Pringle crossed to the piano.

She was the wife of a professor at the University, but had come to Australia as governess to the children of a former governor. She had a flute-like and extremely cultivated voice in which she explained the meaning of Wolfie's music, but inadequately, as she had no idea of its source of inspiration.

"I want you to forget," she said, "that you are in Mrs Radcliffe's delightful ballroom, and to imagine that you are in some woodland on a spring morning, perhaps in a forest in my beloved Bavaria, or even in one of those strange sad glades of saplings above the river at Warrandyte."

The twins looked at each other and raised their eyebrows. This was their first intimation that Bavaria was Lady Pringle's beloved and that the saplings were sad.

Wolfie was only to play three of his sequence of preludes, as Elsie Radcliffe did not want to give her guests too much of what might be above their heads. Her great social success was due not only to her husband's wealth and that she instinctively chose her friends amongst pleasant people, but to the fact that the main purpose of all her entertainment was enjoyment, whereas the entertainment given by women like Aunt Baba was to increase their own importance. People came away from parties at Elsie's house, not merely with the satisfaction of having been somewhere very "smart", but exclaiming: "Wasn't it fun?"

Wolfie's first prelude did seem to evoke woodlands in spring-time, with young lovers and mysterious clouds of blossom. Even the non-musical thought it pretty and there was adequate clapping.

"It's derivative, of course," said Cynthia. "It has all been done before, but I should say that it is quite competent —Debussy and water."

"Debussy *engloutie*," said Anthea.

I had heard Arthur say that Debussy was influenced by Wagner. I trotted this out. "So you see," I said, "if Uncle Wolfie is influenced by Debussy he is on the right lines."

This intelligent view coming from myself irritated Cynthia, who said: "How is Mr von Flugel your uncle?"

Lady Pringle stood up and said that the next prelude suggested evening in the woods, with the saplings drooping under a gentle shower of rain. Wolfie played this melancholy little nocturne and the most exacting part of the entertainment was over.

There were light refreshments, champagne and coffee, at this stage. The real supper was not to be until later in the evening, after Wolfie had played his third prelude. Everyone stood up and began to move towards the buffet in the billiard room. In the doorway the twins became jammed close to Arthur.

"Well, my dear," he said to Anthea, "did you enjoy yourself amongst the saplings?" He was again posing as the virile man above susceptibility to aesthetic impressions.

"I was drenched to the skin," said Anthea.

In the hall we ran into Aunt Baba, our socially ambitious relative, who, to appear smart, had deliberately chosen to go first to the theatre.

"Good evening, Mr Langton," she said to Arthur, addressing him in this way as she thought it was not smart to have relatives. "I hope the music's over. I couldn't listen for an hour to von Flugel playing. I prefer the jam without the pill."

Cousin Sophie, standing near, overheard this. Whatever her personal opinion of Wolfie, she could not endure that culture should be openly disparaged by the vulgar. She turned and said:

"That is a pity, as your mind is in greater need of nourishment than your body."

66

There was a gasp from those who heard, and only Baba gave a dismayed titter. She had lived for twenty years in dread that Sophie might one day turn and crush her with the whole weight of her social power, and now it had happened. It was true that she had asked for it, but life would be intolerable if we were given all we asked for. And Cousin Sophie, for all her culture, had done the most uncivilized thing possible, she had used the full extent of her force against Baba, whose armour was a pitiful and contrived affair. This perhaps was where she showed that Teutonism of which Lady Eileen had complained, and which later was exhibited in different forms, not only by Freddie, but by Wolfie, by Baba herself, and supremely by Mrs Montaubyn. Arthur, who admired Sophie, looked grieved and noble, and Diana who also heard the snub was indignant, and gave Baba a glance of sympathy, which brought Baba's Teutonism at once into play. She only respected power, and mostly when it was indicated by wealth. She recognized that Sophie had the power, and therefore she believed the right, to snub her. She was dismayed, but thought that her misfortune was due to a proper natural order. She was infuriated by Diana's glance of sympathy. Diana was poor. Diana had no power. Her sympathy was an affront and Baba determined at the first opportunity to "get even with her".

In the billiard room Baba stood at one end of the buffet talking loudly and brightly, like someone showing courage after they have been run over in the street. At the other end Sophie was quietly discussing the preludes with Lady Pringle, and was quite indifferent to the moral havoc she had just created.

I was caught by Mildy and had to bring her a tiny glass of champagne, and Miss Bath a whisky and soda. When we returned to the ballroom for the last prelude I could not escape, and had to sit between them.

By now the party had livened up. This was partly due to the refreshments, and a little to the fact that the news of Sophie's snub had spread and had caused a slight atmosphere of malicious excitement. Lady Pringle again stood by the piano and now everyone musical or otherwise, was prepared to be amused by her references to saplings and showers.

"Mr von Flugel's last prelude," she said, "is the longest, and I think the most important. I must explain that I have not consulted him about my little talks. They are just my personal interpretation. I hope that I am not taking too great a liberty." She bowed to Wolfie, who rolled his eyes at her, delighted that anyone should be talking about his music, whatever they said.

"This prelude reminds me," she went on, "with its glowing colour, its rich and yet idyllic interpretation of the natural world, of the *Thalysia* or *Harvest Home* of Theocritus, and I feel that I cannot do better than to read you some lines from this poem."

She took her pince-nez and pulled out the cord from a round, rose-enamelled case, fixed to her bosom, which contained a spring like a miniature tape-measure. When she placed them on her nose, she looked more like someone about to administer a rebuke, than to read erotic poetry.

"The translation is Calverley's," she explained and began:

"... But O ye loves
whose cheeks are like pink apples, quit your homes
By Hyetis ..."

She described the dalliance of the shepherds, and ended:

"And o'er the fountain hung the gilded bee.
Pears at our feet and apples at our side
Rolled in luxuriance. Branches on the ground
Sprawled overweighed with damsons; while we brushed
From the cask's head the crust of four long years."

Lady Pringle took off her pince-nez and the cord whizzed back into the rose-enamelled disc. She looked at us less severely and said: "Perhaps some of you have passed in a steamer between where, on one side, the afternoon sun bathed the tiles of Reggio in a russet glow, and on the other the dome of Messina rose from the mists into its slanting rays, and you may have wished, as I did, being borne by the relentless churning of the propellor, far from those wine-dark seas into a new country, that the sun would turn back on its course, and dispel the mists which obscured the only glimpse we might ever have of the land of Theocritus and Bion. Perhaps Mr von Flugel's prelude may do that for us."

Considering the actual inspiration of Wolfie's prelude, Lady Pringle had not done badly. She had gone as far as her refinement would allow towards envisaging that kind of voluptuousness in which autumnal richness awakens physical desire, though perhaps with Wolfie the process had been reversed. At any rate she had riveted the attention of her audience, if only by her faint absurdity. She had enlarged their horizon and made them feel that something interesting was going to happen. She bowed to Wolfie and returned to her chair.

Wolfie returned her bow with solemn approval and waited a full minute until there was absolute stillness in the room. He then played a few limpid notes with one hand. He had loosened the first tress of Mrs Montaubyn's hair. He continued to reveal to his highly respectable audience the whole process of his lovemaking, the disclosure of the breasts of Ceres, the visions they awakened of the vineyards of Moselle. The splendid chords which declared the unveiling of the thighs sent a shudder through Miss Rockingham, who flung back her head and closed her eyes. To exclude the presence of Mildy and Miss Bath, and to lose myself amongst the pink cheeks and the purple damsons, I did the same. Wolfie thundered out his mounting joy in the whole natural world, the tension of his desire, the soaring ecstatic climax of his passion, and then at the end returned to the few limpid notes with which he had begun, fallen into a minor key.

Elsie Radcliffe's guests, unaware that they had just been presented with a full-length nude of Mrs Montaubyn, but enjoying its vigour and lyrical overtones, and feeling rather excited, applauded vigorously, and even Freddie said: "That's the stuff to give the troops, what?" The only unappreciative people were Mildy and Miss Bath, who was unable to distinguish music from the noise of a train. Mildy gave a few half-hearted claps, and then pursing her lips, said: "It made me think of horrible things."

I had been in a sensuous dream. There had just been a Wagner opera season in Melbourne, and I had been so impregnated with the motifs of the *Niebelungenlied,* forest murmurs and golden apples, that I was conditioned to absorb Wolfie's music. In fact Wagner coloured my whole life at this period. I knew that the family would laugh at Lady Pringle's high faluting imagery and was prepared to join in, but I thought it exactly right. Mildy's squalid comment angered me, and in the crush at the door I managed to be squeezed away from her, and to rejoin the twins.

"Did you enjoy your afternoon in the orchard?" asked Anthea.

"Yes, I did," I said, blushing.

"I saw you close your eyes."

"So did other people. Miss Rockingham did."

"Are you modelling yourself on Miss Rockingham?"

They found this idea very amusing, and from then on they chaffed me about my supposed admiration for her.

As we went through the dining-room to the marquee beyond, where supper tables were laid, each one for four, Freddie Thorpe joined us and we sat together. John Wyckham came up with Josie.

"May we sit with you?" he asked.

"There isn't room for six," said Cynthia. She turned to me. "You give your chair to Captain Wyckham and take your cousin to another table." Josie and I were exactly the same relation to her, but Cynthia could repudiate her as she had a different surname. I was bewildered, as I had not yet realized that these intermittent slaps in the face were an unavoidable ingredient of the twins' friendship. I rose to go

71

but John with a gesture I did not expect from an aide-de-camp, put his hand on my shoulder and pressed me back on to my chair. I did not know that the almost caress he gave me was because he had just learnt that I was Josie's cousin, and was a transference of his impulse to protect her from Cynthia's insolence. He led her away to another table.

Cynthia looked disdainful. "Mr von Flugel has talent," she said, "but not genius." This was clever, but quite untrue, as Wolfie had genius but not talent. Everything he did was inspired. He drew his music out of the air, or from the ecstasy of his love, and so like that of all geniuses, his work was uneven, as he had not the steady intellectual ability of talent, which can produce competent work at any moment. "That kind of music," she said, "plays on emotions we already have."

Freddie made what was probably the only intellectual criticism of his life. "How can music play on emotions we haven't got?" he asked.

"Anyhow, isn't music meant to play on emotions?" I said. "Otherwise it would just be a sort of mathematics."

"Perhaps mathematics are higher than art," said Cynthia with sterile wistfulness, betrayed by her innate puritanism into repudiating any pleasurable stimulus, though she had long denied the God for whom this sacrifice was intended.

The voice of a jolly girl called Clara Bumpus rang out in a lull in the babel: "Orchard? It sounded to me like a house on fire."

Freddie Thorpe turned to look at her. Anthea might have the accent, but Clara had more the attitude of the girls whom he met at hunt balls in Yorkshire.

72

Three things of some importance had happened in the last few minutes. Anthea had been misled as to the quality of Freddie's mind, Freddie's attention had been drawn to Clara, and John was simmering with passionate chivalry as a result of Cynthia's attitude to Josie. He found a small table for two in a narrow space behind the dining-room door.

"Is that young man your cousin?" he asked.

"Yes. He's my mother's nephew. That's his father over there, sitting by Lady Wendale."

"But I thought he was the twins' cousin."

"So he is. We're all cousins."

"But they said to him 'your cousin' meaning you."

"Well, you see, they only like people who are very clever."

"But your father's very clever, and your mother looks very clever too—at least she looks much more than just clever. She's lovely. She knocks spots off anyone here."

"Yes, but we don't know about Molière and that sort of thing."

"The twins like Freddie, and I'll bet he's never heard there was such a person."

"But he's an aide-de-camp."

"What's that got to do with it?"

"Oh, they love aides-de-camp."

"And do you love aides-de-camp?"

"I only know you." She immediately looked confused and they both laughed. They went on eating asparagus and snipe behind the door and enjoyed themselves very much.

Diana was sitting at a table with Jack Radcliffe, Miss Rockingham and Russell Lockwood. Miss Rockingham said that it was remarkable how completely European civilization had been transplanted to Australia. They all assumed that this was desirable, except Jack Radcliffe, who said that Australia should create its own civilization and that it was impossible to reproduce English village life, with its close cottages, its church, its inn and manor house, round a sheep station.

"But we aren't aborigines," said Russell. "We're European, and we have to import the culture of our race."

Jack appeared to think that by culture Russell meant the aestheticism of a small clique.

"I mean something much wider than that," Russell explained, "I mean the spirit that moves a whole people at a given period—Gothic in the Middle Ages, Classical in the eighteenth century, so that the entrances to the palaces or the cottages all had some form of pilaster and pediment."

"We haven't the time for that here," said Jack. "I can't put pediments on the shearing sheds." He affected the manner of the bluff farmer, but he had been to an English university, and he went on: "We haven't the same responsibilities as English landowners. Our social pattern won't produce culture. It has to spring from the soil."

"That's exactly what I mean," said Russell. "All great literature has the imagery of agriculture—like those verses Lady Pringle read."

"Then Australian literature will have to have the imagery of the sheep station," said Jack, trying to dismiss the subject, as he thought it must be boring to Diana and Miss Rockingham, who, however, were very interested.

"Why have you no responsibilities?" asked Miss Rockingham. "You are the aristocracy of your country."

"Yes, but without responsibility. That's why we spend all our time at parties and the races. Our social pattern won't produce a functioning aristocracy any more than a culture—and you can't have one without the other."

He did not entirely believe all that he said, but he did not like Russell, or did not approve of him, because he spent money made in Australia amusing himself in Europe, and because he assumed that European life was so obviously superior.

The conversation at their table and that of Cynthia suggests that everybody at this party was concerned with improving the intellectual outlook of Australians, but the steady hum of voices which filled the marquee and the dining-room was composed of discussions of the dance last night, the winners at Caulfield that afternoon, the ball on Friday, what Sophie had said to Baba, the possible winners at Flemington on Saturday, *sotto voce* declarations of love and requests for more wine.

Towards the end of supper John and Josie came up to Elsie at the next table, and Josie said: "Please could we dance?"

"There's no music, darling," said Elsie.

"Daddy will play for us, won't you?" she asked Wolfie, who was at Elsie's table.

Diana heard. She turned round and said: "You mustn't ask Aunt Elsie"—as her children called Mrs Radcliffe—"to stay up all night."

But Miss Rockingham, whose graceful movements were only perfectly revealed when she danced, said with

75

the deep and gracious intonation of a royal command: "I'm sure Mrs Radcliffe will put up with us for a little longer. She has given us such a delightful party that she can't blame us if we don't want it to end."

Elsie, Miss Rockingham and the Wendales went back to the ballroom. John and Josie followed them, stopping at our table to say we were going to dance. There was an exodus from the supper rooms, and as it was thought that the Government House party had left, the older people began to say good-bye. Mildy caught me in the hall.

"We're going now," she said. "Have you said good-bye to the Radcliffes?"

"He can't go yet," said Anthea, "we want him to dance."

"The car is waiting," said Mildy in a weakly resentful voice. "I told him half-past eleven."

"Let him wait," said Anthea. "He's not a horse." This was a reference to the fact that all through the childhood of our generation we were hurried away from parties because "the horses must not be kept waiting". Anthea also thought it an amusing display of indifference to the convenience of "the lower orders", implying that they were of less consequence than animals. "If you like," she added as she turned away, "we'll bring the curate home."

"That is a rude girl," said Miss Bath, in her thick deliberate voice.

"I'm awfully sorry, Aunt Mildy," I said, "but I *can't* miss the dance."

Mildy, who had been disappointed of her every hope of the evening, that she and I would be laughing together, rather apart from everyone else, with a slight air of conspiracy about us, as if it all had an amusing side which no one else could see, was speechless. I took advantage of the dumbness of her grief to escape, with a hurried good night to Miss Bath, who doubtless said: "That is a rude young man." I escaped but I felt guilty, with a brief twinge of sadness when I heard from outside Mrs Radcliffe's chauffeur shouting into the gloom, where horses stamped and cars glistened behind their dim lights: "Miss Mildred Langton's car."

Diana and Russell lingered on at the supper table, to condemn Jack's attitude in language more forcible than they could use to his face.

"He's just being perverse," said Diana. "He talked like that because he didn't want to appear pretentious before Miss Rockingham."

"We *are* Europeans," said Russell.

"Of course we are. According to Jack we can't produce any culture, and we mustn't import it. Australia's just to be squatters going to the races." Although at that time the squatters were respected for their wealth, they were regarded by many people much as Oscar Wilde regarded the fox-hunting squires, though their sheep were at least not uneatable.

"Do you think that the life here must appear provincial to people like, say, Miss Rockingham?" asked Russell.

"You ought to know that better than I do."

"It's odd, but since I've returned here, I've already begun to accept Australian standards, and I can't really judge it objectively. Probably what we think important in our childhood must always remain so. But I don't see why

Australians should be too modest. I mean Australians of our sort—the others aren't at all modest. I suppose that we're rather like Russia at the time of Peter the Great. At a court ball you'd find people in the most exquisite French clothes mixed up with barbaric nobles in their native dress."

"I wouldn't mind if the squatters were barbaric nobles," said Diana. "They wouldn't be dull. D'you think this party's like a Peter-the-Great ball? Are there many barbarians?"

"Not at all, except that young aide-de-camp, and he's English."

"What, the one who was with Josie?"

"Oh no. He looks delightful. I mean the other one. I think he's called Thorpe."

"You're not disappointed in Australia, then?"

"Not at all. It would be absurd to say so here. This party's beautifully done, interesting and amusing and with a kind of friendly feeling."

"Elsie's parties are always fun. You think you'll stay in Australia? I hope you do."

When she said this he gave her a grateful glance from his sensitive eyes. His perfect manners were a gilded cage in which he kept the fluttering bird of his emotions. They were not a cold-blooded Chesterfieldian cult, not the animal training which had produced Freddie Thorpe. This feeling of emotion restrained within perfect manners made him attractive to women. The trouble was that when he opened the door of the cage, the bird, confined for so long, was unable to spread its wings.

78

"If you want me to, I expect I will," he said. "Wherever one lives outside Rome, one is in a province, and this is as nice a province as any."

"How d'you mean?" asked Diana.

They were the last people in the room, and the waiters began rattling plates at other tables as a hint for them to go.

"If I begin to tell you now, these men will probably go on strike," he said.

"Yes, I suppose we ought to join the others," said Diana.

In the little gallery she stopped him, and said with a hint of accusation which their advance in intimacy justified:

"You didn't call."

For a moment he was taken aback. "I'm the new arrival," he said. "I thought that your husband would call on me first."

Diana smiled. "You've seen Wolfie. Can you imagine him paying formal calls?"

"Perhaps I was optimistic."

"Well, will you call? It's not like this you know." She waved her hand at the arcaded corridor, with its niches and marble urns filled with spring flowers.

"I should like to, very much."

"No, wait," she said. "Perhaps it would be better if we met somewhere else. I'm sure that you are full of ideas that I want to hear, and I want to talk about the places we both knew in Europe. If Wolfie's there we talk of nothing but music. Couldn't we have tea again in that place? Or is that an awful suggestion?"

"I would love it," said Russell.

They went on into the ballroom where we had pushed the chairs against the wall, and had been dancing to Viennese waltzes played by Wolfie. Now there was a slight excitement, as Miss Rockingham was going to dance a tango with Lord Wendale. She was standing by the piano, explaining the rhythm of the tango to Wolfie.

"It goes like this," she said, playing a few notes with one finger, "tum-tum-ti-tum."

"Please again," said Wolfie.

Miss Rockingham repeated the notes and Wolfie sat still for half a minute while the Spirit of the Tango hovered round his head. Then it touched his brain and quivered along his nerves to his finger-tips, and he began to drum out a passionate Argentine rhythm. Miss Rockingham nodded and turned into the waiting arms of Patrick Wendale. They came with solemn twirls down the room, but he was only an accessory to her splendid movements. Her heavy lids were lowered, her equine nostrils dilated, but a faint smile lightened her heavy jaw. Her two long ropes of large pearls swung out in an elaboration of the graceful lines of her own body. She looked sensual and yet dignified and above all extremely satisfied. Like Russell she had always wanted the best, and now she was exhibiting her own first-rate ability, which was to dance, and especially to dance the tango, with its undulating movements and genuflections.

Arthur said that she "looked like David dancing before the Ark", but Russell standing with Diana at the door, watched her with the close attention he gave to any artistic performance. When she stopped he began the clapping, and she bowed to him. She then went over to talk to Elsie

Radcliffe, and in a moment had turned herself back from an odalisque into an English gentlewoman.

Diana felt a touch of uneasiness at this performance. It was not exactly jealousy, as it was altogether away from her line of country, a little too exotic. Wolfie began again his Viennese waltzes and she danced with Russell. Anthea was dancing with Freddie Thorpe and Josie with John Wyckham. There were half-a-dozen other couples. Wolfie ogled the dancers with a mixture of paternal benevolence and concupiscence.

This seemed to us by far the best part of the evening, though it had all been lively and amusing. The influence of Elsie's house prevailed, and even this party to which many people had come with trepidation, thinking it would be too "cultured" for them, and which Wolfie had thought would advance his musical reputation, had turned out to be tremendous fun, with Wolfie doing most to provide it.

At last Cousin Sophie stopped discussing counterpoint with Lady Pringle, and told the twins that they must not keep the cab waiting any longer. Lady Wendale apologised to Elsie for staying so long, but added: "It was a wonderful party. The nicest we've been to since we came here."

In the hall I waited for Anthea to implement her promise to drive me home, but she appeared to have forgotten it, and when I suggested to Cousin Sophie that they might drive round by Mildy's house, she said: "Oh no, it's much too late."

I looked crestfallen and Miss Rockingham turned on me one of those rich amused smiles which she bestowed on the young.

"We can give him a lift, can't we Dolly?" she said.

To my surprise and delight I found myself driving home in the enormous Government House car, whereas the twins still used the horse cab to which they had gone to children's parties. This was the climax to a glorious evening. As I walked up Mildy's path I buried my face in a flowering shrub.

There was a light in Mildy's "living-room" as she called her drawing-room, thinking this smart and modern, though as Arthur pointed out, one lives in every room except a mortuary chapel. I imagined that she had left the light on for me, but when I came in I found her sitting before a few red cinders, being too dispirited even to put a log on the fire. She did not look up, but sat perfectly still, emanating a sense of ill-usage.

"I've had a marvellous evening," I said. "I came back in the Government House car with the Wendales and everybody."

Mildy appeared to find great difficulty in speaking. Still without looking up she said: "That was ..." there was a long pause and then with a faint hiss she brought out the word "nice".

To dispel the atmosphere of morbid depression I spoke loudly and cheerfully: "The twins didn't give me a lift after all. Cousin Sophie said it was too late, so Miss Rockingham said they would, which was a slap in the eye for the twins."

This acted as a restorative to Mildy. "There," she said, "you see they're absolutely selfish. Anthea stopped you coming with me in the nice car I hired for us, and then she would have left you to walk home. I hope you'll

82

have nothing more to do with them, now you know what they are."

"But that's absurd," I exclaimed. "You can't part for ever from someone because they don't give you a lift in a cab."

"It's not only that. They've always despised us, and its not very loyal of you to be friendly with them."

"Loyal to what?"

"To—to us," said Mildy. I did not know whether she meant to the peculiar bond which she pretended existed between herself and me, or to all of us who were not the descendants of her uncle Walter, whom her father had dubbed the Enemy. I did not know that she had extended the application of this word to include all girls and even young men of my generation, who might deprive her of my company. The twins therefore were doubly inimical.

"You spent the whole evening with them and you've learnt your lesson."

"But I haven't," I protested. She was much too upset to be restored to reason by a breezy manner.

"Now you're being rude," she said.

"I'm sorry. But I don't see that it's rude to say that I won't stop knowing the only girls that I do know, except Josie, who's like a sister." This was turning the sword in Mildy's wound.

"I'm sorry you don't find it entertaining here, but doubtless you can find somewhere more amusing. You might live with the twins."

"Actually they did ask me tonight," I said hotly, but added with honest weakness, "though I don't think they meant it."

Mildy was in that neurotic state when her sensitivity responded only to the stings and ignored the assuagement.

"You'd better go then," she said in a trembling voice. "I've tried to make you comfortable, but apparently I'm not rich or smart enough. You want someone who can drive you home in a horse cab."

I was horrified at the implication of ingratitude, and also at the idea of leaving Mildy's house as the result of a quarrel, not only because my father would be annoyed, but because I was dimly aware that there was something ridiculous in sharing an emotional quarrel with my aunt, and that the twins would be very funny about it.

"You've made me wonderfully comfortable," I said. "I thought you wanted me to enjoy myself."

"So I do, but in a sensible way."

"What have I done that's not sensible?"

She searched round for something other than not spending the whole evening between herself and Miss Bath. "You shut your eyes and put on an affected artistic manner when Wolfie was playing that horrible music."

With her inverted reasoning, she did not understand that the last way to endear herself to a young man was to expose his adolescent absurdities.

"I'd better go to bed," I said in a subdued voice. Mildy took this as an acceptance of her rebuke, and proferred her cheek, barely concealing the queenliness of the great courtesan of her fantasy, under the modest demeanour of an aunt, receiving the dutiful kiss of a nephew.

Afterwards she referred to this as "that horrid evening when we quarrelled".

Although during my conversation with Mildy the visions, illuminated in my mind as I stepped from the Government House car, flickered and grew dim, becoming utterly black at the moment of our kiss, as I lay awake soothed by the luxury of the bed which she had bought for me, they began to glow again, and I saw before me brilliant routes into experience. As we have noted, the illuminations of young people, though dazzling, follow each other in quick succession, and are more in the nature of hallucinations. To older people they are more serious, and Diana felt that in some way the party had shown her the journey in life that she wished to make, but for which she had long ceased to hope. This was due to her conversation with Russell.

CHAPTER FIVE

The next day the evening paper gave an account of the
party, but only mentioned that "during the evening
Mr Von Flugel played the piano". This was not exactly a
public recognition of Wolfie's genius, but in Saturday's *Age*
there was a long article by Lady Pringle on the importance
of the music of Wolfgang von Flugel. He was so proud
of this that in the evening he took it in to read to
Mrs Montaubyn, who did not understand a word of it.
He also gave her a description of the grand party given
in his honour, which only filled her with resentment that
she had not been invited. She was sure that Wolfie could,
if he wanted to, introduce her into circles which she felt
that her money and her name entitled her to enter. He was
treating her as if she were a street woman, whereas she had
not "gone with" anybody since she had met him, and so
considered herself highly respectable, especially as she never

took money from gentlemen, but was more apt to bestow it. A woman with a flat on the same floor, with whom she sometimes came up in the lift, had been amused and attracted by her, and a few days after Wolfie's visit, Mrs Montaubyn confided to her that she wanted to "get into society" but did not know how to set about it.

"Oh, you want to write your name at Government House," said the woman, partly to avoid introducing Mrs Montaubyn to her own friends, and she explained how and where to do this.

Diana was not very hurt that Wolfie again went out for the evening and left her alone. She was expecting Russell to ring up and ask her to meet him at the tea-room. She was sure that a friendship would develop between them but had no clear idea of what its nature was to be. Certainly she had no idea of being unfaithful to Wolfie. Her upbringing was such that it would appear ridiculous to her that a woman already a grandmother, though barely forty years of age, should have an emotional relationship with a man not her husband.

All the same she did not see why she should not, now that the spade-work of her duty was nearly finished with the children grown up and going their own ways, enjoy some refreshment of her mind in new friendships. She had not before considered such a possibility, as she had not seen the direction from which it could come. But now she had met Russell.

She had been brought up amongst people whose chief pleasure had been in the use of their minds, in a perpetual flicker of wit, and in the consideration, though not at a deep level, of ideas. They were prepared to discuss intelligently, with what capacity they had, any idea that was presented to them. Wolfie hated to use his mind. It was painful and perhaps impossible for him to do so, except in transferring his emotions on to musical scores. He lived instinctively and he detested logic. When Diana used it to try and induce him to behave with responsibility he told her she was not womanly. At first, after the excessive cerebration of her relatives, she found him restful.

Now she longed for a little quick intelligence, and she believed that Russell could provide the exact variety she needed. At the party she felt she could have gone on talking to him for hours, and she wanted to meet him again soon, while that impulse was at its height. She expected him to ring up the next day, but she did not hear from him till the middle of the following week, and then not by telephone but by post. His letter came in the afternoon, at the same time that Mrs Montaubyn, with a toss of her head and a suspicious glance at the sentry, was entering the lodge in St Kilda Road to write her name in the Governor-General's book.

Diana felt nervous as she opened the letter. She knew it was from Russell, though she had not seen his handwriting, as far as she could remember, until now. He wrote formally inviting her and Wolfie to luncheon at Menzies on Friday. He apologized for the short notice, and began: "Dear Mrs von Flugel".

Diana laughed, but she felt flat. She sat holding the letter and asking herself what she had expected. Had she expected that he would call her Diana? She wondered if he were afraid of her. Perhaps she should not have suggested their meeting alone in the tea-room. Then she felt impatient with his excessive formality and decided that she would not go. She went out so little that the party had gone to her head. He lived in that kind of atmosphere and probably talked to most women as he talked to her.

"I've nearly made a fool of myself—as usual," she thought, and she went over to the writing table to refuse the invitation when Wolfie came in. She felt a sudden affection for him.

"Mr Lockwood has asked us to lunch at Menzies on Friday. You don't want to go, do you?"

"Who is Mr Lockwood?"

"We knew him as children. He was at the party."

"Then we must go."

"Why? I don't particularly want to."

"There will be nice food, and it is good for me to eat in public," said Wolfie.

They discussed it for a little longer, and Diana wrote accepting the invitation, beginning: "Dear Mr Lockwood". Then she thought: "Why should I copy his ridiculous formality?" and she took another sheet of paper and began "Dear Russell". Then she thought that he might think that she was trying to force an intimacy, and she finished her letter on the first piece of paper. She did not know that Russell had also used two sheets.

The other guests at the luncheon were Sir Dugald and Lady Pringle and Miss Rockingham, who in spite of her exalted associations was only a plain "Miss", so that Russell put Lady Pringle on his right and Diana on his left, with the result that Miss Rockingham sat opposite him, making it appear that she was the hostess, and presumably his wife. The waiter evidently thought so, which did not disturb her in the least, either because she never allowed herself to show that anything disturbed her, or because she was so used to deference that she did not notice it, or because with that wickedness which had made her deliberately mention her likeness to a horse to embarrass her friends, it amused her to behave as if she were Russell's wife, but with a subtle air of unconsciousness which would prevent anyone from saying that she was doing so. Also like a hostess, for the first half of the meal she devoted her attention to Sir Dugald on her right, and for the second half to Wolfie on her left.

Lady Pringle talked all the time in her fluty voice of the cultural future of Australia. "We have the Mediterranean climate," she said, "and it is that climate which has produced everything of value in Western civilization. Even the culture of the East, in Persiah and Chinah has developed on that latitude. It is certain that Australiah has a great cultural future." These sounded like Russell's ideas and Diana wondered if he had been talking to Lady Pringle in the same way that he had talked to herself.

Russell made efforts to include Diana in the conversation but Lady Pringle, having blossomed overnight into a music critic, thought everything she had to say must be of value, and it was difficult to stem her flow. Diana and Wolfie, who was enjoying his food but was sulky because he was not being admired, were practically ignored, and she wished that they had not come. When Miss Rockingham released Sir Dugald and turned to Wolfie, with whom surprisingly she seemed to be enjoying herself,

Diana was no better off, as Sir Dugald talked across her to Russell.

By the end of the meal she felt that she almost disliked Russell, and was impatient for the moment when they could leave. She wondered why on earth he had asked them, and thought that he must have regretted the promise of close friendship contained in his manner at Elsie's party, but was obliged to do something about it, as non-committal as possible.

Miss Rockingham, who naturally assumed that she was the most important guest, at last said: "I have to go to help Lady Eileen lay a foundation stone," and they rose from the table. When she had gone Sir Dugald went down to the cloakroom. Lady Pringle, to cover his retreat talked energetically to Wolfie. Russell turned to Diana: "I'm so sorry to have let you in for this," he said. "I hope you didn't find it too awful."

"Oh no. It was very pleasant," she said, for the moment bewildered.

He gave a distressed smile. "It couldn't have been, but it's served its purpose. I'd no idea the Pringles were so overpowering. I really must apologize."

"Please don't. Thank you very much for asking us." As Sir Dugald had returned, she held out her hand to say good-bye.

"Don't go yet," said Russell. "Wait till they've gone. We haven't made any arrangement to meet."

He turned to the Pringles and by thanking them for coming practically compelled them to go. Diana admired his social agility, but with faint misgiving. If he could do that why could he not manage his luncheon table better? Perhaps he had deliberately appeared indifferent to her before the other guests? All kinds of ideas passed through her mind in the minute she was standing alone. What had he meant by the party "serving its purpose"? He could only have meant that it was to establish publicly that he was a family friend. That would be why he had asked Miss Rockingham. She had thought it must be from his love of the highest, but it had been to make their "family friendship" widely known. Everything Miss Rockingham did was noted, and in the dining-room, because of her, glances had been directed towards their table. By this evening half of the people they knew would have heard that she and Wolfie had lunched with Russell. Then Diana thought: "How silly! I'm making it all up." But her dry feeling of irritation had disappeared, and when Russell turned towards her with a complacent smile at his skill in getting rid of the Pringles, she shared his amusement.

"Now let us sit down and talk comfortably," he said.

"I must be at the Conservatorium at three o'clock," said Wolfie.

"Are you going too?" Russell asked Diana.

"No, I'm going home."

"If I run," said Wolfie, "I shall catch Sir Dugald. In his car I shall not need to take the tram."

He bowed to Russell and hurried after the Pringles.

"Are you going home by train?" asked Russell. "May I walk part of the way with you? I'm going to the club."

She waited while he fetched his things and in a few minutes they were walking down Collins Street together.

92

"Lady Pringle has become very authoritative," he said. "Is she always like that?"

"I don't know her very well," said Diana. "She's interested in Wolfie's music, and she's more his friend." As she said this, she realized that it was to let him know that she and Wolfie led partly independent lives. "I think she is rather stimulated by her talks the other night."

"It will pass off, perhaps," said Russell, amused. "A single success is a mischievous thing. Without repetition it's worse than failure."

"But that doesn't apply to you."

"D'you mean I'm incapable of success?"

"No, of course not, but you don't do any of the things that put you at the mercy of the public."

"One is at the mercy of one's friends, who are more important than the public. And there are other things besides art in which one can fail."

"What sort of things?"

"Well, in trying to avoid the second-rate."

"In people?"

"No, people aren't as easily labelled as that. I mean in living."

"I shouldn't think you've failed in anything."

"That makes me sound very vulgar. Even so, I wish it were true."

At the corner of Elizabeth Street Diana stopped to say good-bye before turning down to the railway station.

"Must you catch this train?" he asked. "I was going to suggest that we had tea somewhere."

"I was going to do some gardening."

93

"Shall I come and help you?"

She was pleased at this offer, and surprised at its simplicity. It showed a new facet of his character. She looked at his good English clothes, and general smart appearance.

"You don't look dressed for gardening," she said. "It would be better if I had tea with you."

They decided to walk to the kiosk in the Fitzroy Gardens, and went on up the hill. When they were brought their strong tea, and dry dull cake he said: "Australia should have been colonized by French or Italians, or some people who know how to live in this climate."

"Then we shouldn't be here."

"No, that would be dreadful," he said. "All the same, there ought to be a restaurant here with a French chef. It ought to be the thing to come here—like dining in the Bois."

"D'you think you will stay long in Australia?" she asked.

"Why? I intend to live here."

"But your mind is in Europe. You like Australia now because you are thinking of all the European things that could be done to it. There will never be a French chef in the Fitzroy Gardens. When you realize that, will you want to stay?"

"I don't see why there shouldn't be. We must put the idea about."

"They wouldn't like it—all those rich Toorak people."

"Then they needn't come."

"They rule the roost, now, and their aim is to be as like correct upper-middle-class English people as possible.

94

They have no idea of an aristocratic culture—of your ideas and Miss Rockingham's."

He gave her a quick look when she mentioned Miss Rockingham and she wished she had not done so.

"I mean," she went on, "they have to build their house in good classical proportions before they can add a rococo façade. You have to be a gentleman before you can afford to be eccentric."

"I must say I like rococo façades," said Russell. "When d'you think you'll come to Europe?"

"You say *come* to Europe. That shows you are living there in your mind?"

"All civilized Englishmen lived in Italy in their minds. Shakespeare did, but his heart was in England. One's mind may be in Europe but one's heart in Australia. Anyhow, isn't your mind in Europe as much as mine? No one whose mind was fixed in Australia could talk of façades."

"Yes, but I talk of going there, not coming there."

"That's simply due to your geographical, not your mental situation."

"Are you advising me to go there, then?"

"No, certainly not. At least, not yet. Not while I'm in Australia."

"How long will that be? I suppose that depends on the chef in the Gardens."

They went on talking, half-seriously, half-chaffing, looking down the sloping lawns, where the elms and other English trees were sprouting in their fresh spring green. The scene was quite un-Australian, and though familiar to Diana, combined with Russell's conversation, it reawakened her desire to visit again the other side of the world.

He walked with her to the station. Under the dome they ran into Wolfie, who did not show any surprise at seeing them still together. He explained that he had caught up with the Pringles, as if they had spent the whole afternoon wondering anxiously whether he had had to take a tram to the University. When Diana said that Russell had taken her to tea in the Fitzroy Gardens he bowed and said: "Most kind." In his presence they did not like to make arrangements for a further meeting, but Diana said: "Do ring up and come out to see us."

In the train Wolfie talked about the lunch party for a few minutes. He said that he liked the oysters, but the chicken was overcooked, and that he would have preferred hock to claret. He complained too, of Lady Pringle's monopolising the conversation.

"She was not modest," he said, "but I had pleasure with Miss Rockingham."

For the rest of the journey he hid himself behind the evening paper. Diana thought about Russell. She talked with him more easily than with anyone she knew, although she had only seen him three times since his return. She found talking to him extremely refreshing to her mind, after a married life deprived almost entirely of mental, if not of emotional contact. She had long given up trying to reach intellectual understanding with Wolfie. In one way she understood him perfectly, as one understands a charming Labrador, which whimpers at the door to go out, or cheerfully sweeps a coffee cup on to the floor with its tail, or

96

complacently eats up all the butter left on a low tea-table. But Wolfie did not understand her. She thought: "I mustn't begin saying my husband doesn't understand me, especially to Russell."

She was by no means sure, of course, in spite of their easy conversation, that she understood Russell. His attitude rather implied that he wanted her to do something, to go to Europe or somewhere. She would say that to him the next time they met. This European-Australian business seemed to form a sort of pattern to which they were fitting their relationship. But how could she say so soon that there was a relationship between them? Yet she had never, in the whole course of her life, become so quickly on easy terms with a complete stranger. Their childhood's association had left no tie, though perhaps an intimate knowledge of early background did make for a certain ease. She wanted to see him again soon, not only for the pleasure she had in talking to him, but to discover what he was really like. He said things which were not in keeping with the first idea she had of him, which was of a conventional but intelligent, perhaps rather precious bachelor with social ambitions. Even if he had been only that she would still have liked him, but would have felt that they could not have much contact. But he was more than that. It was nice of him to offer to help with gardening.

It did occur to her at this stage that if she were often seen with him "people would talk", but she had never bothered very much about what people said. She was not "in society". She did not go automatically to all the smart parties. She had friends and relatives, like Elsie and Maysie and Sophie who were regarded as the cream of society, but her association with them had no connection with social functions. She was independent of their approval and would have given any of them tea in the kitchen if it were convenient, whereas many people "in society" if they had Sophie to dine, would have been on tenterhooks lest their parlourmaid should make a mistake with the wine.

During the next few days she found that she was always a little excited when she answered the telephone. When five days had gone by since his lunch party and he had not rung up, she began again to have the doubts about him which she had when he did not call after their first meeting. He could not be simple. Offering to help with the garden must only have been a sophisticated affectation of simplicity. She made up her mind that if he did ring up she would put off any appointment he suggested.

He rang up the following day and asked her if she would go round the National Gallery with him, and have tea there. He sounded perfectly natural, with no hint of apology or suggestion that he should have rung up earlier. Diana, in spite of her resolution, accepted.

She thought she had been very stupid. Of course it was natural that he should wait a week before inviting her again. What on earth had she expected? That they should immediately spend every other day together? That was the frame of mind which had been responsible for what the family called her "idiocies" as a young girl. She always expected everything, superlatively, at once. It was in fact the frame of mind that made her marry Wolfie, and she had paid for that—though she loved Wolfie, and could not now imagine life without him.

She met Russell three times in the following three weeks, once in the Gallery, once on a wet day in the tea-room, and once he drove her out to Heidelberg in his car, and they had a picnic tea on the river bank, boiling a "billy" over a fire of sticks. She enjoyed that most of all. At each of these meetings their conversation continued much on the same lines, absolutely easy, lively and intelligent, with a good deal of chaff, and always the Australian-European argument cropping up, so that it seemed to have almost the character of a flirtation.

At the end of these three weeks he left for Tasmania, where there were festivities at this time of year, with the fleet at Hobart. Diana found herself criticising him for going there, for doing the correct social thing, though she had often done it herself in times past. Again she thought how absurd it was to expect him to stay in Melbourne during the blazing heat of January, when most people he knew would be away, simply to have tea with her once a week, and anyhow she would be away herself, as she had arranged with Steven and Laura to exchange her house for Westhill during that month. This enabled Steven to bathe and Wolfie and Diana to have some mountain air.

CHAPTER SIX

On the week-end that Mildy went reluctantly to Westhill, leaving me alone to keep my engagement with the twins, she followed her usual inverted reasoning and left arrangements for me to have delicious meals while she was away, thinking this would endear her to me. Whereas if she had wanted me to long for her return, she would have given Mrs Trotter the day off, and have left the larder full of cold mutton and rice-pudding, saying: "That'll teach the little brute to think he can enjoy himself without me." So that when she returned I could only exclaim about the marvellous week-end I had had.

There was a further slight strain in our relations in the middle of the week. Sometimes on the fine evenings of early summer, my heart full of Wagnerian magic, I would walk all the way out to Toorak along the river bank. On Wednesday as I was crossing Prince's Bridge, an open car drew up beside me, and a very nice voice said: "Hullo, can I give you a lift?"

It was John Wyckham. I was delighted to be offered a lift by an aide-de-camp, and accepted eagerly, although I thought that he would only take me as far as the Government House gates, which was not in the direction of my walk.

"I met you at the Radcliffes'," he said. "D'you remember?"

"Rather."

"Aren't you a nephew of Mrs von Flugel's?"

When I said I was he asked if I often saw my cousins.

"I see Josie fairly often," I said, "she goes a lot to Warrandyte. My brother has a studio there."

"Is that the place with the sad saplings?" he asked smiling.

When we reached the Government House gates he said he would run me home. He asked me more about the Flugels. He said that he liked Australians. They were so friendly. He asked me if I was one.

"Yes," I said. "But I've lived some time in England. We have a place in Somerset."

"Oh, you're one of us," he said.

I was highly flattered at being told by a member of the Government House staff that I was "one of them" and by the change in his manner to a kind of freemasonry.

Before he put me down at Mildy's gate he said that he would "like to see those sad saplings" and asked if I would drive up with him one day and show him the way.

"Yes, but it would have to be a Saturday," I replied, ashamed of the regular hours of my labour.

"We must arrange it." He smiled with great friendliness as he drove away.

Mildy, the victim of her inordinate affection, was watching at the window for my return. She was pleased that I was early, but suspicious of my means of transport.

"Who was that young man?" she asked.

"John Wyckham."

"You don't mean Captain Wyckham?"

"Yes—why not?"

"Oh dear, how unfortunate!"

"What in the dickens is unfortunate?"

"You can't possibly keep up with people like that."

"Can't I have any friends?" I demanded angrily.

"I want you to have friends," she said, her voice thick with untruthfulness, as she thought she was my adequate friend, and also my brother, sister, mother, spouse and all those relationships which are attributed to the Deity in certain hymns, everything in fact except aunt. "I want you to have suitable friends—some nice Australian boy." But she would only have welcomed an Australian boy if he had not been too nice, and if he had had some idiosyncracy which we could have laughed at together, when he had gone home. Miss Bath had a nephew of my own age, with whom I often asked her to arrange a meeting. When I met him a few years later, I found that he too had wanted to meet me, but that Mildy had always put him off, saying that I was working very hard, or that I only liked English people.

"I'll be dead before I ever meet anyone of my own age," I said bitterly.

"Now you're not being yourself," said Mildy.

For two months from the middle of December, the people who had met at Elsie Radcliffe's party were scattered over three states. Cousin Sophie took the twins to Tasmania, the Pringles went to a wooden bungalow called Helicon perched on a hillside above Ferntree Gully, where it was surprising that they were not roasted alive in the heat, or roasted to death in the frequent bushfires which ravaged the neighbourhood in those days. Some of the squatters went to their stations in the Riverina. The Radcliffes went to the Western District. The Governor-General and his staff stayed some of the time on Mount Macedon, but also went for a tour of stations. It was said that Lady Eileen always took pink curtains for her bedroom on these tours, as a way of keeping Sir Roland's fidelity, but this seems improbable as they would not have fitted the different windows.

There were two or three more dances between the party and this exodus, at which Anthea met Freddie Thorpe, and at which she danced with him the maximum number of dances which convention allowed. Josie also met John again at a dance and at a tennis party at Macedon, where she had been invited for a week by one of Diana's old friends. Then all these promising associations seemed to evaporate in the heat, but those whom they concerned were conscious that they were in the atmosphere, ready to condense and fall again with the return to Melbourne in the late summer.

Mildy and I went up to Westhill for Christmas. Brian came across from Warrandyte, and Miss Rickson our former governess was there, and in terrific heat we ate roast turkey at midday and wore paper caps and snatched raisins out of burning brandy, and Mildy made a great fuss of avoiding the mistletoe.

Then we went down to Diana's house on the seafront at Brighton, and the Flugels went up to Westhill. I stayed with my parents, partly because I preferred to be with them, and they liked to have me when it was possible, but also because I could bathe from the house before going to my work in the morning.

Mildy could not accept that it was more natural for me to be with my parents than with her, and for that month went off to stay with Miss Bath at a boarding-house in Healesville, to make it appear that it was only due to her absence, for pride was one of the chief ingredients of her love for me, as perhaps it is of most love, but more normally the pride results from the love, from its public acknowledgement. But Mildy's initial impulse was to own me to satisfy her pride, which perhaps was natural, as she could hardly have been proud of Miss Bath, her only other close associate. Also I had been flung into her lap. It would have been as absurd to fling a young antelope into the cage of a hungry tigress and expect her not to eat it. And yet Mildy could not simply satisfy herself by eating me. She was hedged round by all kinds of inhibitions and proprieties, and I must have caused her agonies of suffering, which were no less real because they would appear ridiculous to the outside world, and any glimpse of which only made me irritable, though I priggishly accepted all the luxuries she provided for me. I was in the contemptible position of someone who accepts favours, while repudiating the affection which bestows them.

Diana at Westhill was living in the scenes of her past, before the worst experiences of her life, when she was still full of preposterous hope. For half of the month she was alone there with Wolfie, as Josie was at Macedon for a week, and for another week went to Warrandyte to stay with her artist friend Frieda Felpham, where life was amusing with the young art students who came to stay with her and with Brian, a few hundred yards away.

Diana was a good deal alone, as Wolfie spent much of his time at the piano, and she could only take in a limited amount of music. My parents now used a motor car, but there were still horses on the place, and the old governess-cart, jinker, wagonette, and even the Waterpark landau were still in the coach-houses. Sometimes she harnessed a pony and drove along the rough country roads, where the bell-birds made their strange tinkling sounds in the gum-trees, to see old family friends at Harkaway or in Berwick. Often when the heat of the day was over, she would walk out on the hill from which the house took its name, while below her, beyond twenty miles of plain, was the golden expanse of the bay, with possibly a line of smoke from one of those steamers which had become a symbol for her.

In this solitude and in these surroundings, she felt that she had a clearer view of the whole design of her life, if it could be said to have a design. Being here, alone with Wolfie, and visiting these old friends familiar from childhood, brought back the expectations she had had in those days. Looking down towards the distant suburbs of Melbourne and the shores of the bay where she now lived, brought into sharp contrast her expectation and her achievement. One evening when the whole countryside was still, and there was no sound except the distant rattle of milk-cans down at the Burns's farm, it suddenly seemed to her that her life had been given back to her again, for herself to shape the years that remained. The children no longer required her. Even Josie who still lived at home, was half the time staying somewhere else. Why should she not take what was left, and do something with it? She and Wolfie were practically free. With increased dividends and Harry self-supporting, their financial situation was better than it had ever been.

They could go to Europe. When they came back they could sell that white elephant of a house at Brighton and build a little house in South Yarra, but with one very big room where Wolfie could have concerts as Josie had suggested and where she could entertain her friends. She said to herself "Wolfie and Josie" but in her mind was also Russell. She was sure that he would advise and help her in her plans. That he should have arrived just at this time, when her life had become more free, appeared almost to be an omen. He gave her the feeling that he wanted her to do something with her life. She was sure that their friendship was now established. She thought a good deal about him and she was aware that although the steamers on the bay were possibly coming from Europe, they could also be coming from Tasmania.

At last, in the middle of February, we all returned to our normal homes, and our lives became condensed again. The chief moment of condensation was at one of Arthur's Sunday afternoon tea-parties at the end of the month. All the usual habitués turned up, and a few extras. It was usual to ring up beforehand and say that one was coming, when Arthur would describe the other guests whom he was expecting, often in ribald terms, never failing to describe Miss Bath as "the wrong end of the magnet".

This was the first time that Diana had come since the afternoon that Wolfie had kissed Anthea. Arthur, although he chiefly wanted to see his old friends, also liked a sprinkling of quite young people to give a sense of life and to provide decoration, especially girls with pink-apple cheeks. At the Radcliffes' party he had been charmed by Josie, and invited her to come whenever she liked. It was she who, with the indifference of young people to the quarrels of their elders, an indifference that could save the world if it became international, persuaded Diana to ignore the two years' breach, and come to Arthur's on this afternoon. Sophie's presence at Elsie's party had already been a sort of reconciliation.

Wolfie did not come as it was felt, though not stated, that it would be wiser for him not to meet the twins on the actual scene of the crime. His strong sense of propriety did not allow him to visit Mrs Montaubyn on Sundays, so he went out to have tea and supper with a German friend at Kew.

I went with Mildy, who as usual insisted on starting early. Miss Bath appeared a few minutes later, and Arthur, who that morning had said the most frightful things about her on the telephone, comparing her to a brown sow, received her with every sign of affection and pleasure. Her conversation consisted of such remarks as: "When your mother was alive, that table was by the window."

She was soon eclipsed by the arrival of Lady Pringle and Mr Hemstock, who was really one of Sophie's protégés. He had arrived in Melbourne ten years earlier to take up an English lectureship at the University. He was of medium height and looked heavy, but not solid. His eyes were tiny behind very thick gold-rimmed glasses, and a few reddish hairs stood up on his bald head, giving it the appearance of a bladder of lard dusted with cinnamon. His clothes were not very clean as his sight was so poor that he could not see when he spilt his food. His voice, which had a throaty quality, boomed into the room, drenching every corner, and waking a vibrant echo of protest from the piano.

He repeatedly addressed Arthur as "sir", beginning his sentences: "I perceive sir ..." He liked referring to "My Lord so-and-so" but unfortunately in Australia, except for one or two at Government House, there was a shortage of lords, and he had to content himself with lord mayors and colonial bishops. He ignored Mildy and myself, and stood booming at Lady Pringle and Arthur in a way that compelled them also to ignore us. He hoped to be regarded as Melbourne's Dr Johnson.

Cousin Sophie arrived with the twins and Russell Lockwood. They had met frequently in Tasmania, and she had invited him to luncheon on this, his first Sunday back in Melbourne. They brought a burst of life into the room. The twins kissed Arthur and exclaimed "It's lovely to be back! We've had a marvellous time!" They looked somehow larger and more expensive than before they went away. Sophie gave a gleam of satisfaction at seeing Mr Hemstock, but tinged with annoyance that he had been brought by

Lady Pringle. She greeted Mildy with rather less cordiality than she had shown to the servant who opened the door, and Mildy sat with the dejected air of a snubbed kitchen maid.

"Why d'you let them treat you like that?" I muttered angrily. She only smiled in a meek and infuriating manner, as she enjoyed my rebuke, thinking it created the tension of a lovers' quarrel. Cousin Sophie brusquely detached Mr Hemstock from Lady Pringle and sat with him in a corner, from which came blasts of erudition. Lady Pringle consoled herself with Russell, and the twins turned to me. They had been dancing a great deal with naval officers, and their manner, never very gentle, seemed to have acquired a new rather brutal heartiness.

"How's your social life getting on?" asked Anthea. When they were not pretending that I had a passion for old ladies, they gave me the role of a suburban struggler into Society.

"I haven't had any," I said, but added with the awkwardness of young people who try to reveal with nonchalance a fact of which they are proud, "but I'm going to the Government House ball."

"Are you taking your aunt?"

"I expect she'll come."

"And will you dance with Miss Rockingham?"

"I don't really know her."

"We must make Mother introduce you. You like horses and rocking-horses are safer," said Anthea.

In their corner Cousin Sophie and Mr Hemstock were discussing the pronunciation of the Greek letter *rho*. Cousin

Sophie suggesting that it was like the "r" in the French word *rue*. Lady Pringle who loved this kind of conversation and who was annoyed at Cousin Sophie's possessive attitude to Mr Hemstock, turned abruptly and said:

"I was at a meeting of an Anglo-French society in London, addressed by a Frenchman. All the French people were laughing, and the English didn't know why. Afterwards I asked a Frenchman and he told me that it was because the lecturer was speaking like an Englishman who is supposed to have a perfect French accent." She then turned back to Russell.

Cousin Sophie looked stunned by the cruelty of this, far more insidious than her own brusque assaults. She flinched away from its implications and began to talk about Swinburne, but in the sudden silence, caused by the cessation both of Mr Hemstock's booming and her own high-powered English voice, Anthea's reference to Miss Rockingham rang out clearly. Russell gave her a swift glance of concentrated dislike.

Fortunately at that moment Diana arrived with Josie, and unaware of the situation they had saved, they were surprised by the extreme cordiality of their welcome. To Russell, scorched since one o'clock by culture and wit, culminating in Anthea's outrageous remark, they breathed of soothing and gentle humanity. Their eyes met immediately she entered the room, and his delight was obvious at this unexpected meeting.

Cousin Sophie recovered herself sufficiently to say to Diana: "We so enjoyed the party at Mrs Radcliffe's. The house is charming." Any praise given by the Enemy was to something beside the mark, to avoid encouraging conceit. To a painter they would say: "I did enjoy your exhibition. I met so many old friends there," or to a novelist: "I thought the wrapper of your last book excellent."

Diana thanked her for admiring Elsie's house and turned to Russell.

"I didn't know that you were back," she said.

"I only arrived on Thursday. I was going to ring you up this evening."

This gave Diana a comfortable feeling.

"I have a great deal I want to talk to you about," she told him. "I have been up at Westhill for a month. There was nothing to do, and I've been thinking about the things you said."

"Which things?"

"About avoiding dull living, for one thing. But I'll tell you."

The tea was brought in just then, and they had to move.

After tea I went with Josie and the twins into the garden, which was supposed by the ladies who came to Arthur's parties to be very English, as it had a sundial, a birds' bath, an oak tree with a wooden seat round the trunk, and lavender hedges. But many of its shrubs and flowers, guavas, hibiscus and passion-flowers are not usually seen in English gardens, while even those which are seemed to be penetrated by the dry brightness of the air, so that the garden had a unique, more aromatic quality, just as the twins themselves, though brought up so carefully to be English gentlewomen, had caught a slight savagery from the hot sun, which combined with their erudition, made

111

them I think a good deal more entertaining than the girls on whom Cousin Sophie had intended to model them. Of the three, Josie had more the air of being used to English lawns.

Russell and Diana followed us into the garden. Cynthia offered to show him round.

"Mrs von Flugel and I both knew this garden before you were born," said Russell, smiling but firm, and he went with Diana through an archway on to the far lawn.

"Squashed flat," said Anthea cheerfully.

Cynthia looked pained and went indoors to talk to Mr Hemstock.

"You'll be drowned in alexandrines," Anthea warned her. The twins were beginning to separate on the different currents of culture and social ambition. Cynthia was becoming more conscious that her illuminated route led to Cité Université while Anthea hoped that hers would land her somewhere near the Faubourg St Germain. When her sister had gone in through the glass doors a change came over Anthea. She turned to Josie with simple friendliness, asking her questions about herself, not from impertinence but with genuine interest, and suggesting that they should meet more frequently. Anyone meeting her now for the first time would have thought it impossible to imagine a more charming rosy-cheeked, good-hearted girl, and this was doubtless the side she showed to Freddie Thorpe. But the twins, instructed from the cradle to believe in salvation by wit, had formed a team to annihilate their more slow-witted friends, and when they were together they were galvanized by loyalty to their purpose. They did not realize that although salt is a weed-killer it can also destroy

112

the flowers, and that one cannot create a garden with its exclusive use, especially the garden of friendship. We began to amuse ourselves by arranging arabesques of petals on Arthur's bird-bath.

On the other lawn Diana and Russell were remembering the garden as it used to be when they came to Lady Langton's children's parties. They had a slight disagreement and Russell claimed that his memory was the better, as he had left Australia while it was still clearly defined, whereas Diana had seen the garden at every stage of its development, and was less likely to remember accurately which of these stages it had reached at a given date.

On their way back into the house they stopped to look at our arabesques.

"You want to put some yellow petals amongst them," said Diana. "Every arrangement of flowers needs a little yellow." We followed her advice and the birds' bath looked much prettier.

"You touch everything with genius," said Russell.

We were all a little surprised that Russell said this, but we looked at Diana with slight wonder, and a new kind of respect. There was a moment of peaceful happiness as we stood round the little stone pool.

We followed them into the house, where there was a very different atmosphere. Mr Hemstock was relating an anecdote.

"I met my lord Bishop of Yackandandah in Collins Street yesterday," he boomed. "I said to him, 'My lord bishop, you are reported as having, on the second Sunday after Epiphany, split an infinitive in your pro-cathedral.'

To which my lord replied, 'Mr Hemstock sir, it's preferable to splitting hairs,' which I thought considerably prompt. In fact I laughed at my own discomfiture."

As no one followed his example, Mildy, wishing to be kind, said: "How very amusing." Unfortunately her voice was rather whining and plaintive, owing to her feeling subdued in the presence of Sophie, so that her comment far from sounding appreciative, gave an effect of acid sarcasm.

Mr Hemstock bellowed at her: "I'm glad you find it so. I'm glad you have the capacity for amusement. I did not imagine that you would recognize an infinitive sufficiently clearly to be able to split one."

Mildy was so humble in manner because she thought that in this way she would placate and gain the friendship of people whom she believed superior to herself. When she was quite convinced that someone was not superior, she could spread the dragonfly wings of her native wit. Looking at the top of Mr Hemstock's head, where the sparse cinnamon growth stood erect, she said brightly:

"No, I couldn't split an infinitive, but I could split a few hairs."

Everyone pretended not to understand the reference, but this broke up the party. Cousin Sophie collected the twins and went home, taking Mr Hemstock with them. Arthur realizing that he would have no one with whom to talk over the ghastly incidents of the afternoon, invited me to stay on to supper.

"Oh that is disappointing," wailed Mildy. "You must come home. I've got meringues for you."

114

Arthur had walked to the gate with Lady Pringle, and I was able to make a pleasure appear an inescapable duty.

"I must stay," I protested, "I said I would."

"Never mind dear," said Miss Bath, "I'll come and eat your meringues."

"You couldn't eat them all," said Mildy. "You'd be sick."

Miss Bath merely stared at her with the impassivity of those wooden dolls, weighted with lead, which, whatever knocks they receive, recover their upright position.

"Perhaps Josie would like to come?" suggested Mildy. There was some discussion as to how she would get home. Miss Bath who also lived at Brighton, promised to escort her.

Diana and Russell were the last to leave. He had come in his car, having brought Cousin Sophie and the twins on after luncheon. He now offered to drive Diana home.

"Isn't it very much out of your way?" she asked.

"Not a bit," he said. "I've plenty of time, and if I hadn't I'd make it."

On the way he was interested in driving along roads where he had not been since he was a boy. "All the proportions are different," he said. "I used to think this a short road and it's very long, and I remember that house. I used to think it huge, and it's quite a moderate size."

They drove along the beach road at Brighton.

"This is it," she said as they approached her gate. "The one with the pine tree."

He stopped the car, and looked about him. Then he laughed.

"Are you laughing at my house?" asked Diana, a little piqued.

"No. I'm laughing with pleasure. It's pure Australia— the Australia I remember. The wide veranda, the pine tree, the ti-tree and the bay. It's entirely delightful."

"Would you like to come in and look at the house? It's dreadfully shabby."

"I'd love to."

They went indoors, and he continued to express his half-amused admiration. "It's exactly like our old house in Alma Road," he exclaimed. "This is my Australia. I've plunged back into my school-days."

He seemed reluctant to leave. Diana thought a moment and said: "Are you dining anywhere? Would you like to stay to a picnic supper? The servants are out. It'll be cold, but I could make an omelette."

"There's nothing I'd like more," he declared.

They were in the drawing-room and she asked him: "Shall we have supper in here? We often do on Sunday night. The dining-room is so large and gloomy for two people. But it means carrying the trays all the way up the passage."

"I'll carry them," he said.

She gave him some papers and books, showed him the way to the bathroom, and went to take off her hat. When she came back he was not reading but looking at an old Italian painting.

"Where did you get this?" he asked.

"Mama bought it in Italy. She was always buying old pictures."

"It might easily be a Parmigiano. Did you know?"

"No. I'm afraid I didn't."

"You're extraordinary," he said, "you're full of surprises. You ask me to a picnic supper in a shabby house and there's a Parmigiano in the drawing-room. You're like that yourself. You're full of all kinds of qualities but you just put them away in a dark corner."

Diana laughed. "Shall we have a fire?" she said. "It would be more cheerful, and it gets chilly here by the sea after sunset, even as soon as this."

"I'll light it." He knelt on the hearthrug, put a match to the paper and blew at it gently. Diana pulled out a low wide tea-table and opened it. She went out and returned in a few minutes with glasses, knives and forks, a bottle of hock and a bowl of passion-fruit and oranges. She put the things on the table with the candles from the writing table.

"You take elemental things and make them elegant," he said, looking appreciatively at the table. "That is civilization."

"We haven't the food yet," said Diana. "That's rather elemental."

"Wine and fruit are the essentials."

He followed her to the kitchen, where he admired the huge range and the flagstones, which she had always intended to have removed. She told him what was in the larder, but he said that he would rather have an omelette and gruyère cheese.

"*Fines herbes* or plain or cheese?"

"Not cheese as we're having the gruyère afterwards. *Fines herbes* would be best."

They went into the garden and Diana picked some parsley and chives.

"I'm enjoying this enormously," said Russell.

"I think the elemental things are the most enjoyable," said Diana, "even cooking, if you don't have too much of it, and if you do it *with* somebody, not just *for* them. Will you take up that tray, and a corkscrew you'll find in the right-hand drawer of the dresser, and open the wine bottle and draw two arm-chairs up to the table, and I'll bring up the omelette when its ready and we'll eat it while it's hot."

He did all these things without further questioning, and Diana standing watching the omelette, thought how very pleasant it was to be appreciated. If Wolfie had been here instead of Russell he would have waited in his music room until she called him to supper, and then probably have dawdled till the omelette was spoiled, while if she had asked him to carry a tray or open a bottle he would have affected a complete bewilderment at her request, and found the simple tasks impossibly difficult. The contrast was emphasized when she came to the drawing-room to find Russell standing ready, having on his own initiative lighted the candles on the table.

"It's a perfect omelette," he said, "I knew it would be."

"Did you have a nice lunch?" asked Diana.

"Oh yes!" He smiled. "Brilliant. Sparks flying everywhere. It was fun, but scarifying. A sort of electric massage to the brain. Do they keep that up all the time?"

"I think so. But we haven't seen much of them lately." She paused and then said: "Wolfie kissed Anthea."

"Goodness, how brave!"

118

They looked at each other and began to laugh. Diana became almost helpless with laughter. She had known all along that it was funny that Wolfje had kissed Anthea, but nobody had even hinted at it before. There had been a little ironical witty comment from some of the family, but that had only been in private. The public attitude had been informed by the solemn hush that surrounds an obscenity.

"But she is pretty," she said, wiping her eyes.

"I didn't mean that," said Russell. "I meant all the academic thorns round the rose."

"Why academic?"

"That sort of culture's very academic, isn't it?"

"I thought you liked it."

"I do in small doses. I must say your cousins are a wild surprise in Melbourne. I had Rochefoucauld and Madame du Deffand flung at my head all through luncheon. I felt like a boy from the backwoods. But the twins liven it up. Without them all that recherché reference would be rather exhausting. The pleasures of the mind are very dangerous."

"I thought the other sort were supposed to be."

"Oh no. The other sort make people human and kindly, full of goodwill and laughter. The pleasures of the mind make one enjoy sticking darts into one's fellows. What else do the Edward Langtons do? They live for it. Although I enjoy it too."

"I always thought I was rather cultured myself," said Diana. "You said I was—that I made elemental things elegant."

119

"That's not culture—that's civilization. It's entirely different. Or you might say it's culture, but it's not the sort I mean. I mean when some germ comes into your mind, an apprehension, a new glimpse of something true or beautiful—you cherish it. It spreads. It seizes a whole century, a continent—it blossoms into Gothic cathedrals or Renaissance palaces—into Chartres or Leonardo. That's the real thing. But culture—which is just learning about the real culture, about what someone else did so that you can be spiteful to your friends—that's just purgatory."

"Did you say that to Sophie?"

"No. I was too frightened."

"But don't you know as much about Madame du Deffand as she does?"

"Good Heavens, no. I live for pleasure. I don't want to impress people."

"But you do impress people. You've impressed everyone here, even Sophie."

"It's sheer luck—just because I look gentlemanly in public."

Diana laughed again. "Oh dear, I'm enjoying myself," she said.

"Don't say so, or you'll stop. Cupid and Psyche."

"How d'you mean?"

"You mustn't turn the light on your pleasure. It must remain instinctive."

"But one must use one's mind. If you knew how much instinct I have to put up with."

"Do you? I see very little in Melbourne society."

"I mean at home."

"Is Mr von Flugel very instinctive?"

"Entirely—but call him Wolfie."

"I'll try."

"Would you like cream with your passion-fruit? I think there's some over from the apple tart we had for lunch. We always have a pint on Sundays."

"Lovely. Shall I fetch it?"

"You'll have to take one of these candles. There's no electric light."

He took the candle and when he was in the passage she called to him: "It's on the shelf on the right." When he came back she said:

"You told me that I should not say I was enjoying myself, but you said the same thing when we were picking the parsley."

"I was enjoying the external conditions. It's all right to mention that, but you were enjoying your enjoyment. That is dangerous."

"I think that you're more terrifying than Sophie, really."

"Why? I'm absolutely unterrifying."

"You say you live for pleasure, but you do it by very austere rules. All my relatives live for pleasure but they don't know they're doing it."

"Now you've hurt my feelings dreadfully. You've exposed my taint of puritanism, the thing I'm most ashamed of."

"I don't like puritanism myself, but isn't it the bones in one's character?"

"I'm sick of bones. They become so evident in old age."

"You're not old yet."

"I'm forty."

"So am I."

"Oh well, that's comfortable," said Russell.

"But I thought you believed we shouldn't be comfortable. That was one of the things I thought of up at Westhill, that I meant to say to you. You talk rather as if I ought to be doing something, or going somewhere, but I don't know exactly what."

"You oughtn't to hang your Parmigianos in dark corners."

"I'll move it now if you like."

"I mean your personal Parmigianos."

"I don't know what they are."

"You keep giving glimpses of them, but won't exhibit them properly."

"What should I do? Take them back to Italy?"

"Perhaps. Yes."

"That is another thing I meant to ask you. At Elsie's party you said that we were provincial if we didn't live in Rome, but you didn't explain."

"I can't tell you now. You've made me feel like a puritan lecturer."

"But I like being lectured."

"Then it's a bad trait in your character. It's not a Parmigiano. I mustn't encourage it."

"How am I to know what to do if you don't tell me?"

"You're putting responsibility on me."

"If you go round airing ideas you must accept the responsibility for their effect."

"But you are asking me to air more ideas."

"Very well, tell me what you mean about Rome, and I won't hold you responsible for its effect on me."

"It's extremely fundamental. It may change your place in history."

"I didn't know I had one."

"Then I'll tell you. First of all you must believe that the old gods were real. They all had meaning—Cupid and Psyche again."

"But they didn't exist."

"If a thing has meaning it exists. The old gods existed. The Church didn't deny that; it regarded them as devils, but they weren't devils, they were simply unredeemed."

"This is a little difficult for my mind," said Diana.

"It's not really. Just listen. Everything has to be redeemed, including the gods. So the richness and meaning of your religion varies according to the richness and meaning of the original gods who were its *terrain,* in the same way that wine from the same kind of vine alters its character according to the earth it grows in. Wine is a very good illustration. I saw a wine merchant's advertisement in Italy: '*Il vino è Simbolo del Redentore.*' Our religion was not intended to create a new heaven and earth, but to redeem what was already there. That is why it changes its character and value according to its *terrain*. In Ireland Catholicism has its poorest expression because it had such dreary gods to redeem. In Mexico it's most savage, and when you get Calvinism superimposed on some ghastly northern gods the result is diabolical. But in Italy you find all the things that have made us what we are—classicism

123

the basis and Catholicism fused into one and the effect is tremendous. We find our place in history. That is why we can only five happily elsewhere, when we regard ourselves as in a province of Rome."

"I see; at least I think I do," said Diana, "but I am afraid that I don't feel terribly different. You sound rather Roman Catholic, but you're not, are you?"

"No, but I'm European."

"You're not Australian, then. That's what I thought. You'll go back to England."

"If I'm not Australian, I'm not English. Last year I went back to England in July, later than usual. At night I left all that blazing dramatic Italian scenery, the blue and gold and baroque of the Ligurian coast, and woke up in the morning at Sens with the river mists lying on the cool meadows, and the innocent Gothic cathedral a mile away. The contrast was extraordinary. In the evening when I arrived at the house where I was going to stay and passed the village church in the moonlight, and drew up at the Georgian mansion which I had formerly thought so impressive, it all seemed to me remote and touching, a far outpost where the inhabitants of that damp northern island had tried to echo the religion and the splendours of their true home, which for every civilized man is the Mediterranean. But because of that you love it more."

"Now I believe you've revealed yourself."

"What d'you think of the revelation?" asked Russell, and they returned to the level of laughter.

"It's most interesting. Rather richer in texture than I expected."

"Did you think I was shallow?"

"No, not shallow, but I didn't think that you would have quite those ideas—about the gods I mean."

"Don't you agree with them?"

"I think I might when I've assimilated them. But I thought I was going for a nice paddle and you've taken me for a swim."

"One must always go on into deeper water."

"I thought your ideas might save me. Instead of that, apparently, I'm to be drowned."

"You ought to have the best. It's only found in deep water."

"I'm not sure of that. But why ought I to have the best?"

"You're one of the people who ought to. So am I."

"How terribly smug."

"One must be truthful. When I was young I always wanted the best. Everything led me to believe that it was on the other side of the world. Your mother gave me that impression. So as soon as I was free I went there. Then I found that English people expected Australians to be semi-criminal oafs, which is very odd, seeing that half the landed gentry are pretty savage themselves."

"Do you think that of the people here at Government House?"

"They're the other half—the nicest people there are. I mean the female sergeant-majors one sees in Knightsbridge, their feet planted firmly apart and shouting at each other about dogs. Anyhow I thought I must be very gentlemanly if I was to have the best. But just being a gentleman is very dull, though in a way it's necessary, but it's far from the best. The best is finding delight in everything that's beautiful. It's not always gentlemanly. One cannot go about saying this, only when one meets someone worthwhile."

Diana thought that was a nice way of telling her that she was worthwhile. They had finished their supper, but they sat on at the table for an hour or more, sometimes chaffing, sometimes talking more seriously.

They were still sitting there when they heard voices in the hall, and Josie opened the door saying: "Do come in and see Mummy for a few minutes."

Miss Bath appeared in the doorway. She stared at Diana and Russell as if a tiger snake had been coiled up on the hearth-rug. She would have thought it very peculiar to have supper in the drawing-room under any circumstances. If Diana had been with Wolfie she would have disapproved of their lounging in arm-chairs at the disordered but decorative table, with the empty hock bottle, somehow so much more suggestive of wanton gaiety than a mere claret or burgundy bottle, lifting its elegant neck between them. That Diana should be with Russell in this intimate scene was beyond her experience, but by no means her imagination of impropriety.

"I'm afraid I am intruding," she said, in a voice thick with disapproval. This was such a slight exaggeration of her usual tone that Diana did not notice it.

"How kind of you to bring Josie home," she said. "You met Mr Lockwood this afternoon I think."

Miss Bath glanced at Russell. "I did," she said. "Now I had better go."

126

"Won't you stay and have some coffee? Mr Lockwood has been putting forward such startling ideas that I quite forgot to make it. I'll do it now, or Josie darling, will you?"

This stimulated Miss Bath's emanation of disapproval. "I shall go now, thank you," she said. She turned and collided with Wolfie, who had come from Melbourne in the other end of the same train, and had walked home not far behind Miss Bath and Josie.

"You have a party," he said to Diana. "I have missed it. I am sad." He turned tender eyes on Miss Bath.

"I have only just come," said Miss Bath, her voice full of meaning and malice.

"You were not here. Then I am less sad." This was the most charming thing that had ever been said to Miss Bath in the whole course of her life, but she showed no gratification.

"I brought Josie home *just now*," she said, with more insistent meaning.

"All is kindness," said Wolfie, beaming round the room. "We shall have some wine."

"Good night," said Miss Bath, and walked out of the house.

"The poor woman is not happy," said Wolfie. "Her skin is not pretty." He took Diana's hand and stroked it, saying to Russell: "You have been entertaining my wife. That is kind. She does not laugh enough. She is alone much because I must work, and she is so sweet."

Josie came in with the coffee tray.

"Where is Miss Bath?" she asked. "Has she gone? Why didn't you take her home, Daddy?"

127

"Dear, she will be safe," said Wolfie. "She is not beautiful."

"Why didn't you take a cab from the station, Josie," asked Diana, "instead of bringing her all the way round here? She seemed rather cross."

Diana poured out the coffee and Russell stayed about half an hour longer, talking to Wolfie and flattering Josie, which was not difficult, as she responded with a delightful laughing modesty, something like her mother's.

When he left they all went out with him to his car, which Wolfie admired ecstatically. "It shines like the swan of Lohengrin!" he exclaimed.

As Russell drove back to Melbourne he smiled to himself, thinking over the evening he had just spent, so unexpected and so enjoyable. He had returned to Australia because he wanted to feel at home and this was the first time he had done so. Everybody had been very kind, and he had been invited to many pleasant dinner parties, but he had the impression that his hostesses were showing him how civilized they were. He could not imagine one of them telling him that she bought more cream on Sundays, and sending him to fetch it. He was delighted, too, at Diana's complete unconsciousness of the obvious cause of Miss Bath's ill-humour; themselves. The immediate ease with which they talked together was extraordinary. He could say anything he liked to her, and she accepted it. He wondered if it was because they had known each other as children, but they had not been particularly close friends in those days. He had even thought she might not remember him. It was a shame that she was stuck out there in that rambling barn of a house, even if it had its attractions, and what a husband Wolfie was for a woman like that! Although he rather liked him, he could not help feeling jealous of the way she accepted his absurd caresses, with kindness, without embarrassment or the loss of any dignity.

She had said "Come again" but he was not likely to find her alone again. That was what happened, he thought, the greatest pleasures of life suddenly blossomed, without planning, and the exact conditions could never be reproduced. He would never again help her prepare a meal in her huge flagged kitchen, or gather herbs in the garden, or lounge in arm-chairs over supper, arranged on a tea-table by the fire, and talk half-serious nonsense. He felt rather melancholy at this realization. But of course they could often meet and talk in other places.

At supper in Arthur's dining-room, I listened to a commentary on his guests.

"What an unfortunate afternoon," he said. "I thought the jaws of Hell were opening—Hemstock and Miss Bath on the same day. Thank God she performed one useful function, and took Mildred away. Otherwise I should have had to ask her to stay."

It was cruel that Mildy could never know of my loyal retort: "Aunt Mildy's jolly amusing sometimes. We have great fun together."

Arthur ignored this as it gave me the moral ascendancy. "Did you ever see anyone eat like Miss Bath?" he asked. "She gets crumbs all over her face, but she tidies herself up afterwards with the efficiency of an assiduous charwoman.

129

Her mind hasn't developed since she was seven, when she was told she must eat tidily at a party, and because she's clean after eating she imagines that she's a social asset."

"If you think she's so awful, why d'you invite her?" I asked.

"Her mother was one of our oldest friends," said Arthur loftily. It was this method of choosing his guests that gave his parties their particular flavour. Miss Bath sitting next to Cousin Sophie or Elsie Radcliffe, gave the same piquant solidity we feel in an old country house, where a garish beadwork stool is beside a fine Chippendale chair, and next to a Gainsborough portrait is a watercolour of the vicarage garden by Aunt Maggie.

I realized that if I were priggish I would spoil the conversation.

"Don't you like Mr Hemstock?" I asked.

"Like him! That white slug? I can hardly bear to shake hands with him. No man should go about with a hot water-bottle tied to his stomach, especially at this time of year."

"Does he?" I exclaimed.

"Yes. Couldn't you hear it splashing? People think it's indigestion but it's really the bottle. Very few people who go in for culture are healthy."

"But I thought you liked culture." His whole house was arranged to give vistas and to produce soft effects of colour. The chairs on which we were seated were embroidered with a mosaic design from the Baths of Caracalla.

"I hate talking double-dutch about pronunciation," said Arthur. "Hemstock's the son of a grave-digger. He got a scholarship to Oxford and thinks it's grand to be educated, in the same way that Miss Bath thinks it's grand to be clean, whereas everyone else takes it as a matter of course."

"Is he really the son of a grave-digger?"

"Something like that. It sounds like it."

"It sounds to me more like a seamstress."

"His mother may have been a seamstress. Have you read his poems? Lechery clothed in pomposity."

"Does Cousin Sophie like that?"

"Women only half know what they're doing. The more respectable they are, the more they are drawn to the roué. Look at Lady Pringle with Wolfie."

"But Uncle Wolfie isn't a roué. He's awfully kind."

"Whatever makes you think roués aren't kind?"

"Well, you couldn't be kind and not treat a girl fairly," I stammered, blushing slightly. Again on the wings of my innocence I soared into the moral ascendancy.

"I'm glad you think so, my boy," said Arthur, looking noble.

To get away from awkward subjects I said that I thought Mr Lockwood very nice.

"He's too precious," Arthur replied. "He spends his life in Europe chasing beauty and grandees, instead of settling down here sensibly and marrying a girl of his own sort. As this was exactly what Arthur would have liked to do and had done for a short time, he spoke with great moral indignation. "Australia needs to be developed by strong wholesome men," he said, and he went on to give me an address which might have been delivered by the Minister for Immigration, if there was one at the time.

Although it had been said of Arthur that he began life as a conscious hypocrite, and ended as an unconscious one, this may not have been a true diagnosis. The virtues which he originally affected, he may have come in time to value and was therefore no longer a hypocrite. He may even have originally admired them, but have been prevented from practising them by the demands of expediency and youthful passion. In fact the hypocrisy in later years may have been in the affectation of brutality and cynicism, with which he tried to conceal the excessive kindness of his heart. For everything he did, if not what he said, was kind. Even when he flung Miss Bath and Mr Hemstock to the wolves, it was to give me the pleasure of laughing at their mangled remains. He believed that it did them no harm, and might possibly make them objects of pity, instead of bored dislike.

So now, when he saw the great fertile lands of Australia peopled by bronzed wholesome men and women, he was not being a humbug, as he had come to realize that this would give many people happy lives. He also took into account that they would doubtless have beautiful sons and daughters, also that it was far more fun to be aesthetic against this background. To derive pleasure from decadence or from any pose it is necessary to have a strong bourgeois society. There is no kick in being unconventional in a madhouse.

When we moved into the drawing-room he was still in the exalted frame of mind of the Minister for Immigration, which led him to sit down at the piano, where far from breaking into a patriotic march, he delicately began a Chopin nocturne. From this he broke into the impassioned

132

rhythm of a litany. "I heard this at the Brompton Oratory during the *Quarant' Ore*," he said. "Cardinal Newman was there." He went on to give a kind of musical resumé of his life, making frequent comments on the things he played so that his performance would have made a good wireless programme. He played some old-fashioned dance tunes and said: "I remember your grandmother dancing to this at Bishopscourt, sixty years ago. How beautiful she was in her wide floating dress. Nowadays girls look like cows hobbled so that they won't kick over the milk-pail." Although his nostalgic reveries were interspersed with these ribald attacks on the younger generation, his face had an expression of immense and noble sadness. Towards the end he played "Oft in the Stilly Night" and then again the dance tune.

Arthur was so instinctively an artist, that he would make of something, on which he had entered casually, a creative whole. If he had been asked to give a performance like that which I had just been fortunate enough to over-hear, he would have been embarrassed, have fussed about what pieces to choose, have forgotten the best, and would finally have refused. He had the genius to follow his inspiration, but not the talent to produce it in his conscious mind. This was a failing of all the family, even of Diana. They only showed their best in casual moments, in an impromptu charade or an improvised meal, and so always remained amateurs.

When he again played the dance tune, I asked him what my grandmother was like as a girl. He turned on the piano stool.

133

"She was something like Diana," he said, "but her hair was not dark. It was a warm golden colour, and she had an air of authority. She was much more sensible than Diana, but in some ways she had the same kind of life. Of course, she was rich, which made a great difference. She had to give all the time to people who took her unending generosity for granted. Though your grandfather was a very different character from Wolfie," he said, which was not entirely true. "Wolfie has stripped Diana of every comfort and pleasure, and then he bites the hand that feeds him." He thought a little and then qualified this. "He doesn't mean to bite the hand that feeds him. He just thinks 'That's a nice piece of meat. I'll have that too.'"

CHAPTER SEVEN

The Government House ball, to which I was so pleased to tell the twins that I was invited, needs, like Mrs Radcliffe's party, a little introduction. Two people were rather surprised to receive invitations.

Sir Roland Cave, aware that his appointment was a consolation prize for his failure to enter the Cabinet, could not endure any suggestion that it was not fundamentally important as well as highly decorative, and he was often irritated by the feeling that his staff thought they were there simply to amuse themselves. He kept a strict eye on the smallest details of Government House activity, and even had the menus submitted to him before every dinner party.

One morning he prowled into the room where Lord Francis was drawing up the list of guests for the ball.

"Who's this Mrs Montaubyn?" he asked.

"I'm not sure, sir," said Lord Francis. "I think she's English."

"You shouldn't ask people if you don't know who they are. And I don't want all the English tourists invited here. They don't go to Buckingham Palace at home."

"Montaubyn *is* a name, sir," Lord Francis objected mildly.

"Look it up."

Lord Francis pulled out a Court Directory, but could not find any Mrs Montaubyn, though there was a baronet of that name.

"Look him up," said Sir Roland.

Lord Francis yanked out a peerage and turning over the pages muttered: "Gough—Grafton—Hay of Park—Hood—Kinnaird—Limerick—Manvers—Monck—Montaubyn—um-um-um—here we are. James Perry Montaubyn, second son of fourth bart., B. A., Corpus. Canon St Andrew's Cathedral, Sydney, N.S.W. Married Emily McCarthy, one son, Aidan Perry, killed Spion Kop, poor devil—married Gladys Cumfit. That's the one—She's Mrs. A. P. Montaubyn."

"Very well," said Sir Roland grudgingly, "but you want to vet these people more carefully."

Lord Francis was pleased that His Ex. had suspected someone of such unimpeachable standing, and Mrs Montaubyn received a card.

The other person to be surprised at her invitation was Mildy, who had not been asked to a dance of any kind for twenty years. It was probably due to her having a man of the same name in her house. She was pleased, but said: "Of course I shan't go."

Mistaking her common sense for that poor spirit she so often showed when brought into contact with "grand people", I protested peevishly, and at last persuaded her to go. She had foreseen that she would have a far worse evening than at the Radcliffes' party. There I had spent some of the time with her, but at a ball I would be dancing continuously with the twins and other girls, while she watched bleakly from the wall. She did not know that my insistence was an attempt to strengthen her character and not at all to a desire to have her with me. The eternal hope in her breast began to flutter again. Bright blue and pink fantasies came into her mind. She saw the proud moment when we arrived in the Government House ballroom, and our friends would say: "Here are Guy and Mildy" and they would chaff her about looking so young. Perhaps I would dance with her, not more than twice, as we must be sensible.

"Very well", she said suddenly, "I'll go. I'll get a new ball dress for it." In her eye was an excited gleam. She began to talk about her new dress, and as I thought its purpose was to enable her to hold her own vis-à-vis Sophie and the twins and not to make her appear a suitable girlish companion for myself, I encouraged her. Nearly every evening, between the morning the invitations came and the night of the ball, she talked at dinner about the progress of the new dress.

The occasion of this ball was the arrival in Port Phillip Bay of an English battleship, with an Anglo-German prince on board—a relative of Queen Victoria's. To the twins, even more exciting than the prince, was the fact that one of the officers on the ship was Lord Saltash, a young unmarried peer, who was a cousin of theirs, but not of ours. Cousin

Sophie had a letter from his mother, asking her to be kind to him, but it was like trying to catch a whale in the ocean to be kind to it. Cousin Edward managed to entice him to dine at the Melbourne Club, and instructed by Cousin Sophie gave him a further invitation to dine at her house on the night of the ball.

On the day before this function Lord Saltash rang up to say that he was awfully sorry that he could not come as he was on duty, the duty being, she discovered later, to dine with Freddie Thorpe and Clara Bumpus. This unbalanced her dinner table, and the only person she could think of who would accept these last minute fallen crumbs was myself. She rang me up in the evening. I had never heard her so amiable on the telephone. Her invitations were generally commands delivered by one of the twins. She even apologized for the short notice. I was extremely gratified and thought she must have heard something to my credit, and as I was twenty years old, though unfortunately looked younger, I wanted to get married, and I thought she might regard me as an eligible suitor for one of the twins. My imagination was nearly as idiotic as Mildy's, to whom I now went back and said excitedly:

"Cousin Sophie has asked me to dine tomorrow."

"But that's the night of the ball," said Mildy.

"Yes, but before the ball. They'll take me."

"You haven't accepted?"

"Of course I have."

"Oh!" wailed Mildy. "This is too much."

"But surely you don't expect me to refuse?" The idea of going first to a dinner party and then to a ball on the same evening, appeared to me an enlargement of experience which only a lunatic would expect me to avoid.

"How am I to go?" asked Mildy.

"In the car of course, as you intended."

"Alone." This terrible hollow sound fell flat and dead into the room. It shook my egoism, but I was not prepared to abandon reason. Mildy sat with her hands in her lap, staring into the now empty fireplace, and in the same condition of speechless despair in which I had found her on my return from the Radcliffes'.

"I shan't go," she said at last. I was horrified at this sudden end to all the eager anticipation of the last three weeks, but also indignant at the blackmail.

"That's absurd," I protested. "I'll meet you at the ball. It's only ten minutes' drive." In saying this I showed that I recognized her desire to be with me, and accepted it as a fact in our conversation so that in spite of myself I was obliged to be a party to a kind of semi-lovers'-quarrel, taking the role of the neglectful young man. This gave Mildy a slight satisfaction and she prolonged the argument. She was not devoid of the rationality, or even astuteness inherited from her legal ancestors, and finding me so upset, and to some extent at her mercy because of her refusal to go, she saw that she might derive more satisfaction from that than from attending the ball, where she again realized that she would spend a miserable and neglected evening. The apparently enormous sacrifice she made by not going, her expensive new dress wasted, would provide her with material for reproach and blackmail for weeks, possibly months ahead, and in addition to referring to the night of the Radcliffes' party as "that horrid evening when we quarrelled", she would now be able to talk of the night of the ball as "that horrid evening when you left me alone, and went off with the twins, and I couldn't wear my new dress".

The next evening when I came home, before I went up to change, I begged her to come. I said that although Cousin Sophie had promised to drive me to the ball I would not go with her, but would come back and collect Mildy, but nothing would move her. She wore a faint sweet smile as she said: "No. I must be sensible. I mustn't be jealous of the twins."

When I left she kissed me good night rather lusciously and said: "Enjoy yourself," with the result that in the hansom on the way to Cousin Sophie's house I felt guilty and miserable; but these feelings could not last long in the twins' company, unless provoked by themselves.

Cousin Sophie's servants were so ladylike, rather more so than her daughters, and had so thoroughly assimilated the atmosphere of the house, that if I passed one in the street, from a vague familiarity I thought she must be one of our numerous relatives, and expected her to stop me saying: "Aren't you Laura's youngest boy?" One of these now showed me into the drawing-room, and Mildy's sorrows evaporated from my mind.

The drawing-room was rather like that of an English vicarage, furnished with negative good taste. On the walls were watercolours and prints of the Winged Victory and the Temple of Vesta. In spite of Cousin Sophie's hatred of vulgarity, and her anxiety to conceal the extent of her husband's income, if she knew it, there were a few evidences of wealth. On the occasional tables were one or two objects of value, and there was a photograph of the Dowager Lady Saltash, and signed photographs of impressive-looking Governors' wives, with tiaras and dog-collars, and with coronets on the silver frames. The most conspicuous pieces of furniture were two grand pianos, on which the twins played duets, mostly from *The Ring of the Nibelungen*. Whether it was because it was played so much by the twins that I came under the spell of this music, or whether it was the music that put me under the spell of the twins, it is hard to say. But for me all that year before the war echoed with the music of Wagner, which filled my life with enchantment. On summer evenings the river at Warrandyte became the Rhine, and it was in the saplings that Siegfried listened to the bird, and blew his hunter's horn: Because of this music the bludgeonings of the twins was nothing beside their beauty, and when I heard the motif of the golden apples, my heart was pierced with the thought of Anthea. When I was with one of the twins in some woodland place, with a pear tree shimmering in the moonlight, I heard Siegmund's cry at the approach of spring. When a year later I went to the war, it was the song of the Rhinemaidens I heard in my ears, wailing for the gold that was lost for ever. The gold for me was this year about which I am writing, and it certainly does not seem to have been particularly enjoyable.

Cousin Edward was the first to come into the drawing-room. Although I had been here three or four times since the Radcliffes' party, I had not been alone with him before, and I felt a little nervous, as I thought that he might think I wanted to seduce his daughters. In the minds of the innocent are these curious pot-holes.

"I hear Mildred's house is very pretty," he said, illustrating the attitude of the Enemy, who heard about us, but who preferred to have little first-hand information. There was a babel in the hall and the twins burst in.

"Oh you!" said Cynthia crossly. "I thought it was Mr Hemstock."

"You're only *faute de mieux*," said Anthea, "*faute de Saltash*. The peerage has failed us."

"It was very good of you to come at such short notice," said Cousin Edward, gravely courteous. I did not know whether to be mortified at finding myself a substitute, or gratified at being thought an adequate one for a peer.

"Has Father been probing into your prospects?" asked Anthea.

"I don't think I have any," I said.

"We'll give you some—vistas anyway. We'll stretch your mind."

"It sounds like torture."

"All growth is painful," said Cynthia.

"One doesn't go out to dinner to grow," I protested.

"Of course you do," said Anthea. "Eating makes you grow, doesn't it? Talking makes your mind grow at the same time."

"It's quite Greek," said Cynthia. "Mind and body growing together."

"In fact dining out is a classical education," declared Anthea.

142

"I thought it was for enjoyment."

"Not here, it isn't. It's just hell."

"Anthea!" exclaimed Cousin Edward.

"Well, all our visitors leave in tears—utterly shattered. If they don't, we think the evening's a failure."

Mr Hemstock and the two other guests were announced. The latter were a young married couple from Cambridge, both graduates. They were touring Australia in a second-hand car to learn the marriage rites of the aborigines. Cousin Sophie had invited them and Mr Hemstock to meet Lord Saltash, as she thought it would be nice to have an all-English dinner-party. It took her forty years to learn that the English aristocracy do not come to Australia for cultivated conversation in quasi-vicarages, of which they have ample for their requirements at home, but for race meetings and rowdy fun in rich houses.

"Good evening, sir," boomed Mr Hemstock. "Good evening, Miss Cynthia. Good evening, Miss Anthea."

"I think you know our cousin, Guy Langton?" said Anthea.

Mr Hemstock glanced at me, and evidently did not think the question worth answering.

Cousin Sophie, who before her marriage had spent much of her time in vice-regal courts at Dublin Castle and elsewhere, never entered the drawing-room until all her guests were assembled. The reverberations of Mr Hemstock's voice warned her that she might now appear. Dinner was announced almost immediately and we went in.

"A ball is quite an occasion for me," said Mr Hemstock as we sat down. "I am not a devotee of Terpsichore, nor shall I tempt the goddess by pretending that I am."

"I certainly shan't," said Cousin Edward, politely putting himself on the same level of decrepitude as his guest. "I'm much too aged, and to be aged is to be damaged."

"Oh Father!" exclaimed Anthea.

"It's in the *genre* of his generation," said Cynthia.

"That's exactly the same kind of joke," I said.

"*Il ne faut pas enseigner les poissons à nager,*" said Cousin Sophie. Her pronunciation was too good for me to be able to understand her, and I looked nonplussed.

"That means, don't teach your grandmother to suck eggs," said Anthea, who was firmly convinced that any kind of refinement was middle class, perhaps her one point of intellectual contact with Freddie Thorpe. Cousin Sophie gave a smile of almost tearful apology to the Cambridge couple, who were very earnest and sat bewildered throughout the meal, as their conversation was limited to primitive sex and camping equipment.

"Anyhow, who gave you permission to intervene?" Cynthia asked me haughtily.

"You are inclined to forget, Cynthia, that you are not Dr Johnson," said Cousin Edward, with the cruelty which some parents show to children who deviate from the pattern they had in mind for them.

Mr Hemstock, at the mention of Dr Johnson, gave that involuntary, imperceptible start which an Egyptologist will give at hearing the word "Luxor", or an Anglo-Catholic

144

at the word "ferrola" or a snob or a cricket enthusiast at the word "Lord's".

At the end of dinner the port decanter came round to me, but I was talking to Anthea on my left and did not notice it. Mr Hemstock boomed: "The oporto is to you, young man."

When I had translated this into modern English I showed that I was offended at being roared at, so he may have been surprised at the alacrity with which I helped him on with his coat as we were preparing to leave for the ball. He did not look pleased, and would have been less so if he had known that my attention was largely due to a wish to hear his hot water-bottle splash. I was rewarded by a faint gurgle, but was not sure that this was not, as Arthur had denied, the natural rumblings of indigestion.

The Enemy were possessed by a ruthless determination that no one else's convenience should interfere with their own. It was unknown for one of them to say: "Please don't bother to call for me. It will be so much easier for you if we meet at the theatre." A more familiar sound was: "I couldn't possibly do that. It would be tiresome."

The transport to Government House consisted of a hired car which would just take five passengers—the twins at last had struck at going to parties in a wagonette—and the grubby two-seater of the primitive sex students. There was no room for me, and although Cousin Sophie had said she would take me, she now merely told me that I could ring up for a hansom if I liked. The Cambridge man, seeing my dismay, told me that I might stand on the step of his car.

I accepted thankfully but he did not moderate his speed to my precarious situation. Also at that time I had the idea that it was smarter to go to dances without an overcoat, giving the impression that one always just walked out of the house into a rich warm limousine. As he whizzed round corners I hung on grimly, rubbing my white waistcoat and shirt-front against the canvas hood, impregnated with the fine brown dust of some Australian desert, so that when I entered the ballroom they looked as if I had just fished them out of the dirty linen basket.

"What on earth have you done to your shirt?" demanded Anthea. "You'd better go home and change it." Owing to my appearance the twins only gave me one dance each.

This made me very disconsolate and I wished that I had not gone to their beastly dinner party. I thought of Mildy with tenderness and sympathy, and considered ringing her up, and saying I would come for her. Then I could change my shirt and she would pay for the taxi. But I decided that by the time I returned to the ball it would be too late to fill my programme.

I saw Aunt Baba arrive and stand inside the door, waiting for George to come from the cloakroom. As she was not technically the Enemy I thought she would be nice to me and I went over to her. She did not answer my greeting, but gave a vicious glance at my shirt-front.

"What on earth have you been doing?" she said. "For goodness sake don't stand by me."

I left her and stood by myself against the wall. By now I was almost in tears, and wondering what I should do, when I became aware that a woman of about forty, with golden curls massed on her head, was watching me with an expression of the most benevolent kindness. Our eyes met and she smiled, and I felt a sudden human warmth suffuse my body, and diffident, ingenuous, with my heart opening like a flower in the sun, I moved towards her.

"Cheer up, ducks," she said.

This caressing word fell on my wounds like healing ointment. Such easy humanity, such absence of priggishness and wit, such indifference to my dirty shirt, made me feel that I had entered a nobler world where rich and natural rhythms were not disturbed by the tricky agility of the mind. There was about her a suggestion of high summer, of the orchards and vineyards to which Lady Pringle had referred, in the richness of her curls and her ruby velvet dress, in the many gold bracelets on her plump arms, and the necklace of gold vine leaves, very beautiful, but recalling rather those labels which are sometimes seen on the necks of decanters, lying on the soft powdered folds of her bosom. She was, of course, Mrs Montaubyn.

With that foolish confidence which I was apt to show to anyone with a kind face I asked her: "Do you think my shirt-front looks awful? It got smudged driving here. My cousins say I should go home."

"Don't you worry about your shirt-front, dear," she said. "It's your face that matters and that's as sweet as two pippins."

"Oh!" I said, a little startled. "Well, it's jolly nice of you to say so."

"Jolly nice, eh? Are you one of the swells?"

147

"Which swells?"

"All the swells that hang round the governor and Lord Tomnoddy. Haw! Haw!"

"I don't hang round anyone," I said. "I don't get a chance."

At this she inflated with silent laughter, ending in a wheeze.

"What you want to hang round is a pretty girl. And I'll bet you do with that complexion. You're English aren't you? That's where they get it—the Scotch mist and all that. I bet you have your fun and quite right too. We're only young once, I say. Don't you worry about your shirt. You have a good time and tell your cousins to go and you-know-what themselves."

"Oh, thank you," I said much cheered. "I will if I can."

I saw Diana, followed by Wolfie and Josie come into the room. "There is my aunt," I explained. "I must go and say hullo to her."

"Ta-ta, ducks. See you later," said Mrs Montaubyn. She followed me with her benevolent gaze, and I led it straight to her quarry. I saw Wolfie staring at her with horror, and thought he must be annoyed with me for speaking to someone of that kind, though it would be most unlike him. He turned at once and talked to the Pringles, who had arrived just behind them.

"Hullo, Aunt Diana," I said, "what a lovely dress you have." It was of black net and had little gold flowers sewn all over it. I asked the inevitable question about my shirt-front, but being used to Wolfie's, her standard was not high and she did not think it mattered.

"There's a most extraordinary woman over there," I said, "but she's awfully nice really."

"She looks kind," said Diana. "She has beautiful hair."

We drifted towards the queue that had been formed for the guests to be presented to their Excellencies and to the prince. We passed within two yards of Mrs Montaubyn, who ogled us expectantly as we approached. Wolfie, breathless, terrified and pompous, explained some musical theory to Lady Pringle, and tried to look as if he did not see her. I smiled at her but she was no longer concerned with me. As we walked past without any other recognition, the bright expectancy faded from her eyes, and she looked hurt, and rather puffy. She joined the queue a little behind us. Wolfie was so obviously ill-at-ease that Diana asked him what was the matter. He said that his collar-stud hurt him.

We had not moved far away from the prince when Mrs Montaubyn was presented and I heard her name. She was so intent on giving him a glance in which loyalty to the throne and amorous invitation were simultaneously expressed, that she stumbled as she made her curtsey, for which she had not been prepared. John Wyckham, with that readiness for any emergency which is essential to an A.D.C., put out a hand and steadied her.

"That lady is called Montaubyn," I said to Diana, who was amused.

"She suggests a name of some substance," she said.

Wolfie opened his mouth twice like a gasping fish, and then urged us to come away, as we were causing a block. For the time being we lost sight of Mrs Montaubyn.

A little later the guests crowded round a cleared space to watch the quadrille which was danced by their Excellencies and the governors of other states and their wives, who were in Melbourne for the races and for the prince's visit. As the wife of the Governor of New South Wales had sciatica, Miss Rockingham took her place. I was jammed in the crowd between Diana and the twins. A man behind us exclaimed *sotto voce*: "Great Scott! Who's that woman like Salomé?" The comparison was with Miss Maud Allan who had recently been in Melbourne, and the reference was to Miss Rockingham, whose sorrowful, sagging eyes showed no consciousness of the people watching her, nor of the grace of her own movements. In the grand chain she wove her way through the opposing line of governors, and as she took each hand she gave a slight inclination of her noble equine head, which brought it into the perfect lines of her body.

"I see Miss Rockingham's having a preliminary canter," said Anthea, fortunately before Russell Lockwood had edged his way over to join Diana. He admired her dress, saying that she looked like Persephone in mourning. Cynthia pricked up her ears at the hint of culture.

"When was Persephone in mourning?" she asked.

"In the underworld, of course. As she had no real flowers she had to make them out of gold from Pluto's mines."

"What a nice thing you've made up about my dress," said Diana. "We've been watching Miss Rockingham dance. She's wonderfully graceful."

"Yes, she is," said Russell, and he watched her for a minute or two with more than casual admiration. Anthea had the sense to say nothing more about horses.

The quadrille ended and the crowd drifted apart. Mrs Montaubyn appeared again. She looked appraisingly at the twins and said:

"Having your fun, ducks? That's right." She then moved away.

"Who on earth's that?" demanded Cynthia.

"She's called Mrs Montaubyn."

"Do you *know* her?"

"Not exactly," I said, unwilling to disclaim anyone who had been so kind.

"Then why did she call you a duck?"

"I suppose she thinks I look like one," I said.

"Your nose isn't the right shape," said Anthea.

The general dancing began and I was occupied with my youthful partners, but I noticed that in the intervals Mrs Montaubyn appeared to be circling round any group I happened to join, like some gorgeous bird of prey preparing to swoop. Or I may have been to her like the pilot fish that leads the shark, if this is true natural history. She had seen me greet Wolfie, and thought that through me she might force him to acknowledge her. He was no longer in sight, but was sitting in the men's cloakroom, mopping his head and sighing.

As I had only just begun to go to dances, I did not know a great many girls, and I had some gaps in my programme. During one of these, I was standing at the buffet eating ices, when Uncle George joined me.

"Hullo," he said, "Baba said your shirt looks as if you'd been using it to clean a motor car."

"Does it?" I asked.

151

He gave it a judicious glance. "No, only a bicycle," he said.

At this moment I became aware of a presence on my other side, and of a whiff of brandy, strong enough to assert itself above all the smells of food and drink and women's scent in the supper room. I turned and found Mrs Montaubyn beside me, and I realized that the necklace of golden vine leaves was not inappropriate, though she had not chosen it herself, but had inherited it from her mother-in-law, who had often worn it to most temperate dinner-parties given by the Archbishop of Sydney.

"Where's your girl, ducks?" she asked.

"I haven't got this dance," I said.

She nudged me and whispered huskily: "Introduce me to the gentleman."

"Oh, Uncle George," I said, "may I introduce you to Mrs Montaubyn? My uncle, Mr Langton."

"How d'you do," said George, without looking at her, and he walked away.

"Stuck-up old love-child, isn't he?" said Mrs Montaubyn. She tried to appear indifferent, but in her eyes was once more the hurt expression of a child who is puzzled to find itself the victim of social injustice. In her simplicity she had imagined that when once she had arrived at the ball, all would be gaiety and good-fellowship. Feeling myself under a cloud because of my shirt-front, and all the time haunted by a picture of Mildy, perhaps sitting up for me, while in her room the new ball-dress was spread uselessly on her bed, and being ashamed of Uncle George's behaviour, and also hating anyone not to be happy, I felt much sympathy for her.

"My uncle is not really like that," I said, "but his wife's very jealous."

She looked at me suspiciously.

"Really," I assured her. "I bet he'd much rather talk to you than to Aunt Baba. I know I jolly well would."

She pinched my cheek, and I looked round in dismay, but the music had begun again and the supper room was nearly empty.

"You're a real pal," she said. "I'd dance with you only I'm not a cradle-snatcher. My toes aren't half itching, all the same."

Mr Hemstock, taking advantage of the dancing, had come in to have a quiet guzzle.

"Look," I said. "There's a man I'd like to introduce to you."

"Which, dear?" she asked, turning. "What the gig-lamps! I'd rather die a virgin." I was both too polite and too unsophisticated to ask if this were still possible. "I must say I would like a dance," she continued. "Come on, ducks, I'll dance with you. Who cares what these stuck-up sods think?"

Although I cared a great deal what the stuck-up sods, particularly Cousin Sophie and the twins, thought, I did not see how I could properly refuse. I was full of sympathy for her loneliness and I thought that by dancing with her I might make a kind of act of reparation to Mildy. Also I thought that no gentleman could possibly refuse a request of this kind from a lady. I did not realize then, or until many years afterwards, that to be a gentleman one must put strict limits to one's chivalry, that is if one wishes to remain in the class where gentlemen are supposed most usually to be found.

And so, feeling that I was in one of those dreams where we are naked or grotesquely clad in a public street, I followed Mrs Montaubyn back to the ballroom, and with courteous diffidence allowed her to fold me to her bosom. We may be reasonably sure that this act of pure compassion was seen with delight by the holy angels, but my relatives did not share their view. Mrs Montaubyn had already attracted notice by her prowling round the ballroom, and her roving expectant eye. Baba said furiously to George: "Look at Guy dancing with that woman. He must have gone mad. Can't you keep your relations out of the gutter?" Even the more tolerant thought I was a little off my head, and the twins found further support for their assumption that I had a leaning towards older women. Like many plump people Mrs Montaubyn was light on her feet, and she responded to the slightest touch, like a racing dinghy to the tiller, so that we danced very well together, which made my behaviour appear more outrageous. Mrs Montaubyn was aware that it was a little odd of me to dance with her, and when the music stopped, from a good-natured wish to save me further embarrassment, she merely said: "Thanks, ducks. That was good-oh," and she turned on her heel to begin once more her lonely prowl.

Anthea passed me with Freddie Thorpe, and deliberately ignored me. My next dance was with Cynthia, and I was almost afraid to claim it. To my surprise she was quite pleasant. She had just begun to realize that the social exclusiveness in which she had been brought up, was not intellectual, and she took an enlightened view of my performance, though questioning me about it rather as if it were a case-history.

The twins frequently surprised me in this way. Just as I had decided that Anthea was the kinder and more naturally friendly of the two, she would administer a devastating snub, while Cynthia, as now, would be understanding. The reason was that Anthea was guided entirely by her feelings and personal convenience at the moment, while Cynthia's actions were always directed by her mind, which at this time was in process of change. Anthea thought: "He has a dirty shirt and he likes dancing with old women. How squalid!" Cynthia's first reaction was the same. Then she thought: "Am I possibly prejudiced? Is there any reason why he should not dance with old women if he likes?" And she began that train of questioning, of re-assessment so beloved of the intelligentsia, which having become an obsession, has led to the distintegration of our whole tradition of art and religion and moral values.

At the far end of the ballroom was the state drawing-room, opening into a corridor near the main entrance to the house. The ballroom had its own entrance by which people arrived for large parties. In the intervals between dances a few people found their way into this drawing-room, but for much of the time it was empty. At about eleven o'clock Russell and Diana went in there. They had met twice since he had had supper with her at Brighton, and at both meetings they had continued more or less the conversation of that evening. Whenever they met they at once burst into this animated exchange of ideas which they only broke off with the greatest reluctance. The slight stiffness and uncertainty of their first meetings had quite worn away.

"You talk," said Diana, "not as if we *were* somewhere, but as if we had to *go* somewhere. After all most people have to live in the countries where they're born, and they quite like it."

"Poor things," said Russell.

"Not at all."

"Well, let me think. I know that there's an answer to that. I've got it. Only our bodies were born in Australia. Our minds were born in Europe. Our bodies are always trying to return to our minds."

"Well then, suppose we go to Europe. Our minds want to return to our bodies in Australia. Besides, it's largely things we go to Europe for. Our people are in Australia. Perhaps you like things more than people."

"That's absolutely wrong. I came back to Australia because I like people more than things."

"And now you want to get back to the things again."

"I didn't say I did. You say it."

"You always talk of them. So do I. I want them too. But you keep showing me the moon, and saying, 'Look, isn't it wonderful? That is what you ought to have.' It's not within my reach."

"I don't see why we can't have people and things too. One makes one's love of things obvious. It's not so easy with people."

Baba looked into the room, saw them sitting there, gave no sign of recognition and went away again.

"Are we discontented with our lots?" asked Diana.

"Yes," said Russell, and they laughed.

"What have we to be discontented about? We are sitting in a very grand room—a little ugly perhaps—we both have enough to eat, warm clean clothes, and a ball every now and then."

"You don't mention the real things."

"What are they?"

"Human relationships."

Diana could not think of anything to say. She had many human relationships, whereas Russell, in spite of his poise and air of success, had none as far as she could see. She loved Wolfie and her children and with them behind her it was easy to play about with ideas, but perhaps it all meant more to Russell. Certainly she found her human relationships trying at times, and the thought of an escape to a wider life was attractive, and from her secure position, amusing to play with. Russell was trying more urgently and seriously to relate himself to some environment.

Josie came into the room with John Wyckham and introduced him to her. He had already met Russell and said: "How d'you do, sir?" This was the first time that Russell had been called "sir" by a young man on his own social level, and it gave him a shock.

"Captain Wyckham's taking me to see the house," said Josie. "He was up at Macedon. I told you about him."

"Did you, dear?" asked Diana.

"Didn't she tell you about me, Mrs von Flugel?" asked John. "I told her to, and to say that you should bring her to more dances. I spend half my time looking for her."

157

The two young people stood talking and laughing for a few minutes. Diana had a feeling how very pleasant it was to be there. She was proud of Josie, and both John and Russell were not only nice looking, but had an easy gentleness of manner, which made this brief conversation almost an illustration of that civilized life which at one time she would have thought a normal existence, but which living with Wolfie had made elusive.

"That is an exceptionally attractive young man," she said, when they had gone on.

"Yes," said Russell. "A little too self possessed, like all the aides, though very different from that other fellow."

John showed Josie various rooms in the private part of the house, and then led her into a small sitting-room, and shut the door behind him, standing with his back against it.

"Now I've got you," he said.

Josie laughed. "I'm not frightened of you," she replied.

"Why not?"

"Well, because of your face."

"What's wrong with it?"

"Nothing serious. That's why I'm not frightened."

"Has it got minor faults, then?"

"A few, I expect. Everyone has."

"You haven't."

"Yes, I have."

"I can't see them. May I look closer?"

"No. You're dreadful."

"D'you mean I look dreadful?"

"No, of course not."

158

He left the door and came over to where she was standing by a sofa.

"Sit down here," he said. "Now then, explain yourself."

"What must I explain?"

"Why you keep out of my way."

"But I don't."

"Yes, you do." He counted on his fingers. "Mrs Radcliffe's party, one; full of promise, no result. Two dances after that; full of promise, no result, that's three. Tennis Macedon, four. More tennis Macedon, five. One impromptu dance Macedon, full of promise, no result, six; tonight, seven. Seven times between November and March. It's ridiculous. I see some girls night after night. Why don't you come to more parties?"

"Because I'm not asked, I suppose."

"Who doesn't ask you? They must be mad. Why don't they ask you?"

"I don't know. Perhaps because I'm not rich."

"That's a good thing. I hate rich people."

"Then I'm glad I'm not rich."

"You do mind whether I hate you or not?"

"Of course I do. I don't want anyone to hate me."

"But me, particularly?"

"I don't know."

"You don't know anything. Where d'you go when you don't go to dances?"

"I stay at home, I suppose, or I go to Warrandyte."

"What! the place with the sad saplings? Where is it? I don't believe it exists. It's magic. It's something you disappear into. Perhaps you're not real. Perhaps you're a vision."

"I am real and it's on the river. I'm going there on Saturday for a fortnight."

"Then I won't see you at any dance for over a fortnight? Look," he said. His confident provocative manner fell from him and he looked very humble. He touched her hand gently.

The door opened and a footman put his head into the room.

"Captain Wyckham, sir," he said. "There'a drunk lady in the ballroom, and his Excellency says would you and Captain Thorpe put her out."

"Where's Captain Thorpe?" asked John, dazed.

"I can't find 'e, sir," said the footman.

"Good Heavens!" John thought a moment. "You'd better tell them to send a car round at once—to the house entrance, not the ballroom."

"Yes, Captain Wyckham, sir," said the footman, and he disappeared.

"Wait here," John said to Josie. "I'll be back in a few minutes." He went off to cope with Mrs Montaubyn.

As the night wore on this lady's control of the itching in her toes weakened in inverse ratio to her consumption of alcohol, but her contempt for the stuck-up sods grew stronger, so that partly to relieve the itching and partly as a gesture of independence, she joined the dance in an unsteady *pas seul*. By now there were few of the five hundred or so guests at the ball who were unaware of her presence, and it was at this point that Sir Roland sent for the aides-de-camp to lead her away.

I had managed to secure another dance with Cynthia, but again I was a substitute for Lord Saltash. This young man had been introduced to her by her father, and he had booked a dance, but when it came round he was sitting on the servants' staircase with Clara Bumpus. Like the other dancers we kept clear of Mrs Montaubyn, whose steering was uncertain, so that all the time there was an open space of floor round her, and when the music ended, she was standing in the centre of it with Cynthia and myself at the fringe.

Diana, after Josie and John left them, remembered Baba's glance into the drawing-room. She would ignore malicious gossip but she did not think it sensible to provoke it.

"I suppose we really ought to go back," she said. "I wonder where Wolfie is. I've hardly seen him all the evening. He must be in the supper room."

When they came into the ballroom, Russell left her and she joined Lady Pringle, who was standing near the wall watching the dancing. When the music stopped Mrs Montaubyn pulled herself up only a few yards from them. She took the open space around her as further evidence that she was being avoided, which was now true. As a boy may be mercurial and a woman Junoesque, Mrs Montaubyn was a kind of Ceres. It was this which made Wolfie find in her the peace and beauty of his native vineyards, and which had drawn me when I was rejected by the artificial, to the soothing mother-comfort of the natural world, which she shed in a soft glow. But she was, as Russell would have said, a Ceres unredeemed, and she was now nature in an angry mood. Her necklace of gold leaves had gone back-to-front and the ruby clasp gleamed like a warning light at her throat. She stared about her like some baited animal, and scanning the circle of her tormentors, as she regarded them, she saw first of all Diana, and then her eye fell on me. She beckoned me with a peremptory movement of her head, very different from the fond glances of a few hours earlier.

I hesitated, but Cynthia, either obeying the impulse of the twins to put me in any ludicrous situation, or else still preserving her attitude of detached curiosity about human behaviour, or else from the sheer impulse of *un crime gratuit* gave me a slight push towards her and said: "Go on."

Mrs Montaubyn, fuddled as she was, had recognized Diana and Lady Pringle as the women who had come into the room with Wolfie, and whom I had left her to greet. She fixed me with an eye from which all maternal concupiscence had fled, and nodding towards them, demanded:

"Who are those two?"

"They are my aunt and the wife of one of the professors," I said, an instinct warning me that it would be wiser not to give their names, but there was no escape. If alcohol had blunted some of her perceptions, it had sharpened others.

"What are their names?" she asked more threateningly, and I had to say:

"Mrs von Flugel and Lady Pringle."

"Which is which?"

"Lady Pringle is the one with the pince-nez and the green beads," I said.

She took a few unsteady steps towards them.

"Where's Dingo?" she asked Diana.

Although at times it was hard to realize that Diana

and Mildy were sisters, they had one point of resemblance, which was that when they became aware that someone was impertinent they became clothed with an unconscious and sometimes annihilating dignity. With Mildy this seemed like a gift, suddenly bestowed from on high as she showed no trace of it in her ordinary demeanour, and it made people say that she was treacherous.

Diana gave a glance at Mrs Montaubyn, said "I'm afraid I don't know anyone of that name," and went on talking to Lady Pringle. This aloofness further angered Mrs Montaubyn.

"You're Mrs von Flugel, aren't you?" she said.

"Yes," said Diana, looking at her more attentively.

Lady Pringle, seeing Mrs Montaubyn's inflamed and truculent face, with the moral cowardice of the respectable slipped away, and did not hear the rest of the conversation, if it could be called that. No one else could hear, as fortunately Mrs Montaubyn did not shout in her cups, but became quiet, foul and malevolent.

"So you think you're too good to know me."

"I've never given the matter any thought," said Diana coolly. "I have no idea who you are."

"You ask Dingo who I am. He knows all right—the dirty yellow-livered little love-child."

It flashed into Diana's mind that by Dingo she meant Wolfie, but even then she did not imagine that there could be any close connection between them. She did not move as she thought it better not to appear to be running away, possibly with this woman following her down the room.

"I think you are making a mistake," she said.

Her cool manner, her poise, the perfection of her appearance infuriated Mrs Montaubyn. She let out a stream of sibilant back-street abuse. Then she turned to go, but as she turned she swayed round on her heel to add another insult. She did this a second time, and found the rhythm of the movement agreeable. A faint smug smile appeared on her face as she swayed to and fro, with each backward turn giving a vituperative after-thought, the last of these being: "And tell Dingo not to come to bed in his socks."

At that moment John appeared. He was horrified to see this tipsy trollop obviously, if quietly, abusing Josie's mother. He went up to her and said: "May I take you to your car?"

Mrs Montaubyn, interrupted in the pleasant swaying that had kept her on her feet, stood unsteadily, and as before, when she had curtsied, John put his arm under her elbow. She stared at him, and seeing the blue lapels and the gold buttons on his tail coat, she thought he was a policeman.

"That's right, ducks," she said. "Take me to my carriage and pair, take me to my fairy coach, take me to my bloody Black Maria."

Without much difficulty John led her out through the private part of the house, to the car he had ordered. So Mrs Montaubyn, attended by an aide-de-camp, drove home in state, a height of grandeur she had not contemplated when she set out for the ball, though it is possible that as the car was very large, and had a crown instead of a number, she thought that it was a Black Maria. Her evening cloak was sent in by a footman the next morning, which made the manager of the block of flats where she lived, who had begun to question her desirability as a tenant, treat her thenceforth with particular deference. At breakfast Sir Roland, with that inaccurate justice of which Lady Eileen had complained, bullied Lord Francis for having sent a card to Mrs Montaubyn.

To return to the ballroom. The scene had happened at the beginning of an interval, but Sir Roland sent a message to the band to play another dance immediately, as he did not want people standing about gaping and discussing what had happened. Diana was bewildered at Mrs Montaubyn's assault until her last remark, when, like a violent wave breaking over her, she was struck by the knowledge that this woman was Wolfie's mistress. When John had led Mrs Montaubyn away, she found that she was trembling and she felt an urgent need to sit down. She walked along by the wall, avoiding the dancers, some of whom glanced at her with interest, back to the drawing-room.

At first she was too emotionally upset to reason about what had happened, but she was aware that it meant the disruption of her life. She had known that Wolfie was not a highly moral character, and there had been the unfortunate incidents when he had petted his pupils. She had overlooked these as she believed that they were largely paternal. He said the society of young people was necessary to his music. He liked young girls but she had believed that he treated them more or less with respect. She had been a young girl when he had married her. She was one no longer, and if they were necessary to him, she had

165

supposed she would have to put up with it, as long as it did not become too serious.

But Mrs Montaubyn was a woman of her own age, and one of unspeakable vulgarity. That Wolfie should prefer her to herself was not only a hideous insult, but argued some depravity in his character, which she had not suspected in all the twenty years of their marriage. She had only seen Mrs Montaubyn drunk and muttering filthy language, and had no idea that she could awaken poetic images of the happy autumn fields.

She sat trying to compose herself, and wondering what she could do, when Russell came into the room. He had seen the incident and Diana, looking white and shaken, escape back here, and as soon as he could, he followed her.

"What a horrible thing to happen!" he exclaimed. "Whatever made that frightful creature fix on you?"

"I don't know," said Diana, trying to smile. Then she suddenly thought that she could tell him. He was the only person she could tell. She could not tell the children. She could not tell her relatives as they were always against Wolfie and she still had that loyalty to him. She could not even tell Elsie for the same reason. But Russell was new on the scene. He was detached from it all, and yet because of their childhood's association he was not a stranger, but had an intimate knowledge of the family from the beginning.

"At least, I do know," she said. "That woman is Wolfie's mistress."

He stared at her incredulously. "She can't be."

"But she is," said Diana.

"How long have you known?"

166

"Five minutes."

"What! Did she tell you?"

"Practically."

"What are you going to do?"

"I don't know. I'm knocked a little flat." She gave a nervous laugh.

Russell sat down beside her.

"Good God!" he exclaimed. "It's insanity. I can't believe it. You—and then a woman like that. Isn't there any reason in life?"

"I don't think there's been much reason in my life," said Diana bleakly. "Or what there was has gone."

They sat in silence for a minute, then Russell turned to her abruptly and said:

"Diana, come with me."

"Where?"

"Anywhere. Away from here—from this idiotic society. We'll go back to Europe. You want to go. Come with me. We'd be happy together. Every time we meet is better than the last. The first time I saw you coming down Collins Street, before I realized who you were, I saw you were different from all the rest."

"I'm not as different as all that."

"You are to me. When I'm with you I feel quite differently alive. The crab's shell I live in falls off. I say what I like and what I feel. That was lovely getting our supper together the other evening. We could do that always."

"It would be heaven," said Diana.

"It would. You see you know it would."

"But you might become tired of getting supper with me."

"Then we'll go and dine in the Bois."

"Ah, Russell, it's too much. It's too late."

"It isn't too late."

"I've become a provincial mouse. I don't think I could lead that sort of life now."

"You're not a mouse. You're a lioness, or a panther with golden spots." He touched one of the flowers on her dress.

Diana laughed wretchedly. "I don't feel like a lioness. I feel like a mouse in a trap."

"I'm opening it for you. I'm taking the pressure from your bruised paws." He lifted her hands.

Diana laughed again. "You are kind. You are funny," she said.

"Say you'll come."

"It would be heaven."

"Then take heaven. You've had enough of the other thing—all your grace and all your gifts wasted. All the things you do taken as a matter of course—making the elementals elegant. Always giving wonderful gifts to people who take it for granted. I've seen enough myself, and I've heard."

"You've heard?"

"Perhaps I shouldn't tell you. But everyone says how badly you've been treated."

"Oh, I didn't know that." Her mind seemed to go away from him. He watched her expectantly as he felt that she was following some process of reasoning. He saw a flash of anger in her eyes and then she said: "Very well. I'll come."

"We'll have the moon—the people and the things," said Russell.

They sat side by side on the sofa for a long time without speaking. They had to assimilate the decision they had made.

Josie waited for John in the little sitting-room but when he did not return, she thought she had better go away as, if Lady Eileen or one of the household came in, it would be rather difficult to explain why she was there. On her way back she went through the state drawing-room and found Diana and Russell.

"What's the matter, Mummy?" she asked, seeing something unusual in Diana's expression.

"A horrible drunken woman was rude to your mother in the ballroom," said Russell, to save Diana the difficulty of answering.

"Oh yes," said Josie. "John went to ask her to leave. Did he?"

"Yes. I think he's taken her home."

Josie looked relieved at this explanation of his not returning.

"Where's Daddy?" she asked.

"I don't know. Will you find him darling?" said Diana. "We ought to go home."

"Must we, yet?"

"You're mother has had a rather dreadful experience," said Russell. "She's a bit shaken."

"Oh Mummy, I am sorry," said Josie and she went off to find Wolfie.

When she had gone, Diana said thoughtfully, "There are a lot of complications."

"We can cope with them."

"Yes. When can we meet? Not tomorrow—say Friday. I can't think clearly now, only of the—the elementals."

They smiled, looking into each other's eyes, almost questioningly, as if seeking mutual reassurance. They made an arrangement to meet in the National Gallery on Friday at three o'clock, and Josie came back to say she had found Wolfie.

Wolfie, who had spent nearly the whole evening in the cloakroom explaining to the attendants that he did not feel well, was given a ribald account of Mrs Montaubyn's departure by a friend who had come in to collect his hat. He added as an afterthought:

"By the way, I believe she was talking to your wife."

"Dear Goodness! Dear Gott!" exclaimed Wolfie, horrified.

On the way home he waited for Diana to give some account of what had happened, but she did not mention it, and only spoke to Josie, asking her about her partners. When they arrived home, after seeing Josie to bed, she went to her own room and moved her things into the room which formerly had been Daisy's, and made herself up a bed there. Wolfie made no comment on this. He did not dare speak first as he might give away something that Diana had not discovered. Occasionally from time to time she had moved into another room, if one of them had a cold, or in summer when she said that the east rooms were cooler.

Cousin Sophie, to ease her conscience, offered me a lift home. But she may not have felt that her conscience needed easing, as she had told me that I could ring up for a hansom to come to the ball, and if I had demurred she might have said, as I had to Mildy: "What is ten minutes' drive by yourself?"

When she dropped me at Mildy's gate and drove off with the twins, I stood, reluctant to open it. A gibbous moon had now appeared in the sky, and before me the house stood dark and silently reproachful, a casket containing unconsoled grief. My own misfortunes during the evening had made me sensitive to this. Until now, Mildy's blackmail had not come off. Her tremendous sacrificial gesture of staying away from the ball had passed unnoticed. No one, not even George or Diana, had asked where she was, and if I had not dirtied my shirt and been ridiculed for dancing with Mrs Montaubyn, I would not have thought of her either. Now I felt the emanation of her grief from the dark little house, which looked so sad and sweet in the unwholesome moonlight. On either side of the path was a crab-apple tree, and with the shadowed pseudo-medieval gables of the house beyond, the garden looked like an illumination from the very rich hours of the Duc de Berri.

While leaning on the gate I was subject to a curious experience, an enlargement of the understanding, extremely painful. I saw Mrs Montaubyn and Mildy with, as it were, the eye of God. I understood that the degradation of the former and the folly of the latter were irrelevant to their true natures, and had come upon them like physical sores, under which they were bewildered and pitiful. I felt an intolerable anguish at the thought of them. When this passed I went in to bed and slept peacefully for what was left of the night. In the morning I felt no particular sympathy for anybody; but caught the tram to the architect's office, where I continued with the working-drawings of a cement factory.

CHAPTER EIGHT

In the morning Wolfie had to go into Melbourne. He was still afraid of turning suspicion into certainty and did not even ask why Diana had moved her bed. She spent the morning moving her clothes and the rest of her personal belongings into the other room. The housemaid looked surprised, and Diana said: "There's so much traffic now on the beach road. I don't hear it on this side of the house."

Wolfie spent a miserable day and could not give the slightest attention to his work. When he set out for home he felt in great need of female consolation, but he knew that he would not receive it from Diana. He knew that something serious had happened in her mind. She was in a cold, withdrawn mood which he had never seen in her before. Hitherto, when she was annoyed with him, she had been heated rather than cold, or had shown a kind of patient logical exasperation.

He was angry with Mrs Montaubyn for going to the ball and for behaving so outrageously when there. He thought that he would find some consolation in rebuking her, and at least with her he would have the moral ascendancy. Instead of going to the railway station he went up Collins Street and rang the bell of her flat.

She was frightened and ashamed of what she had done, and her fear was worse because she could not remember exactly what she *had* done, but she had a dim recollection of having caused a scene. In the morning she felt very ill and in the evening when Wolfie called, she was a little better but she had not yet dressed and was lying in a loose and lacy tea-gown on her bed.

"Dingo!" she cried with tearful relief when she saw him at the door. He nodded his head gravely and walked before her into the flat. Mrs Montaubyn lay down again on her bed.

"You have been indiscreet," he said.

"Now, Dingo, don't you go on at me. I haven't half got a head."

"It would be wrong if I did not show you your mistake," said Wolfie.

"I know," said Mrs Montaubyn. "I lost my head. Let's forget it."

"When I have spoken, then we shall forget it. You intruded into Government House to embarrass me. That was not good."

"I had a right to be there." She showed a little truculence. "I got a ticket with a crown on it."

"Even so, it was inexpedient of you to come. If you

came you should have been temperate and modest and kept far from me. How shamed I was to see you whom I love, flushed in the skin. You spoke coarsely to my dear wife. You did not behave as one who loved me. Love is the noblest thing. All good that we have flowers from it. From my love for you has sprung glorious music. So it was holy. But what did you do? You took this precious thing which stirred beautiful music in my heart and exposed it to laughter. That was not good. For the most beautiful and the most true grow in secret."

Wolfie had instinctively taken off his coat, and now was loosening his tie, as he stood addressing her over the foot of the bed.

"They cannot be exposed without losing their essence," he continued. "What grows from them may be revealed, the music, the beauty. The flowers may blossom in the gardens of summer and waft their scent, but the roots must remain in the dark earth. What did you do with our love? You revealed what should be dark. You have injured the fibres of our roots. And as more evil grows from evil, you have spread that harm. My life is in danger. I may lose my dear home, my wife and children by your exposition."

As Wolfie spoke of this possibility, it became more real to him. Trembling with distress he hung his tie on the bed end.

"Do you not understand that life must have balance?" he demanded. "So it is music. In the orchestra are many instruments. In our lives are many people. Some are violins and some loud drums. My daughter is a sweet flute. You give me the rich notes of the clarionet, but my clarionet has played out of tune and has attempted to drown all the harmony in stridence. Will you please unfix the stud from my collar? It is tight."

He lifted his chin and bent over her while she performed this service.

"So all is suspense," he said, straightening himself. "It is through your selfish deed. You thought of yourself. That is very wrong. You thought I shall be grand Mrs Montaubyn who visits Government House. So, that would not be wrong with discretion, but with self-evidence it is folly. All is endangered. Now I have been foolish and come to you while the danger is still. But I was alone and I needed my clarionet."

Mrs Montaubyn only half understood Wolfie's rebuke, but she gathered she was forgiven, which made her ignore for the time being the fact that her old grievance remained in an aggravated form. She was further than ever from "entering society" or being introduced to Wolfie's relatives, and he had practically told her so.

"Well Dingo," she said, "I reckon I talk better English than you, but you're more educated in your mind like, and you didn't ought to take advantage of me to say things like that. If I was educated in my mind I reckon I could say some things to you too."

"I had to speak. Now it is forgiven, yes?" He lifted a tress of her hair.

When Wolfie left Mrs Montaubyn it was past dinner time and he had said that he would be home to dinner. He was in a panic. He told himself that he was mad to have let his need of a little consolation further endanger his situation. He rang up Diana from the railway station. He said

176

that he had been kept late and had missed the train. He was having a snack at a tea shop near the station. His anxiety was increased by the fact that Diana, sounding indifferent, only said: "Very well." Normally she would have said: "Oh Wolfie how tiresome! Don't have a meal at that grubby little place. Wait till you get home, and I'll ask Bessie to grill you a chop."

When Wolfie did not turn up to dinner, Diana wondered if he could possibly have left her for good. It was odd that he had said nothing last night or this morning about the incident at the ball, and that he had seemed to accept the barrier which she had raised between them. This would simplify her situation immediately, and yet the possibility gave her a curious empty feeling. Did she want to have it out with Wolfie first? It would be very painful. She should be relieved at the likelihood of avoiding a scene of recrimination and argument. And yet she was relieved when she heard his voice on the telephone, though she answered him with reserve.

She had expected him at about six o'clock, and had braced herself to introduce the subject then. When he did not come her nervous tension increased. She knew that it would be very difficult to keep Wolfie to the point. He would fling red herrings in every direction. When he had not returned by half-past six she wrote down the chief points of her arguments in case she should forget them in emotional recriminations.

Wolfie came in looking nervous, almost sidling round the door, and he gave too voluble explanations of why he was delayed.

177

Diana went with him into the music-room.

"Wolfie," she said. "That woman at the ball last night, Mrs Mont-something, is your mistress."

"Why do you say so?" asked Wolfie, turning sharply.

"She told me, more or less."

"Would she tell you such a thing?"

"She was tipsy. Besides she did tell me. I'm not making it up."

"She disgraced herself," said Wolfie loftily.

"Then you admit you know her?"

"I know her—yes."

"But you never told me you knew her."

"I do not tell you of many of my friends. You are too high for them."

"Why must you have low friends?"

"They are not low. They are humble and worthy."

"Is Mrs Thing humble and worthy? What is her name?"

"She is Mrs Montaubyn."

"She didn't look humble. She was tipsy and she used horrible language."

"I say she disgraced herself."

"She disgraced me too. I felt as if I had been splashed with mud from the gutter."

That Mrs Montaubyn, whom he had left tenderly, within the hour, should be called "mud from the gutter" distressed Wolfie.

"What do you wish?" he asked.

"I want to clear the situation."

"Do you wish me not to see her then? It will not happen again. I have rebuked her."

178

"You have seen her already?" said Diana.

Wolfie gaped for a moment, then he said: "I telephoned to her." Diana knew that he was not telling the truth, but that was a minor detail. She had wanted to keep cool, but she was angry that he should have gone so soon after last night's incident to see the woman. She did not know whether her anger was reasonable or if his visit made any difference to the situation, except that it emphasized its sordidness and made her more determined to hold to her intention.

She glanced at the piece of paper in her hand on which she had made her notes, and she thought how absurd it was to conduct a vital discussion with her husband from notes. But Wolfie touched everything with absurdity. The amusement it caused spread a protective cloud round him which preserved him from the results of his behaviour. She would no longer be amused.

"Listen," she said, her voice shaking a little, "I've never asked very much of you. I had great belief in your music. I still have. I thought that people who can create music or art of any kind should have more freedom of behaviour—that it might be necessary to their work. If a man can write a poem which brings understanding to millions of people over the centuries, we can never pay what we owe him. It was a silly romantic idea perhaps. But that's why I put up with all those girls on piano stools. I didn't like it."

"You do not speak like a lady," said Wolfie.

"Possibly not. But I expect I'm as ladylike as Mrs Mont-thing. I know you like young girls."

"Please!" said Wolfie haughtily, holding up his hand.

179

"Listen," said Diana. "I thought it was troublesome but harmless. I thought, as you said, they inspired your music. When you married me I was a young girl—" She gave a little choke. "I'm not one any longer, so I tolerated the piano stools. But this woman is something entirely different. She is my own age, and you prefer her to me—you prefer that unspeakable vulgarity ..."

At her reference to Mrs Montaubyn, Wolfie clutched his hands.

"What do you want? What do you drive at?" he demanded.

"I want the situation cleared up."

"Do you want me not to see her more?"

"That is no longer my concern. What I'm trying to say is that I don't think that I have any longer the obligation to sacrifice my life to yours."

"And then please?" said Wolfie haughtily.

"I want a divorce."

He stared at her incredulously. "A divorce!" He gave a long sarcastic artificial laugh.

"I'm serious," said Diana.

"You are serious, please? After twenty years of our happy life—suddenly—a divorce! No previous intimidation —nothing! Just five minutes, then please, divorce. I laugh again." He repeated the horrible sound.

"It's not sudden," said Diana. All the things she had endured, his complete indifference to her convenience and the requirements of a household, and the more serious but less explicit worries he had caused her, came seething into her mind and she could have poured out a flood of accusation. But she did not want to widen the issue. She clung to Mrs Montaubyn as her key to freedom. Also she knew that it is possible to love most deeply those who have asked most from us, and if she released this flood, the end might be a reconciliation she did not desire.

"You are serious to ask a divorce," said Wolfie, "because I have one extra friend. She does not harm you."

"She has insulted me in about the most public place possible, in the sight of half the people I know."

"That was a misfortune. It will not happen again. For this one thing you will wreck our life, our beautiful home where we are so happy. Do we not often laugh together? Do you not put your feet on that sofa while I play you lovely melody? Are we not proud together when our children come home to kiss us—our sweet Josie who is gentle like a flower? Is it all to be gone, blown off in a harsh tempest of jealousy? That would be wickedness."

"It is you who have wrecked it," said Diana.

"You say so. But it is not I who will do so. It is you. I do not speak of divorce. Divorce? My wife, my beautiful home, my dear children—broken apart! What shall I do in this desolation?"

"You might have thought of that earlier."

"What must I do? What do you wish? That I should give up my Mrs Montaubyn? Will that satisfy your cruel heart? Very well, I shall do so. I shall not see her again. She will be a sacrifice to your coldness!" He was now in a state of extreme agitation.

"Wolfie, do be calm," said Diana, her own voice trembling.

"I am to be calm before such horror? I am not like you. I have no cold blood."

"I'm not cold," she said, "I don't like wrecking our home. But the children are grown up. We can go our own ways."

"You are glad to leave me. Suddenly, in a day! You are treacherous."

"Is it less treacherous to carry on with that woman behind my back?"

"I do not wish to leave you," said Wolfie. "I have loved you all."

"You don't consider us."

The argument, as Diana knew it would, went right away from the point. She crumpled the paper with her notes into a ball and threw it into the wastepaper basket. Wolfie told her she was like a governess. He became reckless and boasted about Mrs Montaubyn.

"That is why I seek her," he said. "She is warm, generous, a true woman."

"You need a governess to keep you clean," said Diana bitterly. "You couldn't catch a train without one. But I'm not going to bother any more to keep you clean to go off to disreputable women."

Then, as they continued to bicker, they fell into the idiom of their private conversation, Diana using inadvertently though ironically certain witticisms which were family jokes, and something began to happen. Their entangled fibres, those long-established tendrils of feeling began to assert themselves, and they made irrelevant whatever words they flung at each other. Diana was afraid to stay with him, lest the whole discussion should dissolve in emotion. She knew that this was the only opportunity she would ever have to escape from her long exploitation into the kind of life which until now had seemed an impossible dream, and she must not risk losing it. She made a gesture of exasperation and went to her room.

The next afternoon she met Russell at the Gallery. There were not many people about and they met in one of the side galleries where they were not likely to be interrupted. Russell looked at her with affectionate concern and asked: "Any developments?" She compared his attitude with Wolfie's, whose demonstrations of affection were almost entirely a form of self-expression.

"Only in my own mind," said Diana.

"What are they?"

"I told Wolfie I wanted a divorce. He just let out a stream of emotion, pleadings and reproaches. I knew he would. I even made notes beforehand on a piece of paper, so that I could keep him to the point, as if I were going to address a public meeting. But it was useless. He won't hear of a divorce. I don't know the legal situation. Can I divorce him on the strength of that woman?"

"I'm not sure. I don't think so," said Russell. "I think he'd have to desert you as well."

"He has about as much intention of deserting me as a limpet."

"Then what are the developments in your own mind?"

"I'll tell you, but I don't know what you'll think of them. You asked me to go away with you, but you didn't say when or how. We didn't think of any details."

"No, but that's what we're to do now, isn't it?"

"Yes. Well I thought the obvious thing was for me to divorce Wolfie. But apart from the legal side I don't see how it's possible. How can you divorce someone who insists on living with you in your house? But even that isn't the real difficulty. Supposing that I could obtain the divorce, it would take a year, wouldn't it, before I was free?"

"I imagine something like that."

"What could I do for that time? I can't go on living at the Brighton house with Wolfie, and he won't leave it. I would have to take a flat somewhere. It would all be confused and ludicrous. And then if, during that year we met frequently, that might affect the divorce proceedings, mightn't it?"

"I suppose it might." Russell looked a little pale. "Do you mean you want to call it off?" he asked diffidently.

"No. Oh, no!" exclaimed Diana. "I wasn't leading up to that at all. It's only that I want to tell you everything. Please don't misunderstand anything I say. I don't think you will, that's one of your attractions." She smiled. "You can't think what a great relief it is to speak to a rational mind. This is what I want to say—the thing I hope you won't misunderstand. But you must know it if we are to be together. It is not easy for me to make this break. It is in a way chopping off a limb. I mean because of the children and all my friends and associations here; but I am ready to do it because I want to be with you. All the rest of me will be more alive, and it will be worth the limb, but I want it chopped off sharply, not slowly torn away, with each separate ligament yielding its full capacity of pain."

184

"Then?" asked Russell.

"You said would I go away with you. I don't know if its unwomanly of me to ask you—Wolfie said I was unwomanly—but did you mean now?"

"I mean as soon as you possibly could."

"I hoped you meant that; that is what I want to do. But I thought that you might want things arranged so that we remained—well—respectable."

"You don't think I would give up a year of life with you for respectability?" He meant this, but also he was enjoying the prospect of giving society a slap in the face. He had made too many sacrifices to it and he felt that this would restore his manhood. He was tired of hearing old ladies say that he was such a nice man.

"But you have so much to lose—in that way, I mean."

"My dear, I have nothing," exclaimed Russell. "You will be sacrificing real things for me. I shall only be giving up rubbish for you. I wish I could give up something real. I only gain it."

She felt a wave of gratitude to him for his apparent understanding of what it would mean to her to break with her home and family, and his complete absence of resentment at her mentioning it.

"You don't mind my being logical, or trying to be?"

"Mind it! I love your understanding and your clear-sightedness. If you only knew the relief I have in talking to you," said Russell.

"But I have the same relief with you."

"Our minds were turned out of the same mould."

"I'm sorry that there are so many complications attached to me."

"You mustn't think that. Anyhow, Andromeda wouldn't have been such a prize if she hadn't been chained to the rock." They laughed. "You are exactly what I came out to Australia to find," he added.

"Did you come to Australia to find someone?" asked Diana.

"I didn't realize it, but I believe that is what I did."

"Why did you have to come out here?"

"I've told you. I wanted someone of my own kind. I'm not really English, you see."

"We're getting back to spiritual homes. Where will ours be?"

"Where we are together," he said. She made a gesture of assent.

Opposite where they were sitting was a painting called "Winter Sunlight" by Walter Withers. It was of a little white wooden farmhouse on a grassy hill.

"That is the Australia I love," he said.

"So do I, but why?"

"I think because it's pure Australia. It's not anything else. It's innocent. If there is to be an Australian civilization it must begin with that—not with importations."

"Is that our place in history?"

He laughed and said: "It might be."

"Shall we find a little house like that? In Western Australia perhaps?"

"We couldn't live there, because when we found that we were peasants we'd try to show that we were intellectually superior to the other peasants. We're both European. For us this tie has never been cut. There are Australians whose life has begun here. They're the true Australians. They've never known anything else. Our sort are just carrying on the kind of life they brought with them. It's better to go back to the source.

"But you wanted a chef in the Fitzroy Gardens?"

"That was before I knew you properly."

"Am I a substitute for the chef?"

"You will be sometimes, I suppose," he said, chaffing her.

They talked about food for a little while, what she could cook, then Russell said:

"Listen. We must make our plans. If we're not careful we'll never get anywhere, because whenever we meet, we just talk."

"I know," said Diana. "It's because I've been gagged for years. And I love talking to you."

"I love it too, it's wonderful. We have years ahead; now we must arrange to secure them."

"Yes. I'm sorry."

"It wasn't your fault."

"I began about the chef."

She continued to explain to him her situation. She really supported her family, as Wolfie's earnings were small and he spent them exclusively on himself. Harry was now practically earning his own living on the station in Queensland where he was a jackeroo, but she might have to give him some capital later. Daisy was married to one of the Bynghams, a painter. They were dreadfully poor and she had to give her an allowance. Then Josie had to have an allowance and she could not leave Wolfie entirely dependent on his own resources. As she said this, she gave Russell an anxious glance. Would he object to all this, she asked him. She could keep about a third of her income, which would be enough she hoped to prevent her being an expense to him. He looked at her with gentle surprise.

"Why shouldn't you be an expense to me?" he asked. "I want you to be. I want to give you beautiful things. I shall be so proud of you. And we are to be married."

"Yes, but until then I thought ... I don't know. Perhaps I'm a little puritanical after all."

"Your attitude is absolutely unpuritanical," he said. "It has no trace of the righteous meanness of the puritan."

"You take all my problems as if they were your own."

"They are my own."

"The cut-off limb is not yours. You should be free."

"I don't want the amputation to hurt you."

"When I'm with you I shan't feel it. I don't feel it now, except for Josie," she added.

Josie, she thought, was her most difficult problem. The two girls loved Wolfie, as he had shown them playful affection since childhood. Daisy now had her husband, but it would be a dreadful blow to Josie if her parents were divorced, and in those days divorce was also a social cataclysm. Harry would be shocked but not hurt in the same way. All the respectability that should have been spread evenly over the family seemed to be concentrated in him, and he despised his father because he was not commonplace. She tried to think that in the long run it might be better for Josie to live with her and Russell in an orderly and civilized household in Europe, than with Wolfie sinking into more careless bohemianism. She did not like using money in this way, but she thought that she might make it a condition of the settlements that Josie was to live with her. She asked Russell if he would mind, if say in a year's time, Josie joined them in Europe.

"No, I would like that," he said. He had been very taken with Josie on the few occasions he had seen her, at the Radcliffes', at Arthur's and at the ball, and thought it would be nice to have an attractive girl about whatever house they might have.

"Well, I think we've cleared a lot of ground," said Diana with relief.

"Yes. Now we have to decide when we'll go."

"I'll have to see how long it will take me to fix things. Two or three weeks, I suppose. Would that be too soon?"

"I could go tomorrow. I'm very lightly settled here."

Diana felt that even if all her affairs were in order she could not leave so suddenly. In one way she wanted to be off as soon as possible, as she felt treacherous staying in the house and knowing her intention. But she needed a little time to accustom herself to the idea—to brace herself.

They arranged to meet again on the following Monday. Then Josie would have gone to Warrandyte and would be away a fortnight. Wolfie had shown no change of attitude. His manner was wounded and aloof, and yet she felt that all the time he had an eye on her, ready to melt in reconciliation. She told Russell that she found living under these conditions a strain and that she was going up for a week to Westhill. While there she would ask Steven to drive her over to Warrandyte to spend a day with Josie. He and Laura would want to go to see Brian's new studio. From there she would return to Brighton, say on Wednesday week. Would Saturday be a good day for them to go? She often gave the servants that night off, as Wolfie was always in Melbourne then. Josie would be away until the Monday.

They discussed the details of their departure, and finally decided that he should call for her in his car at about seven o'clock on the Saturday. She would spend the night alone at the George, a respectable hotel in St Kilda, in those days a sort of equivalent of Brown's Hotel in London, and they would set out in the morning by car for Adelaide where they would take a ship for Naples. He would book the passages.

"I wish this fortnight was over," said Diana. "It will be dreadful saying good-bye to Josie, without telling her that it's for so long."

"A year soon passes," said Russell.

"Yes. And it will be a wonderful year."

CHAPTER NINE

On the Saturday ten days after the ball, there was a dinner party at Government House in honour of the prince. Sometimes, on the invitation cards sent to Cousin Sophie were the words "and the Misses Langton" but on other occasions, as for this dinner party, only one Miss Langton was invited. When this happened the twins took it in turn. For this dinner it was Cynthia's turn, but in spite of its being such an exceptionally desirable invitation, she gave her option to Anthea because of Freddie Thorpe. Although the twins put on such a tremendous façade of assurance to the world, in the virginal privacy of their rooms they made these little adjustments and subterfuges. Before a party of cultivated people where they were anxious to sparkle, they mugged up their Rochefoucauld in a book of quotations beforehand.

Anthea was not very satisfied with her place at the dinner. Sir Roland's gold plate was magnificent but it could not be stretched to serve everyone at such a large party, and she was at the end of the table where people had to eat off mere china, though this was blue and gold Worcester. There had been some competition to sit next to her, but if she had known the reasons for it she would not have been very gratified.

Freddie went to Lord Francis and asked to take her in. Lord Francis said that he would see what he could do. Then John came and asked for the same privilege and as Lord Francis liked John better than Freddie, and as he thought Anthea too good to be married to Freddie for her money, although for a moment's idle amusement he had given him his rather misleading information about that, he put her beside John, who had only asked for the place so that he could find out more about Josie. He began by asking about myself, who he knew was Josie's first-cousin. This astonished Anthea, especially when he said that he would like to meet me again.

"That's easy enough," she said. "If you come to supper tomorrow he'll be there. He's one of our tame dogs, and always comes on Sunday night."

Beside having to eat off china, and having John instead of Freddie next to her, Anthea had another disappointment during the evening. Lord Saltash was at last introduced to her. He looked at her in terror and at the first opportunity escaped. This was because when he had been introduced to Cynthia, she, anxious to show the high standard of Australian culture, had asked him: "Do you think that if Fénelon's pupil, the duc de Bourgogne, had come to the throne, the course of French history would have been different?"

192

Anthea did not know this, and behind her façade her pride bled a little, but she had spirit, and she made jokes about the elusiveness of peers.

The chief attraction at the twins' on Sunday night, apart from the pink apples of their cheeks, were the charades which we acted after supper. If Mr Hemstock was present, these were very cultured and portrayed incidents of Greek mythology. At other times they were ribald lampoons of our relatives. Cousin Sophie and any visitors good naturedly allowed themselves to be dragged from her sitting-room to guess the word, probably something like "Archimedes" or "palinode".

On the night after the Government House dinner, when John Wyckham was present, Anthea had thought out a rather indelicate theme which she called "putting salt on the tail of Lord Potash". It described the efforts of Cousin Edward to lure a young peer into the bower of his beautiful daughters. I was forced by the twins, much against my will, to act the part of their father. Unfortunately, as when I danced with Mrs Montaubyn, I did it very well. When the charade was over, Cousin Sophie said severely:

"Am I to understand, Guy, that you were impersonating your host?"

I do not know whether Cousin Sophie had any Teutonic blood, but this was another example of inexact justice. She thought it in very bad taste for the twins in the presence of an A.D.C. to do a charade illustrating their wish to acquire aristocratic English husbands, but she did not want to emphasize it by reproving them, so she turned on me. As it happened John was much too modest to compare himself with a member of the House of Lords, and he thought the charade very funny, which it was.

The twins did not own up that they had forced me into the part, not from cowardice, but because they thought the injustice of Cousin Sophie's rebuke amusing. I stood revealed as a horrible little cad, and imagining it would be unforgivable to put the blame on others, my chivalry again led me into disgrace.

John, who knew what had happened, came over to me and said with great friendliness:

"When are you coming to show me the way to Warrandyte?"

My face was suffused with gratitude, and I exclaimed:

"Oh, I can go any day. At least any Saturday."

The twins laughed at my humiliation at having to admit that I went to the city every day, though Cousin Edward had to do the same, whereas neither my father nor any of my uncles had ever been into an office in their lives, unless it was to ask a lawyer to arrange a mortgage. But the twins never bothered about their own plate-glass windows when they heaved their bricks.

"We can show you the way," said Anthea. "You needn't wait till Saturday."

"Saturday would be the most convenient day for me," said John. This did not prevent the twins from attaching themselves to the excursion, which they imagined, as I did, was simply to satisfy John's curiosity about "the sad saplings" mentioned by Lady Pringle. He gave this impression. He did not appear very pleased at having to include the twins.

Mildy had three attitudes, any of which she might adopt if I were going out without her. One was of wounded and bitter reproach, one of melancholy resignation, when she said "I suppose I mustn't be jealous of the twins". The third, also of resignation, but cheerful and almost jocular, was used on the few occasions when I went out with another young man. "I'll stay in and rest my old bones," she would say, "while you two boys go and enjoy yourselves."

On Saturday John was to call for me and then go on to collect the twins. Before he arrived Mildy said: "I shan't mind so much today as I shan't actually *see* you go off with the twins. I must say I rather like Cynthia. She is much less offhand in her manner than Anthea." She made an exception of Cynthia, as she saw that she did not particularly want to be smart, and that she had intellectual tastes which she was sure before long would make her dowdy, unattractive and even forbidding.

Mildy did not come to the gate to see us off as she was nervous of meeting anyone from Government House, but she waved merrily from the window.

While driving from Mildy's house to the twins', John said: "Your cousins are very amusing but rather frightening. They terrified Saltash."

"I thought it was the other way round."

"Isn't he your cousin too?"

"Not mine, only the twins'."

"Is he Mrs von Flugel's cousin?"

"No."

"Are all your relatives so cultured?"

"They all do charades, but not with Greek words, and Aunt Diana can't be rude in French."

"I'm glad of that," he said laughing. "Have the Flugels a place at Warrandyte?" he asked more diffidently.

"Oh no. My brother has a studio there. We'll go to tea there. I've told him that we are coming. He always has rows with the twins. It'll be rather amusing."

"Good Heavens! The twins in battle array must be terrific."

"Brian beats them."

"He must be a bit of a warrior."

"Oh no, he's an artist."

"I thought Miss von Flugel said she stayed sometimes at Warrandyte," said John. "Where would that be?"

"She stays with a Miss Felpham. She's awfully kind. She's a painter too. Josie's jolly nice," I said, "I think you'll like her."

"Oh, yes," said John noncommittally, and he appeared to lose interest in the subject.

It was odd how often the twins interfered with the comfort of my means of transport. One might almost have believed that some supernatural influence was responsible, as they did not do it intentionally. It began to function when they came out to the car, but more strongly, later in the afternoon. John's car just had room for two beside the driver, and a small hard dickey-seat opening at the back. If the twins had not invited themselves I should have travelled in comfort beside John. As it was, I bounced about on the hard little seat clutching my hat with one hand, and the iron support with the other. Although I was only twenty, and owing to the unusual seclusion of my upbringing appeared and behaved as if I were a good deal younger, if I had not worn a hat on a country excursion, the twins would have thought it wildly eccentric, and Cousin Sophie would have thought it clear evidence of immorality. The white dust scurried up from the road behind us and settled in a fine powdered film on my clothes. I could not take any part in the conversation, of which bright fragments were blown back to me. As we approached Warrandyte we drove through some barren, yellow clay country where the gum-trees had been felled and the stumps had sprouted with new blue-leaved growth.

"Are those the sad saplings?" asked John.

"Oh no. They're much sadder at Warrandyte," said Anthea. "Those are rather jaunty."

Brian had bought an orchard with a paddock and a wood, about five acres altogether, which lay in a small valley. The orchard was divided from the paddock by a stream, dry at this time of year, and the wood was beyond the paddock. He had built his studio-cottage on the far slope. It was of wattle and daub, all local material. It had a terrace with a pergola to make a ceiling of grape vines, but they were only just planted. As we alighted from the car, the twins' high-powered English voices burst with an effect almost of violence on the limpid Australian air, and warned Brian, two hundred yards away, that we had arrived.

"We've come to see the Latin Quarter of the Bush," said Cynthia as we reached the terrace where Brian came out to greet us. After introducing John, I followed him indoors to help him bring out the tea.

"You didn't tell me you were bringing the twins," he grumbled.

"They are a confounded extension," I said.

"Who's that fellow? Did you say 'Captain'?"

"Yes. He's an A.D.C."

"Good God! What a party!"

"He's awfully nice, really. You wouldn't think he was a soldier."

This attitude towards soldiers was fairly usual then, and had nothing to do with being politically "left". The most extreme Tories like Arthur would say: "Soldiers are notoriously stupid." Unless they were young and handsome aides-de-camp, who had a social cachet, they were never invited by Cousin Sophie, and if by chance some travelling English relative with military rank had to be asked to dine, the moment the door closed behind him, the twins would pretend to faint with the exhaustion of their boredom. The English relative, on the other hand, when he arrived home would say: "Australia isn't as crude as people think. I went to one or two quite possible houses in Melbourne. I had a very enjoyable dinner with Edward Langton. We had a Chateau Yquem with the pudding and his wife is a lady, though his fillies need a touch of the whip."

"He doesn't look bad," Brian admitted, but he disliked aides-de-camp as a species, thinking them smug and brainless, and it is true that Freddie Thorpe was a more typical specimen than John. He also thought Melbourne society ludicrous.

"Parties are fun," I objected.

"Yes, but they don't have them for fun. They have them for competition. Only a half-wit thinks he's important because he's been to a party."

While we had tea on the little terrace the twins made a rather unfavourable assessment of the merits of Brian's cottage. Cynthia thought it too picturesque. After tea we went into the studio to look at the paintings.

"You didn't invent that method," said Cynthia. "Why don't you experiment with more interesting ways of using paint?"

It was surprising how soon in that remote place she had caught the atmosphere which was to corrode the soul of her generation.

"You didn't invent shoes," said Brian rudely, "but you don't go barefoot."

John began to fidget. He led me ostensibly to look at a picture at the other end of the large studio, but then he said: "I'd like to go and look at those saplings." When I was about to tell Brian, he stopped me.

"No. Don't interrupt them," he said. Brian and the twins were now in the throes of an intellectual slanging match, and when John and I went out they took no notice.

At the back of the studio a flight of steps, cut in the earth, led into the wood.

"There are the saplings," I said. "D'you think they look very sad?"

John gave them a brief glance. "Where is Miss Felpham's cottage?" he asked.

"Just over there. We can walk to it along that track if you like. It won't take five minutes."

"I'd like to do that. I haven't seen this sort of place before. Only sheep stations. It's very pretty here, like something in Hans Andersen."

We set out along the narrow track through the wood. I went first to show the way. We had not gone fifty yards when I saw Josie coming towards us. She was wearing a linen dress, an old straw hat, and was carrying a pot plant and a garden fork.

"Here's Josie," I said, and forgetting that I had seen them together before, I added, "I'll introduce you."

They took no notice of my introduction but stared at each other, Josie with surprise, and John with a sudden liveliness in his eyes. They did not even exchange any conventional greeting. John said:

"Where are you going with that plant?"

"It's a daphne," said Josie. "Miss Felpham has given it to Brian. I'm going to plant it." She looked a little nervous and amused.

"I'll help you. No, we won't do that yet." He turned to me. "Would you be a good chap and take this to your brother?" He took the pot from Josie and handed it to me. "And this too." He gave me the fork. "I have a slight argument to finish with your cousin."

Josie appeared to acquiesce in this, so I took the pot and the fork back to the studio.

"Now then," said John when they were alone. "Will you please explain yourself?"

"What must I explain this time?"

"Why you didn't wait where I put you?"

"I didn't have to," said Josie, "I'm not a sentry or Casabianca. You didn't come back."

"I had to take the drunk lady home. You knew that."

"I didn't know that you had to take her home. I thought that you just had to put her out in the garden."

"What? To cool off?"

"Something like that, I suppose. And I thought someone might come in and find me there alone."

"They'd be jolly lucky if they did," said John.

"You're awful."

"You keep saying that. Do you really think so?"

"Was the drunk lady very difficult?"

"No. I just heaved her into a car, dumped her on her doorstep, and rushed back, but you'd flown. If you knew the trouble you'd caused me you wouldn't be so pleased with yourself."

"I'm not a bit pleased with myself."

"Well, you look it."

"What trouble did I cause you?"

"I had to sit for a whole dinner beside Anthea—on the cultural qui vive for an hour and a half. The mental strain was terrible."

"What did you do that for?"

"To find out how I could meet your cousin, the chap who's just taken in the pot. Then I had to do charades with the twins the next night, because he would be there."

"Why did you want to meet him, particularly?"

"So that I would have an excuse to come up here to find you. So you see what I've gone through."

"Thank you," said Josie.

"Is that all you can say?"

"What should I say?"

"You should say you are sorry for causing me so much anxiety and trouble."

"But I'm not."

"Good Heavens!"

"It's very nice to meet you here, out in the fresh air."

"Then you're glad you've met me."

"You shouldn't force me to make extreme statements."

"I don't call that extreme."

"What do you call extreme?"

"I'll tell you when I've got a bit more confidence," said John.

"I hope you don't get too much, because you've got a good deal already."

"D'you think I'm rude?" he asked, a little crestfallen.

"No. You make me laugh."

"That's not very polite."

"I don't mean at you. I mean when I think about you."

He was quiet for a moment. "I laugh when I think about you, too. But not always. Sometimes I feel awfully upset."

"Why?"

"Because I'm afraid it'll be a long time till I see you, and that before then you'll meet someone else who makes you laugh more than I do."

"Don't you want me to laugh?" asked Josie a little shyly.

"Not about anyone else—not in the way you laugh about me. That is, if it's in the same way that I laugh when I think about you. I do it because I suddenly feel terribly happy—because you are alive. But I don't suppose that's

202

why you laugh about me. I suppose it's because you think I'm a bit of a joke."

Josie didn't answer.

"Do you remember what I was saying when I had to go to the drunk lady?" he asked.

"Yes," she said quietly.

"I was saying—I was just going to say, I love you."

She looked up at him. Her eyes were full of light, and she was like the flower opening in the sun. He kissed her quickly, several times on both sides of her face. Then they stood back and looked at each other. They laughed and she went into his arms.

They walked about in the saplings for a long time. John said: "You understand that we're to be married?" Josie said: "I gathered you had some such idea." They made a few arrangements. Josie had intended to return to Melbourne on Monday, but John wanted her to come back with him this afternoon. He would drive her to Brighton and he would ask her parents' permission.

"I can't bear any further suspense," he said, and asked anxiously:

"Do you think they'll object?"

"Oh no! They'll be delighted," said Josie.

"I can't see why," said John.

When I returned to the studio about an hour earlier, Brian was saying angrily:

"You mean that I am to abandon every natural talent I have, and all the skill I've acquired through infernally hard work, and every perception of the natural world, to paint like a donkey's tail dipped in whitewash! I've seen the dirty little advocates of that sort of art, soaked in absinthe in the Boul' St Germain."

Cynthia looked pained but not convinced.

"We don't live in the world of the Old Masters," she said.

"Their world is eternal. It's the natural world."

"Perhaps the time has come for us to rise above the natural," said Cynthia.

"How are we going to do that—by fitting ourselves with tin entrails?" asked Brian brutally.

I was horrified at this, as I took the twins at their own and Cousin Sophie's valuation, and thought they should be treated in certain ways with reverence. To distract attention I said:

"Miss Felpham sent you this pot of daphne."

"Where's Captain Wyckham?" asked Anthea.

"He's gone to look at the jolly old saplings."

"I should have thought one sapling was enough."

"He's with Josie. I think they've gone back to Miss Felpham's."

"Let's join them," said Anthea, implying that the air of the studio where they had invited themselves, was heated and stale.

"Would you mind putting the plant out on the terrace?" Brian said, his politeness to his younger brother emphasizing the appalling rudeness he had shown to Cynthia. "I'll see to it later."

We left him in the studio, squeezing out paint, and went round by the road to Miss Felpham's cottage. Cynthia talked about "significant form", a phrase she had discovered in an English review. Anthea looked irritated. These rifts in the twins' combined front appeared occasionally to those who knew them intimately.

John and Josie had not arrived back at Miss Felpham's. The latter, a kind, intelligent spinster of about forty-five, welcomed us with great pleasure and invited us into her orchard to eat peaches. Cynthia continued to talk about significant form. Miss Felpham, a good and sensitive painter, who felt herself a little out of the world, listened with respectful attention, not knowing how flimsy was the source of Cynthia's knowledge. Anthea walked a little further up the orchard and I followed her.

"I hate culture," she said.

"You?" I exclaimed. "Why, you're awfully cultured. You know about Molière and everybody."

"Fat lot of good it'll do me," she said. "I don't want to be a governess and I don't want to marry Mr Hemstock."

"It would certainly be very awkward with his bottle," I agreed.

"What? He doesn't drink, does he?"

"I don't know," I stammered, realizing that my remark had contained one of the candid improprieties of innocence.

"Anyhow, if you're cultured, you can move in any society," I said, priggishly.

"Rot," said Anthea. "The best people haven't got a brain in their heads. Give me money and fun, any day, and you can have Molière."

This brief conversation gave me a comfortable feeling with her and I had the illusion, dispelled within half an hour, that she was a much more good-natured and human girl than Cynthia. She began to fuss about the time. She wanted to return early as she was going to a small dance, ending at midnight, where she knew Freddie Thorpe would be present. It was his influence which had changed her attitude to culture.

When we left to return to the studio Miss Felpham said to Cynthia: "You must come again and explain your theory more fully. I can see that I am becoming rusty up here."

"It's very charming rust, the colour of your zinnias and your ripe peaches," said Anthea, automatically, at the moment of departure, turning on the gracious manner which Cousin Sophie had taught her to use to people who might be thought humbler than herself.

As we came up the slope to Brian's cottage we saw John and Josie, bent over the daphne which they had planted below the rough stone wall of the terrace. They straightened themselves as we arrived. Their hands were earthy but their eyes were lively and beautiful.

"Hullo," said Josie to the twins.

"Where's Brian?" asked Anthea. "We must go."

"He's in the studio, painting."

We went in to find him giving the last touches to a sketch. With that lyrical delicacy of which he was a master, he had painted a woodland glade, in the middle of which was a distorted, angular couple embracing.

"I've been following your advice," he said, handing it to Cynthia. "Here's some paint used in a new way."

"The figures are interesting," said Cynthia. "The

background is pretty, but it's all been done before and far better than you can ever do it."

Josie looked at the sketch. "Oh how horrible!" she exclaimed. "Whatever made you do such a beastly thing?"

Everyone was surprised at the passionate feeling in her voice. Brian looked at her, then at John.

"You are right," he said. He dropped the sketch on the floor, face up, and screwed his heel on the wet paint.

"That was probably the last thing you'll ever do," said Cynthia.

"You don't say that because you think it," Brian replied. "I'm twenty-three. You can have no idea of what I'll do. You only say it to treat me for conceit."

There was too much feeling in the room, and Anthea repeated that we must go.

"Josie is coming with us," said John. "We just have to collect her things from Miss Felpham's. It won't take ten minutes."

"How can she? There's no room," said Anthea.

"I'm afraid that one of you will have to sit in the back with Guy."

"Why can't Josie sit in the dickey?"

"We must divide the relations," said John politely, but there was a glint in his eye. He and Josie went down through the paddock and up through the orchard to his car.

"This is absurd," said Anthea crossly. "Who's going to sit in the back? I shan't. He should have said that he was going to bring her back when he asked us." She turned to me. "Can't you stay the night?"

"I told Aunt Mildy I'd be back."

"Oh, you mustn't fail your aunt, of course. You could walk to Ringwood and take the train." It was seven miles to Ringwood.

"Still one of us would have to sit in the back," said Cynthia. She had suddenly become quiet and kind and reasonable. "It's a lovely evening, I'll walk to Ringwood with Guy."

Although I was not consulted about this arrangement, I was delighted at it. Owing to the limited number of my girl friends it appeared almost miraculous that I should be about to walk seven miles through the summer evening alone with a girl, especially with one of the twins. I thought anything might happen.

We walked across the valley to the road, and Brian, now that his guests were departing, became very polite, and the twins themselves put on their gracious veneer.

The car, trailing clouds of white dust, came round a bend in the road. When they pulled up John signed to Josie to move closer to him, and Anthea got in at the far side.

John asked me: "Are you sure you're all right?" When I said I was, he shook hands with me over the side of the car, and said: "Thank you very much for showing me the way."

Josie said to Brian: "Water the daphne and give it plenty of leaf mould. If you look after it, it may bloom this year and you'll get delicious whiffs when you're sitting outside having your tea."

"You're a delicious whiff, yourself," said Brian, smiling at her.

We all laughed, and John, looking sideways at Josie, let in the gear.

Cynthia and I waited until the dust had settled before following on foot. Brian shook hands with us, and when Cynthia's back was turned he gave me a slow wink before putting his hands in his pockets and strolling back through his orchard, glowing and russet in the evening light.

We walked down the hill, crossed the river on the black wooden bridge and turned towards Ringwood. Cynthia was subdued and did not speak much at first. She recognized, when Brian told her she was treating him for conceit, that it was true. She had trained herself to accept everything she believed to be true, and although at times her intellect impaired her human kindness, on this occasion it had brought it into play. The process was a little painful and it took her about half an hour to recover her usual poise, like a sea-anemone, slowly putting out its tentacles, after a boy has poked it with his finger.

The river was on our left, and the wooded hills rose on either side. At intervals, in a little clearing was a white-washed cottage with a bark chimney, built in the early days by prospectors for gold, who believed it could be found in the sands in the river.

"This is like Siegfried's journey to the Rhine," I said, with my urge to relate my own experience to a parallel glowing with romance and music.

"I don't see much resemblance," said Cynthia.

"We are walking between woods."

"That's not enough reason to drag in Siegfried."

"That's the Rhine," I said, nodding towards the Yarra, "and it's gold has been stolen. Listen, can't you hear the Rhine maidens?"

"No," said Cynthia.

We walked on in silence. The sun was setting and the tops of the wooded hills were greenish bronze, but below the line of light everything was sunk in purple mists. Here I was, alone with a girl in this lovely place. I thought we should automatically break through into some experience of magic beauty, but did not know how it would happen. Vaguely I felt that Cynthia's intellect was the obstacle, and I was rather cross. Perhaps Cynthia herself thought that we were not making much use of our situation, for when we were crossing over a gully, a deep mysterious and aromatic hollow, screened from the road by a wooden fence, she climbed up on the rail and said:

"Tell me a story."

"What about?" I asked, sitting beside her.

"Anything unusual."

"About a girl and a young man?"

"That's very usual."

"This girl wasn't."

"Why not?"

"She'd lost her head."

"That's not unusual. Anyhow, how did she lose it?"

"It was knocked off."

"Is that the end of the story?"

"Not at all."

"But the girl was dead."

"This one wasn't. She walked about without her head."

210

"*Il n'était que le premier pas qui coutait,*" said Cynthia, unable to resist such an opportunity. As I did not understand she continued: "How could she if she was dead? You are not suspending my disbelief."

"She was a nymph and it was magic."

"Well, I don't mind a bit of magic on a summer night," she said, almost with Anthea's intonation. "Go on."

"All the young chaps ran after her."

"Why?"

"Because she hadn't got a head."

"That doesn't seem very sensible."

"It was very sensible. She couldn't tell them to go away and it didn't matter if her face was not very pretty."

"But she hadn't got a face."

"I mean the idea of her face."

"I doubt if the idea of a face could exist in that way."

"Of course it could. I can imagine all sorts of faces that haven't got bodies. Anyhow, she had to agree with everything they said. She couldn't answer them back or boss them, so each of the young chaps in that village took her for walks on successive Saturday nights."

"They must have been very bored," said Cynthia coldly, "and very stupid to go with anyone so brainless."

"It was very agreeable. And though she was brainless she had strong arms and could pull the chaps' hair if they went too far. In fact when they told their friends in other villages, those chaps knocked all the girls' heads off too, and there were no lovers' quarrels in all that country, just peaceful walks on Saturday nights."

"Is that the end of it?"

211

"No, because the goddesses were furious when they saw all the girls going about without heads, and they blamed the first girl for setting the fashion, and they turned her into stone, just as she was grabbing a chap's hair, and he was turned into stone too."

"I don't think much of that story," said Cynthia, and she got down from the fence.

That was the nearest I ever came to a flirtation with one of the twins.

When I reached home, and told Mildy that I had walked all the way from Warrandyte to Ringwood, alone with Cynthia, mostly in the dark, she was aghast. She asked me questions about the time we had taken, to discover what opportunities we might have had for dalliance.

"Did you stop to rest on the way?" she asked, looking intently into my eyes.

"We sat on a fence for five minutes," I said.

She looked both relieved and disappointed, and during the evening I felt her eyes resting on me with suspicion and envy, while her imagination conjured up scenes of wantonness on the Ringwood road.

"Have you a headache?" she asked.

CHAPTER TEN

Diana was waiting in the house at Brighton for Russell to call for her. She felt wretched. She had let the two servants go out after tea, and at six o'clock Wolfie went to Melbourne, ostensibly to a "Saturday night reunion of musicians", a fixture for many years, which she now realized had been a cover for visits to Mrs Montaubyn or her precursors. She half hoped that tonight he *was* going to see her, as it would give stronger justification to her own departure, but she was not cheered by the possibility.

He came to tell her that he was leaving. He did not look smart, but as usual like a village boy who has tidied himself up under protest to go to Sunday School. Normally she supervised his dressing, fixing his collar, pulling his coat straight, and brushing him down; but since the ball she had left him to himself, and he showed signs of her neglect.

A week or so earlier she had lent him a pound as he was setting out on one of these jaunts. He now took a handful of coins from his pocket and picked out from them the only sovereign. He handed it to her saying: "Here is the pound I borrowed from you."

It was unusual for him to return money he had borrowed from her, unless she asked for it, which she only did in an emergency. Clearly he wanted to end their strained relations and to be reconciled. Perhaps, after all, he was not going to Mrs Montaubyn, as, if he gave her the pound it would only leave him a few shillings, not enough to take her out to dinner. She felt confused and ashamed and did not want to take anything from him even though it was her own.

"Oh, don't give it to me now," she said.

"I may have it?" asked Wolfie, looking pleased, both at keeping the money and at a sign that Diana was relenting. This sudden change from an air of pompous guilt to naive pleasure was so characteristic of him that it made vivid in a moment all the long years of their life together, and the anger which she had been laboriously sustaining, became dangerously weak. She thought: "This may be the last time I'll see him," and she went with him to the door, and then, impulsively, she kissed him.

She turned into the empty house which she was to leave in an hour. She had been quietly packing in her room since tea-time. She was not taking many things. The clothes she left behind could be given away. She had written a note for Wolfie and a letter to Josie, and she had nothing to do but wait.

She thought she had been idiotic to kiss Wolfie, and yet she could not feel sorry that she had done so. It would make him think that she was utterly treacherous, when he came back and found her gone. Josie too must think her treacherous, when she found that she had said good-bye to her as if for four days, when it was for a year or perhaps longer. For twenty years she had been the strength and stay of the family. They would be bewildered to find her gone. She felt as if she had arranged to commit a murder.

She went round the house saying good-bye to the different rooms, and in every one she was overwhelmed with memories. She went into Josie's room, and into Daisy's and again felt in them all the love and amusement and anxiety the children had given her. In an hour it would be ended for ever. "I can't go," she told herself. She certainly would not be able to go, she thought, if she continued to give way to these feelings, and she returned to the drawing-room where she lighted a jet in the chandelier, and sat down to reason with herself.

"What will happen if I don't go?" she thought. "Wolfie will never change. People will go on pitying me, Josie may marry soon, and I shall be here alone. Russell offers me the most wonderful life, the sort of life I have always wanted. We get on perfectly together. It would be outrageous to fail him after all his kindness." She repeated these arguments to herself, but they did not change her feelings. "It has been arranged too suddenly," she thought. "I really need more time to become used to the idea." But it was she who had wanted to make the sharp break. "I don't know myself," she thought, and her wretchedness came near to panic.

She could not sit still, and she began to walk about the darkening house again. The walls seemed to reproach her, to send out emanations they had absorbed from the children's lives. All their laughter and their pains seemed to have been absorbed into their surroundings, into the things they used.

The house was full of ghosts, but ghosts of the living, and of the living who were most dear to her. They poured on her, as on myself at Westhill forty years later, with full hands, their treasures and their calamities. It was not, as it has been claimed a house should be, a machine to live in. It was a material substance that absorbed life from the lives and feelings of those who lived in it, and which gave out again to console them for vanished time, the life that it had absorbed. When she left it, she would cut her life in half, and with a sense of desperation, she went from room to room, choosing various small objects to take with her so that her loss would not be absolute. From Josie's room she took a small watercolour of Westhill. It was really Josie's but when she found it had gone, she would know, Diana hoped, that the theft was an act of love. She thought of taking the reputed Parmigiano from the drawing-room, but it might be valuable, and she thought it might be a mean thing to do. There had always been speculations and jokes about it, and she could imagine their dismay, not at its loss, but at some kind of repudiation of one of those many trivial causes of amusement which together added so much to the substance of family affection, when they came in and said: "Mummy's taken the Old Master."

From Wolfie's room she took a blue vase which Harry had given her at Christmas when he was twelve, and she collected photographs of the children from various parts of the house. She took a Florentine pottery bowl which her mother had brought back from Europe for her when she was a child. It was of no value and she would probably be going where she could buy hundreds of such things, but she had known it nearly all her life and it would help to give her a feeling of continuity. She put these things on her bed and looked at the pitiful array; all the material evidence she would have of her past life.

She tried to encourage herself by feeling angry with Wolfie, but she did not feel angry, even when she thought of Mrs Montaubyn. Then she thought of Russell, all his attractive qualities and his kindness, but they seemed irrelevant. She could only think of the children and of her life being cut in half.

While she was standing there looking in desperation at the photographs and the blue vase, the watercolour and the pottery bowl, she heard a motor car stop at the gate. She could not let Russell see these things, and she opened one of her cases and managed to squeeze them in. Then she looked in the glass, and surprised at her tragic face, she tried to smile. The bell jangled down in the back passage, and feeling that she was going to execution, she went to open the door.

Josie and John were standing there. He was carrying her suitcase.

She stared at them for a moment, unable to speak.

"You do look surprised, Mummy," said Josie.

"I thought you were not coming till Monday," Diana explained at last.

"I wasn't but something's happened."

"Nothing unfortunate?"

John and Josie laughed. "We don't think so," she said.

Diana looked at him. "Aren't you—er—"

"Captain Wyckham," said Josie.

"Of course. Won't you come in?" She gave this invitation but she stood uncertainly in the doorway. She wondered how soon she could get rid of him. But then Josie would still be here. Would she catch Russell if she rang up immediately? The situation was appalling.

"I'd like to come in if I may," said John apologetically, feeling that he was not very welcome.

"Did you drive Josie down?" asked Diana, saying anything to give herself time to think. "That was kind of you."

"Yes. Josie and I have something to tell you."

Diana had been so completely submerged in her own feelings and her situation, that for a moment she thought that they must somehow have discovered her intention, and have come to prevent her. But what had this young man to do with it?

"Won't you come in?" she repeated and led them into the drawing-room. She stood under the bleak light of the solitary gas jet and turned to hear what John had to say.

"Aren't you well, Mummy?" asked Josie.

"I'm perfectly well, darling." Diana tried to smile reassuringly. "I was only startled to see you there. You must forgive me," she said to John.

"I hope you'll forgive me, Mrs von Flugel," he replied.

"Why, what have you done?"

"I've asked Josie to marry me."

"Oh! Do sit down." She felt her knees weaken, and did so herself.

"Aren't you pleased?" asked Josie, a little plaintively.

Diana put her hand to her head.

"Yes, I think I will be. I'm sure I will be. It's rather much to take in. I had no idea ... I don't really know you," she said to John.

"He's awfully nice," said Josie. John moved close to her and took her hand.

"I'm sure he is." She felt that if she were not careful she might burst into hysterical laughter. Supposing Russell walked in at this moment? In fact he was certain to, within a quarter of an hour. Then when she thought of him, she realized that it would not matter at all, as she knew that she could rely on him in any situation. He would pretend that he had been driving past and had looked in on the chance of finding someone at home. And she would have a respite. There would be arrangements to make. She would have time to accustom herself to the idea of her situation.

As this dawned on her she felt a tremendous surge of relief, and she was able to give the two young people her entire affectionate interest.

"Now you must tell me everything," she said, "or tell me a little. I don't know anything. I didn't know you knew each other."

"I introduced you at Government House," said Josie. "I told you I knew him."

219

"Yes, so you did. You're one of the A.D.C.s," Diana said to John. "I suppose I ought to ask you questions, but I don't know where to begin. When my other daughter was married, it was to a young man she'd known as a child. He didn't ask our permission. He just married her. I couldn't reasonably object, as I married against my own parents' wishes, and I've never regretted …" She stopped abruptly. She had noticed two or three times in the last fortnight that if she was not careful, her mind continued to flow along the channels it had been accustomed to, before she discovered Wolfie's infidelity. She went on: "I suppose I ought to ask you if you can keep her."

"I haven't any money," said John, looking anxious.

"None at all?" asked Diana, kindly but equally anxiously. She did not want Josie to trail homeless round the world as the wife of a soldier living on his pay. It turned out however that John had an allowance from his parents, from whom he would inherit an estate of four thousand acres in Devonshire, with a house called Wootton Speke built in the fifteenth century, which had been in the possession of his family since the seventeenth. His father had thought that he should go into the army till he married, but he did not like it very much. When he married he was to have a farm and take part in the management of the estate.

"I don't call that having no money," said Diana.

"Yes, but we won't have much until I inherit, and I hope that will be years and years ahead. You would like my father."

Diana smiled at him and said to Josie: "You go and tidy yourself while I ask Captain Wyckham some more questions."

"He's John," said Josie, and she went out of the room.

"I must apologize," said Diana. "When you arrived I was worried about something—a personal matter, quite irrelevant, but at first I could hardly take in what you were saying. Apart from what you have told me I know nothing about you. It's rather strange to agree immediately to one's daughter marrying a young man whom one doesn't know. But I may tell you that I do like what I have seen of you, and that from our point of view you are an extremely desirable *parti*. In Australia so few of the people of our sort have much money nowadays. My other son-in-law is very nice, but he's penniless. I'd rather have that than a rich boor, but naturally I don't want my daughters to starve. What I most want to be sure of is that you really love Josie and that you will do your best to make her happy."

"I wanted to marry Josie the first minute I saw her," said John. "I knew I must. It was at that party at the Radcliffes' when she stood by the door and looked surprised, as if she had just come into the world. I wanted to put out my hand and touch her. I've been looking for her ever since, but she's so elusive. I saw her a few times up at Macedon and I was going to ask her to marry me at the ball, but I was called away to remove that awful woman. Then I ran her to earth at Warrandyte this afternoon."

"But what d'you think your parents will say? They might not like your marrying an unknown girl from the other side of the world."

"They'll be thrilled when they see Josie. This afternoon when I met her she was carrying a pot plant to give to your

221

nephew. We planted it together and she knew all about how to do it. My parents will love that. When I saw her carrying that pot of daphne I knew I couldn't live a minute longer without her. And I'd rather cut off my head than not make her happy," he added, with a touch of indignation. "I only hope I can." His eyes were moist.

"I'm sure you will," said Diana gently.

Josie came back into the room. "Is everything all right?" she asked.

"It's more than all right," said Diana. She took Josie in her arms and kissed her and the warmth of her affection was due not only to pleasure in her happiness, but to the fact that she had been so surprisingly restored to her for a little longer.

The bell jangled again in the kitchen passage, and Diana went towards the door. "Isn't Maggie in?" asked Josie.

"No. They're both out. I'll go," said Diana.

When she opened the front door, Russell, as she expected, was standing there.

"Is somebody here?" he asked quietly. "There's a car at the gate."

"Yes. It's Josie and that young Captain Wyckham, the aide-de-camp. They've just arrived from Warrandyte. They're engaged. It's a complete surprise." Diana stepped out on to the veranda. "I'm afraid I can't possibly come tonight, Russell. I am so sorry, but it's impossible."

He thought a moment. "Yes, of course, I see that." He paused and as if finally convincing himself, added: "It would be quite impossible. Ought I to come in?"

"I think it would be better if you did."

"I could say I was passing and called in."

"I thought you would do that," said Diana. She now felt completely at ease. Half an hour earlier, when she was in despair at leaving her home and her children, Russell had seemed unreal, almost menacing, a slightly sinister, romantic hero. Now that he was here in the flesh, kind and sensible as usual, she was immensely comforted and cheered. She led the way into the drawing-room.

"Here's Mr Lockwood," she said.

"I was in the neighbourhood and called on the chance of finding someone in. I believe I'm to congratulate you," he said.

"Yes, you're the first," said Josie.

"That's a privilege." He shook hands with both of them, giving John a quick approving scrutiny.

They stood talking conventionally for a few minutes, then Diana said: "I'm sorry I can't ask you to stay to dinner, because there's no dinner."

"Why don't you all come and dine with me in Melbourne?" asked Russell.

"At Menzies? We'd all have to change."

"No. At a foreign restaurant. I've found quite a good one."

"That would be lovely," said Josie.

She went with John, and Diana drove with Russell.

"This is a dreadful thing I've done to you," she said. "I told you I had complications, but I didn't foresee this one. It isn't fair that you should have your plans upset by my affairs."

223

"Naturally, I'm disappointed," he said, "but I regard your affairs as my affairs—I don't mean to interfere with— but what happens to you, happens to me."

"You understand so perfectly that I feel I can tell you everything."

"I hope you will."

"Russell, I hope you'll understand what I'm going to say. I'm glad that this has happened. All the time I have been worried about Josie, and this settles that difficulty. He seems an extremely nice young man, simple in a good way. You may think I'm rather unstable. It was I who wanted to go quickly because I felt that I couldn't go on living in the house with Wolfie. But since I came back from Westhill it has not been so bad. We lead our independent lives fairly comfortably. I hope to bring him round to accept the arrangement. You see at first I wanted to rely on anger to make the break, and that's cowardly. I want to make it peacefully if I can."

"That would be better," he agreed.

They did not speak much for the rest of the drive. He seemed rather thoughtful. Diana wondered if he had really accepted what she had said, but she did not feel that he had withdrawn from her. She felt that he was *with* her.

They drew up outside a French restaurant, near the Exhibition Buildings. John, who had been ahead, slowed up and signed to them to pass so that he could follow them and know where to go.

As they went into the restaurant Diana had a moment of anxiety lest they should find Wolfie there with Mrs Montaubyn, but this was a situation which she was spared.

Russell said that this was a celebration, and he ordered champagne. They became cheerful, and John and Josie were lively and amusing, already chaffing each other about how they would behave when they were married. Russell and John appeared to get on well together, and Diana thought what a well-assorted party they made. She had thought so the last time they were together, for those few minutes in the drawing-room at Government House. Everything, after her terrible anxieties of an hour or so ago, was falling into its proper place. New aspects of this development occurred to her at intervals. Josie would be in Europe and they would not be separated. She and John both evidently liked Russell, and nothing could be more desirable than that this should happen before events which might prejudice them against him. Also, she knew the attitude of most Englishmen to Australians, and to produce someone as highly-civilized as Russell as an old family friend, would give a good impression of Josie's background. The four of them together created happiness, and Diana thought that in a year's time, when she had fixed up her arrangements here without too great a scandal, they might be dining together like this in Paris or in Rome, and how wonderful it would be.

When they came out of the restaurant, John said that he could take Diana back to Brighton, but Russell said it would be more comfortable if they took both cars.

When they were again together in the car, Diana was thinking that they would be unable to go before Josie's marriage, so she was surprised when Russell said:

"We shan't be able to go before their marriage."

225

"It seems so unfair to you," she replied.

"It would be shockingly unfair to them if we did."

"Yes. I was just thinking that."

"When are they likely to be married?"

"Assuming his parents agree, I suppose the wedding could be in about three months."

"It isn't long."

"D'you think it's too soon? People will say I'm trying to make certain of him. That's how they talk here."

"They don't matter. I should think three months is about right."

"When am I going to come up against something horrid in you?" asked Diana. "Every time I meet you you show some new goodness."

"D'you want me to be horrid?"

"No, of course not. But I feel I must be imagining greater happiness than anyone can have—anyone of my age. One expects these illusions in Josie and John, though I hope they're not illusions."

"You'll find my faults in time. I'm clever at concealing them. I don't think it shows unusual virtue to expect you to avoid wrecking your daughter's life. Imagine the effect on his people if you eloped before the wedding."

"It would be grotesque—but after the wedding?"

"Then our lives are our own."

John and Josie arrived at the house before them, and had crossed the road and were looking at the sea, across which a sparkling, pale golden path ran to the moon. They came over when Diana and Russell arrived. John had to go.

"I should have been back earlier," he said, "but I think the occasion justifies a breach of discipline. In fact I think it justifies a jolly revolution." Then he turned to Diana and asked seriously: "What will Mr von Flugel say?" Josie replied:

"Daddy will say: 'It is good for a young girl to marry a young man. I am happy.'"

They laughed, Diana a little uneasily.

CHAPTER ELEVEN

John cabled to his parents asking their approval of his engagement to Josie. He did not ask their permission as he was determined to marry her. He knew that they would be dubious about his marrying an Australian girl with a German name, and to reassure them he put in his cable: "No blemishes. Miss Rockingham approves." They replied: "We trust your judgement. Love." Though it was really Miss Rockingham's judgement that they trusted.

The announcement of the engagement caused surprise, and amongst the new-rich Toorak ladies, great indignation. Mrs Vane, whose husband had forked out two thousand pounds a year to enable his daughter to marry an aide-de-camp, though certainly he had been the son of a peer, was dumbfounded that a penniless girl from Brighton, who was not "in society" should get one for nothing. Baba was as angry as Mrs Vane. With her social ambition she might have been expected to be glad if members of the family made good marriages, but she so disliked her "in-laws" and especially Diana, that she could not bear any good fortune to come to them. Also, the only sentence in all Holy Writ of which she approved was: "From him that hath not shall be taken even that which he hath." She had been accustomed to say: "Josie's a pretty little thing, but no one will want to marry von Flugel's daughter. Couldn't she find some useful employment?" She now began to hint that not only Wolfie was disreputable, as Miss Bath had told her that she had found Diana and Russell having supper alone together "in arm-chairs".

Cousin Sophie on the other hand, who might have been expected to be a little piqued as she regarded Government House as her own preserve, showed great pleasure. She might be unable to resist the satisfaction of an erudite *riposte* even if it flattened its victim, but she was never unkind in her intention. Although she knew many people of the kind of whom Baba and Mrs Vane were extreme examples, she never understood them. She thought that they were rather vulgar, but she did not take in that they had no basic reality. They spent their time trying to fit their lives to a pattern which existed on the other side of the world, the original of which most of them had never seen. Cousin Sophie on the other hand had grown up in that pattern, and modified it here and there to suit the country in which she found herself. It was the action of these two processes, the striving by one, and the modification by the other, which led, twenty years later, to the amazing incident of Baba's cutting Cousin Sophie.

Cousin Sophie may also have thought that she could afford to be complacent about Josie's engagement, as she expected very soon to be able to announce Anthea's to Captain Thorpe. He was not the type of young man whom in England she would have thought a desirable son-in-law, but she was sufficiently influenced by the atmosphere of Melbourne to feel the glamour surrounding anyone attached to the Governor-General's staff, and as it was through Government House that she had descended into Australian life, she had a vague feeling that it might also be the door through which her daughters might ascend again to the region she had inhabited in her youth.

She thought very little about money. She had an instinctive regard for exalted rank, but most she valued a cultivated intelligence. She did not bother about the finances of presentable young men. She was not very clear as to how much her husband earned, and she would have been astonished at the idea of a fortune-hunter coming after one of her daughters. She thought that Freddie was attracted to Anthea because she had the manner of a young English gentlewoman. She knew that Freddie was Sir Roland's nephew. She did not know that when Sir Roland's sister married his father, the marriage was deplored, and only allowed because Mr Thorpe was enormously rich. In a few years he lost his entire fortune and committed suicide, and Sir Roland had to pay for Freddie's education, a rather unprofitable expenditure.

Wolfie did not receive the news of the engagement quite as Josie had expected, though there was no question of his withholding his approval. He had not intended

230

to visit Mrs Montaubyn on the evening when he had believed that Diana had forgiven him, but the reconciliation had awakened sentimental feelings, and during the half-hour's journey to Melbourne, owing to the trance effected in his musical mind by the rhythm of the train, he sank into a reverie on the sweet sadness of life, and when he arrived at Flinders Street he felt the need of womanly comfort, and he called on Mrs Montaubyn after all. With the pound which Diana had allowed him to keep he took her to dine at the French restaurant, but by miraculous good fortune they left five minutes before Russell and his guests arrived.

When he returned home a little earlier than usual, he felt ashamed of himself, and wished that he had not been to see Mrs Montaubyn, especially as she had not been very comforting. Lady Eileen had said that Germans are incapable of understanding the effect of their actions on other people, and it was certainly true of Wolfie. He complained to Mrs Montaubyn about the rift in his home life. If he had said how tiresome and ill-natured Diana was, she might have given him all the sympathy he required. Instead of this he sang Diana's praises and said how sad he was that she would not show him affection, and he implied that the responsibility for this rested with Mrs Montaubyn.

When he found Diana and Josie still up, and when they told him of the engagement, he felt more ashamed. This would have been the perfect moment for a reconciliation. He would have liked to be the proud and honourable parent blessing his daughter. He disliked being ashamed, and when it happened, he immediately searched for some way of transferring the feeling to others. He complained that he had not been consulted.

"Captain Wyckham came to ask your consent, but you weren't at home," said Diana.

"He will take her to England. Who will care for my old age?" asked Wolfie.

Josie looked hurt. Diana was so angry that Wolfie should at this moment cloud her happiness with his miserable selfishness that if Josie had not been present, she would have retorted: "Mrs Montaubyn, presumably." Instead, she said: "You might think of Josie, rather than yourself, at this moment."

Wolfie looked surprised and said: "Indeed, I wish her happiness," and he kissed her. Diana could tell from his guilty manner, always insufficiently disguised under a pompous veneer, that he had been somewhere disreputable, and to see him, perhaps with the powder from another woman's cheeks on his face, kissing Josie in her shining happiness, blotted out any kindliness she might have felt for him when she herself kissed him at the door a few hours earlier. People might think Wolfie amusing, but these children of nature could produce at times situations of intolerable squalor. She was hardened in her intention to leave him as soon as Josie was married and had left for England.

She now met Russell with acknowledged secrecy. Before the ball they had accepted without actually mentioning it, that it would be indiscreet for them to be seen much together. But then, as she had regarded her behaviour and her intentions as blameless, she did not think it would have mattered much if their friendship had been noticed, and so she had not been disturbed by Miss Bath's intrusion on them at supper.

After some discussion, cables to England, and arrangements for a new aide-de-camp to take John's place, the wedding day was fixed for the middle of July. As Diana had foreseen, Baba said that this was because she did not want to give John a chance of backing out. She did not like this sort of malicious gossip touching Josie, but she thought that she had no right to delay Russell longer than she could help.

Once again she tried to lead Wolfie up to discussing the subject of a divorce, but at the first hint he was so full of righteous indignation, that she abandoned all idea of coming to a reasonable settlement with him in conversation. He said that it would be a monstrous wickedness for parents to arrange a divorce while their daughter was preparing for her marriage, and Diana herself felt that in more moderate language, there was something in his argument.

She told Russell of Wolfie's reaction, and taking it into account, they made their final plans. John and Josie were to go for their honeymoon to Tasmania. They would only be there for ten days, after which they would return to Melbourne for three days and then sail for England. Diana would leave for England alone a fortnight later. It was quite usual for wives to go to Europe without their husbands, who often could not get away. It would be assumed that she wanted to see Josie settled in her new home, but of course she could not travel on the same ship as an unwanted chaperone with the young married couple. Russell was to leave Melbourne in a ship a week before Diana, disembark at Fremantle and spend a week in Perth, ostensibly to visit friends there, and then join her ship when it arrived. In London or the Continent, they could live how they chose. No one would be interested in what they did. It might be a year before it leaked out that they were together, and by then the divorce and re-arrangement of Diana's affairs might be completed. Josie would be well settled in her new life, and it was almost solely on her account that this elaborate secrecy was planned.

Wolfie might object to her going to Europe or want to come with her, but if it came to the point, she would simply have to refuse to pay his fare. As it happened, when at last she told him that she was going, he took it with surprising docility, partly due to her suggestion that Daisy and her family should come to look after him.

Harry, in Queensland, was the only one who, in his letters, gave an impression of dissatisfaction. Why did Josie want to marry an Englishman, especially an aide-de-camp, who would be sure to think that he had conferred a favour on the family by marrying her? Then he was indignant when he heard that Elsie had again come forward and lent her house for the reception.

"Do we have to live on the Radcliffes?" he asked. "Isn't our own house good enough for him? Or at any rate why can't it be at Aunt Maysie's if you have to be so grand? If we have to live on charity, it's better to take it from relations."

Diana was thankful for Elsie's offer. Her own house was not only far out, but was now very shabby. She had a great deal of expense ahead of her, and she had to sell some shares to pay for Josie's trousseau and the wedding expenses. She had thought of selling some more to have the house done up, but then she thought that would be foolish as it would immediately be wrecked by the occupation of Daisy and her family, who had a new and strange attitude to furniture, almost the same as their attitude to food, that it was not a stable possession but something one used up. Then a year later the house would probably be sold in its ruined condition at a heavy loss.

The obvious person to lend her house for the reception was Diana's sister Maysie. She had a rich husband and a large house in Toorak. But Maysie had been slightly infected both by her husband's and by Baba's attitude to the Flugels, that it was outrageous that they should have anything good. The reason for this was an unconscious loyalty to their own kind, the acquisitive "go-getter" who alone they believed to be entitled to material prosperity. But the real reason why Maysie did not offer her house may have been that not long ago she had prepared an enormous wedding reception for her own daughter, who had run off with her first cousin, leaving the immensely rich bridegroom waiting at the altar, and so causing the greatest social fiasco Melbourne had ever known.

John and Josie did not mind how soon the wedding took place, and Diana was thankful that she had no qualms about it. They were so happy together, so naturally gentle with each other, that she was sure the marriage must be a good one. She knew Josie's character, and from what she saw of John and from what Lady Wendale told her about him, she was sure that he would always be considerate. She believed that their attraction was of the heart and mind, and that they recognized some spiritual quality in each other which drew them immediately together, something far more enduring than physical attraction. When they met, Diana was amused at the way they at once began to talk as if they had never been separated.

The sight of them together could not fail to make her compare their love with her own attachment to Russell, and she saw that the latter was of a much more sober quality. She was glad that it was. She could not have borne her emotions to be as heightened as Josie's. It would have made an absurd situation in the house. Hers would be, as she had already told herself, largely an elopement of convenience, though she did not see how it could be convenient for Russell. She suggested to him that she had the best of the bargain, but he reassured her, repeating that it was amazing good fortune for him to have found her, and he again said that she must have been the reason for his coming to Australia. He said how wonderfully different his European life would be when she was with him. He talked of the things they would do, the places they would go to, and there formed in Diana's mind a picture of the halcyon existence she would lead when her present preoccupations were over.

CHAPTER TWELVE

Anthea had not accepted Josie's engagement quite as complacently as Cousin Sophie. If she had already been engaged to Freddie Thorpe, it would have slightly tarnished the gilt on the gingerbread if one of the Enemy acquired an aide-de-camp a few weeks later; for to the twins we were also the Enemy, an uncouth tribe troubling the fringe of civilization, though they had not actually given us this label. Anthea was not conscious that Freddie's attractiveness for her was largely social, but it would be absurd to deny that girls, at any rate girls "in society", or, to strain charity to its limits, their mothers, are indifferent to the position of the men they marry. She had been anxious to return early from Warrandyte as she was almost certain, from his manner at their last meeting, that he would propose at the dance where she was to see him on that evening, but he did not, and Josie's engagement was announced instead.

237

Anthea need not have been annoyed at this, as it was owing to the announcement that Freddie at last came up to scratch. He had hesitated, partly because he saw so little evidence that her father's income was as large as he had been told, and partly because of Anthea's conversation. Her manner was adequately brutal, and would pass amongst the fox-hunting young women in Yorkshire, to whom he was accustomed, but it was marred by flashes of wit which puzzled him, and by an awareness of the splendid tradition of Western culture from which, in spite of her declaration of independence in Miss Felpham's orchard, she could not free herself, and which he was sure his county friends would think ill-bred. In spite of these disabilities, she was more of a lady than the two other girls he had under review. She would be all right in the hunting field as long as she did not mention Montesquieu. He thought he could cure her of all that by starting her on breeding beagles. If that did not work he would simply tell her to shut up.

He still hesitated when John, on Sunday, beaming like the morning sun itself, announced that he was engaged to Josie. Freddie did not dislike John, but he despised him. He did not go with whores, and he had a delicacy of manner and varied interest which Freddie thought unbecoming in an officer and a gentleman. He was indignant that someone so insignificant and also his junior, should have "beat him to it", and he then decided to "put his money on Anthea" though it was in fact her money that he decided to put on himself.

He went to Lord Francis and asked: "Is it really true that Edward Langton has ten thousand a year?"

Lord Francis, confirming the inexactitude of "has" for "earns", said: "You can take it as gospel, my boy. I had it from the horse's mouth."

Before Freddie went to a dance, almost a week later, he took a piece of writing-paper stamped with the crown of England, and wrote on it "£10,000". He divided this by two, achieving the result of "£5,000" which coincided with the figure at which he had arrived by doing the sum in his head. When Cousin Edward died apparently Anthea would have £5,000 a year, not a bad income to get with a girl who was on the whole presentable. He wondered what allowance she would have until that happy time. The girl who married an A.D.C. last year was given £2,000 a year, and an extra £1,000 because her husband was a soldier, but her father was an exceptionally rich squatter. He was firmly convinced that Australians would pay almost anything to marry their daughters to English gentlemen like himself, and he thought that Cousin Edward would be sure to allow Anthea at least two thousand pounds a year. He folded up the piece of paper, put it in his pocket, and went off to the dance, where he proposed to Anthea and was accepted. They arranged that he should call on the following Wednesday evening to ask Cousin Edward's permission.

After Josie's engagement, Cousin Sophie frequently invited her to the house. Baba said that she only did this because Josie was now going to be "in society". She always imagined that Cousin Sophie's motives were the same as her own would have been, if performing a similar action, which made their mutual misunderstanding complete. If Cousin Sophie was told that she invited Josie to improve her social position, she would have been as bewildered as if she heard that a fortune-hunter was after one of the twins. She invited her from genuine, if slightly patronising, kindness. She thought that as the Flugels were not rich, Josie could not have much knowledge of the kind of well-run English houses where she would soon live. She thought that in her own house she might see a reflection of this, so that when she arrived in England she would not be entirely at a loss. This may have been of use to Josie, although Diana had brought up her children to behave well in most circumstances.

On the Wednesday when Freddie was to come to interview Cousin Edward, it happened that Josie and I were invited to dine with the twins. When Cousin Sophie came into the drawing-room she said to Josie:

"I asked Captain Wyckham, but he couldn't come."

"No," said Josie. "He had to go to the theatre with Lady Eileen and Miss Rockingham."

"I hope they've taken a loose-box," said Anthea, who was in high spirits. Miss Rockingham, with an appreciation very different from Anthea's of herself, had told Cousin Sophie at the Radcliffes' party that she was "an English rose". She had never looked more so than this evening, with her eyes bright and lively, but not hard. Perhaps she was more a Teutonic rose, as she also did not understand the effect of her actions. She had no ill-will towards Miss Rockingham. On the contrary she admired her, and when they met, spoke to her with charming deference, and she had no idea of the cruelty of her repeated jokes about her resemblance to a horse, though they never reached her ears. Josie puckered her forehead and gave a faint polite smile.

After dinner I wanted to do charades, but Anthea objected. There was a fidgety atmosphere in the drawing-room, as everyone excepting myself knew that Freddie might arrive at any moment, and the reason for his visit. Anthea had confided to her mother that she was engaged to Freddie, or would be when they had her parents' permission, and that he was coming on Wednesday to ask it. There was a curious kind of secrecy in the house. Cousin Edward was told by his wife, but did not speak of it to Anthea. He was not very pleased, chiefly at first because he did not want Anthea, the most lively member of his household, to go to live on the other side of the world, however grand a marriage she might make. He vaguely accepted the prevailing idea that aides-de-camp were grand, but he did not like soldiers, having been brought up to regard them as "notoriously stupid" and of Freddie at least this was true. On the other hand he wanted Anthea to be happy. He kept an open mind, but made a few discreet inquiries about Freddie in the Melbourne Club and elsewhere.

He heard about his parentage, but he did not blame him for that. He also heard that he obviously intended to marry for money, which puzzled him, as although Lord Francis's estimate of his income was true, he did not think of himself as rich, as he had not yet accumulated large capital assets. He thought therefore that Freddie must be so attracted by Anthea that he had abandoned his ignoble aim, which made Cousin Edward feel rather kindly towards him, but he also was a little worried and preoccupied during dinner, and as soon as he had drunk his coffee he left the drawing-room and went off to work on some case. He had hardly gone when a parlour-maid opened the door and said:

"Captain Thorpe wants to see the Master private, ma'am."

"Show him into the study, Ellen," said Cousin Sophie.

There was now an atmosphere of constraint in the room, and to ease it, she suggested that the twins should play a duet on the two pianos.

"Oh, yes!" I exclaimed eagerly. "Do play the love music from the *Valkyrie*."

Cousin Sophie smiled ironically.

"I don't want to," said Anthea, and added with that engaging schoolboy vulgarity with which she interlarded her erudition: "Don't count your chickens before they're hatched."

Cousin Sophie ignored this and said with the patience which middle-aged people so often display when their children are mulish: "Very well, I shall play." She showed her perfect good taste by choosing a piece by Schumann, neither joyful nor depressing, and quite unrelated either to Anthea's feelings or to the scene being enacted in Cousin Edward's study.

Freddie, feeling perfectly confident that he had come to confer a benefit, was shown into that large secluded room at the back of the house, lined from floor to ceiling with legal books in pale brown calf, the quartz from which Cousin Edward extracted the gold of his income.

He was seated at his writing table when Freddie came

in. He stood up, shook hands and asked him to sit down. He was irritated by the confidence of Freddie's manner and let him speak first.

"I've come to ask your permission of my engagement to Anthea, sir," he said with what he believed to be manly directness. Cousin Edward gave no sign of the pleasure which Freddie expected his statement to evoke. He was unsmiling and replied:

"I understood that was the reason for your call." He thought a moment, and then continued: "I am, of course, only concerned for Anthea's happiness. I will be quite frank with you and say from my own point of view I would rather she married one of her own country-men. Then her marriage would not entirely separate her from her family. But I shan't allow that to influence my decision."

Freddie did not realize that he had come to interview the cleverest K.C. in the country, whose success was largely due to his ability to see what witnesses were thinking, and who now saw from the slightly surprised and offended look on Freddie's face that he had thought that he was performing an act of condescension. He was half-amused, half-angry, and he determined to readjust Freddie's estimate of his own desirability, which to Cousin Edward was almost non-existent. He was himself not only a K.G. but the son of a High Court judge; he had married into the English aristocracy, in which also lay his own origins, and he believed himself to be highly intelligent. That this brainless son of a bankrupt suicide should expect him to be gratified at the prospect of an alliance between their families, struck him as preposterous impertinence.

"All the same," he went on, "I must be sure that you have the equipment to make her happy. Perhaps you will give me some idea of your ability in this direction."

"We get on well together, sir," said Freddie.

"That is important, certainly, but it is not the only requirement in marriage. You won't mind if I ask you to give me some idea of your financial position and your prospects?"

Freddie's financial position was simple. He had his army pay with extra allowances as an aide-de-camp. He also was allowed fifty pounds a year, which she could ill-afford, by his mother, who lived in a village house in Yorkshire in a perpetual state of anxiety lest Freddie, to secure the luxuries which he believed were his natural right, should do something dishonourable, much more so than marrying a rich girl.

Freddie explained his position but did not mention his debts or his mother's allowance, regarding the latter as in the class of a boy's pocket-money. It made little difference to his expenditure though it deprived his mother of her annual visit to her relatives in the south.

"Then how do you expect to be able to keep a wife?" asked Cousin Edward, looking puzzled, but as if Freddie would doubtless produce some explanation.

Freddie, for once a little ashamed, said that he would inherit money on his mother's death. This was not as bad as it sounded, as he did not at all count on his mother's death for financial relief. It might be expected that Cousin Edward, with his talent for reading people's thoughts, would not have been able fully to exercise it on Freddie's face, which was round and smooth with a low forehead, rather coarse mouth, opaque eyes, and a complete absence of any fineness or subtlety, though with a pleasant look of youth and health. But Freddie's thoughts were simple, and his face was adequate to their expression. It was as easy for Cousin Edward to read them as for a classical scholar to read dog Latin.

Helped by the gossip he had heard, he very soon discovered, though Freddie did not state it explicitly, that he expected to be supported by his wife. He even suspected that he had in mind the three thousand pounds a year obtained in marriage by the last A.D.C., and he gathered that somehow, he could not think how, Freddie must have discovered the extent of his own income. After an urbane but slightly cruel cross-examination under which the moon of Freddie's face had reflected all his expectations, Cousin Edward opened his heavy fire.

"You may have thought," he said, "that perhaps I would make a settlement on Anthea." Again a gleam in Freddie's eyes revealed that this was exactly what he had thought. "Now that I have asked you about your position, perhaps I should explain my own. I am not a rich man, not in the sense that Mr Vane is rich." Freddie started at this further revelation of his thoughts. "My income is almost entirely earned. In ordinary prudence I have to put aside much of it to give security to my wife and daughters. If I were to settle on Anthea anything like the amount Mr Vane settled on the Brayfords, it would be roughly a third of my income. If it were unearned income, that would be, to say the least, disproportionate. But it is not, so it would mean that for a third of my working year I would be using my energies to support you and your wife. I am sure that you will agree that it is hardly reasonable to expect me to do that?" He smiled.

Freddie, equally with Wolfie, hated logic, but although he was far less cultivated and intelligent than Wolfie, he could understand it, while to Wolfie it was simply some sharp unnatural weapon that Diana stuck into him out of malice, to reduce him to despair and bewilderment, and Diana's logic had a family resemblance to Cousin Edward's. Freddie saw perfectly that there was no reason why old Langton should sweat to keep him. He began to sweat himself, and Cousin Edward, seeing his acute discomfort, and aware that he had made his point, began to ease the situation.

"I do not think," he said mildly, "that it is a good thing to marry too early. In your life you have many opportunities of seeing the world before you settle down. It would be a pity to waste them. I don't suppose you have ever considered living permanently in Australia? It has many advantages. One escapes the dreadful English winters." He said this, thinking that if Anthea kicked over the traces and insisted on marrying this young oaf, he might make that the condition of a modest settlement.

"That's the best time," Freddie managed to choke out. "Hunting."

"Yes. Each to his taste," said Cousin Edward amiably. "I like walking in the winter."

"Walkin'?" Freddie stared at him as if he were dealing with a lunatic.

Cousin Edward made a few more general observations, and then, seeing that Freddie was itching to get away, he pushed back his chair.

"Perhaps you would prefer me to tell Anthea that there can be no engagement at present," he said. Freddie made a few guttural sounds which indicated his agreement. Cousin Edward, chatting pleasantly about the architecture of Government House and its resemblance to Osborne in the Isle of Wight, went with him along to the hall, where he handed him his hat and stick and wished him good night. He then put his head into the drawing-room and asked Cousin Sophie if she would give him a few minutes. She left the piano and followed him across into the dining-room, where he closed the door. Anthea looked surprised and perturbed. She went out, and not knowing that her parents had gone into the dining-room, she went first to Cousin Sophie's sitting-room and then along to the study. When she did not find them she came back to the drawing-room and said: "Where's Mother gone?"

In the dining-room Cousin Edward with a hint of blame that his wife had allowed things to go so far, said: "We couldn't possibly allow Anthea to become engaged to that young man. He hasn't a penny and he's quite brainless."

"Have you told him that you won't allow it?" asked Cousin Sophie anxiously, thinking of the shock to Anthea.

"It wasn't necessary. He's after money. When I told him that I couldn't make a large settlement on Anthea, he was obviously anxious to back out. The conversation was rather amusing, an exchange of implications—no naked steel."

"You haven't actually forbidden it, then?"

"It wasn't necessary. I told him I couldn't keep them, and that finished it."

"But why on earth should he expect money with Anthea?"

"I have no idea, but he evidently did."

"Couldn't we allow them a little?" asked Sophie doubtfully. She was distressed at the thought of the engagement falling through, chiefly for Anthea's sake, but also she could never quite eradicate the idea, implanted in her youth, that no Australian could be the equal of an upper-class Englishman.

"A little would be no use. He's got Lucinda Brayford's three thousand pounds a year fixed in his mind. Anyhow I don't want Anthea to marry him. If they were back in England with no money, and he was no longer in the viceregal aura, she'd see him without glamour and he'd bore her to death. I'm blowed if I know what she sees in him now. He's almost inarticulate. It's quite upsetting to think one's own daughter can be attracted to a man like that. Though he's not really bad of course. In a way I rather liked him as he was so transparent. But he's not *homo sapiens*, only a house-trained animal. I suppose we ought to tell Anthea."

He had the inherited characteristic of liking anyone who provided him with amusement, but he held it under strict control, unlike our side of the family who, when they saw Wolfie, burst out laughing, and in gratitude handed him Diana on a silver dish.

"It will be a dreadful blow to her," said Sophie, but

she never dreamed of questioning her husband's decisions. She had not taken in that the decision was really Freddie's, and that if he had expressed his devotion to Anthea and his willingness to work for her, Cousin Edward would have settled a suitable income on them, but in hundreds, not thousands. As it was he had to endure the odium of being thought a stern parent, indifferent to his daughter's happiness.

Anthea, not finding her mother in the drawing-room, went out again. Trying to ignore this disappearance, one by one, of our hosts, I made some remark to Cynthia, but she did not reply and after a moment of indecision followed her sister, and I was left alone with Josie, who also seemed affected by the general uneasiness.

Soon Cousin Sophie came back to us. She said that Anthea was not very well, and would I take Josie to the train. We expressed our sympathy, and with that slight sense of humiliation, inseparable from receiving a request to go, however reasonable it may be, we left without seeing the others, except, just as we were saying good night to Cousin Sophie, Anthea came out from her sitting-room, which opened into a passage at the far end of the hall. The light from the open door shone on her face, which was hardly recognisable in its grief. I had never seen Anthea, except as the English rose blooming with confidence on the breeziest heights of the hedge-row, the most vital creature that I knew. To see her blighted with despair gave me one of those shocks which, particularly when they come in youth, we always remember, as they are an extension of our experience.

"What's up?" I asked Josie as we walked down the drive. She told me that John had told her that Freddie wanted to marry Anthea, and that he was coming to ask Cousin Edward's permission.

"Then why did everyone disappear, and Anthea look so ghastly?" I asked. "You'd think they'd drink their health or something."

"Perhaps Cousin Edward won't allow it," said Josie. "Oh, I do hope it isn't that." She sounded as if there were tears in her voice, as she imagined that if this were so, Anthea must be feeling as she herself would feel if she were ever separated from John. Her fear may have been justified, as the frustration of a purely physical attraction, combined in this case with social ambition, which incurred a wound to pride, can be as painful as the frustration of a love which also suffuses mind and spirit. Though with moderate common sense the pain of the former can be cured in about three weeks.

"Why shouldn't he allow it?" I asked. "I'd have thought that they'd be awfully pleased. Cousin Sophie dotes on Government House and the English."

"Freddie Thorpe hasn't any money at all," said Josie. "He has to marry someone to keep him. I suppose Anthea can't do it. It must be awful for him." The idea was not shocking to her, as she had been used to it from infancy, Diana always having supported Wolfie. Josie also attributed to Freddie the same sensibility, with a corresponding capacity for anguish of soul, that she knew existed in John.

I put her into the train which was to be met at the other end by Wolfie, and I went home to Mildy. I was puzzled that someone with no money at all could live in a palace, spend his time at dances and race meetings, drive about in huge motor cars, have perfect clothes, dine off gold plate, and go about with people who, whenever they entered a room or a theatre, galvanized everyone to attention and awakened the strains of "God Save the King". I enjoyed a certain amount of free high-life myself, but nothing on that scale.

Mildy was usually difficult when I returned from the twins', but tonight as I was back early, she was cheerful, hoping that I had been bored.

"You *are* back early," she said. "Will you have your hot milk now, or shall we have a little talk first?"

"I don't mind," I answered, though I had been taught that this was the rudest possible reply to any offer, and I added: "Cousin Sophie asked us to go."

"Have you quarrelled with them?" Mildy asked with delight.

"No, but Captain Thorpe came. I think it was to ask if he could marry Anthea."

"Oh!" said Mildy crossly. "How mean! They're jealous of Josie so they have to catch an aide-de-camp for themselves."

"It's not that at all," I said hotly. "Cousin Sophie has been terribly nice to Josie. Anyhow, Cousin Edward won't allow it, as Captain Thorpe has no money."

Mildy clapped her hands. "Oh, good!" she cried.

I thought of Anthea, the stricken rose, and was revolted by Mildy in her silly glee. My education had made me very chivalrous towards women, except in moments of sensual reverie, but then my feelings were not directed

251

towards any individual, only towards the headless nymph. I was shocked to find that they could be so unchivalrous towards each other.

I was too disgusted to speak, as I could not have done so with restraint. Mildy, with an uneasy smile which showed that she was conscious of being guilty of an error of taste, but at the same time that she was not going to accept any criticism from me, went out to heat the milk. On the mantlepiece was a large photograph of myself and with the egoism of my age I went over to look at it. While I was wishing that my nose was shorter, I noticed a smudge on the mouth, from which it was evident that Mildy had been kissing the photograph. I was furious and rubbed the smudge off on the seat of my trousers.

Yet Mildy was more deserving of sympathy than Anthea who still had many prospects of kissing something more living than a nephew's photograph. Having been sent to Europe to recover from Wolfie's mild avuncular embrace, for this more serious convalescence she was only sent to Fiji where she stayed a few months with the High Commissioner, who had married one of the Bynghams. After the outbreak of war, she forgot Freddie in the excitement of there being a German battleship loose in the Pacific.

It was thought necessary to get her away before Josie's wedding, which it would have been painful for her to attend, as Freddie was to be best man, and it would have been "marked" if she had stayed away. In spite of her absence the wedding did aggravate her humiliation, as Freddie as best man was made more aware that John had "beat him to it", and he proposed to Clara Bumpus, the second girl on his list, who accepted him with alacrity. She was altogether more satisfactory than Anthea, as her father had considerable capital assets, on which he drew to show his gratification at the alliance. Also she was unlikely to embarrass him by quoting Montaigne, Madame du Deffand or Voltaire at a hunt ball, as she was no more than himself aware that any such people had existed.

CHAPTER THIRTEEN

One of Diana's chief preoccupations during the three months between Josie's engagement and the wedding, was to keep in existence the barrier between herself and Wolfie. This was made more difficult by an event which, if she had known of it, she would have thought could not possibly effect her in any way. The manager of the building where Mrs Montaubyn had her flat, dismissed the liftman and engaged another, a retired professional footballer. This handsome man was eight years younger than Mrs Montaubyn and his fine muscles had not yet turned to fat. When one day she walked unsuspecting into the lift and found herself in that confined space with such a splendid specimen, she gave a faint wheeze of wonder and desire, and turned on him glances similar to those she had given me at Government House, though warmed with something of the reverence of invitation with which, on the same evening,

254

she had looked at the prince. In the next few days she found many occasions to use the lift, and at the end of the week she invited him, when he was off duty, to come into her flat.

Mrs Montaubyn since the ball had become increasingly irritated with Wolfie. He maintained his air of moral superiority to compensate himself for the disgrace he felt attached to him at home, and for which he implied too often that she was to blame. He also boasted about Josie's engagement, exaggerating the grandeur of the life she would lead in England and again, with Teutonic unawareness of effect, implied that it was a life of which Mrs Montaubyn could not even touch the fringe. She would have parted with Wolfie for good if she had not been doubtful of her ability to attract another man into her life. The new liftman relieved her of this anxiety. Far from being patronising, he was naively impressed by the luxury of her flat, and he said frequently: "I never thought I'd go with a real lady."

When Wolfie rang the bell on Saturday evening, Mrs Montaubyn, also with Teutonic indifference to the effect of her words, half opened the door and said: "You can clear out Dingo. I've had enough," and she slammed it in his face.

Wolfie wandered desolate about the streets of Melbourne. He walked through the arcades and looked in the windows, but he did not see what he was looking at. He could not go home to Diana, shut off from him behind her cool efficient manner. It would only emphasize his terrible sense of isolation. Also she would ask him why he was back so early.

He usually went by train to Brighton station but there was now another way; to go by train to St Kilda and take

255

the electric tram from there. To go by his usual route, by which he had returned so often and so happily from evenings with Mrs Montaubyn, he thought would sharpen his distress, and after an hour of aimless wandering he took the train to St Kilda. It was still early and instead of entering the Brighton tram, he strolled down to the esplanade.

He went into some tea gardens, where the ti-tree was festooned with coloured electric bulbs, and he drank a lemon squash into which had been tipped an ice-cream. After that he paid sixpence to go into the Palais de Dance, where he sat bouncing a little in time to the music, and sighing as he watched the happy couples. From there he went on to Luna Park, a huge fun fair at the end of the esplanade. In this, was an erection called the Helter-Skelter, a tower round which descended in a spiral, a trough of highly polished wood, down which one might slide at a few pence a time. Wolfie thought it looked very dangerous but he was feeling so desperate that he decided to allow his suicidal impulse threepence-worth of gratification. He mounted the tower and came whizzing down through the fresh night air, a sensation so exhilarating that he bubbled with laughter. But what most eased his depression was the kindness with which the young man at the bottom of the slide took his elbow and helped him to his feet. It was for just some such human touch that he had been longing for the past two hours. He went up the tower again. He stayed in the place until closing time, and every now and then he went back to have a slide down the Helter-Skelter for the moment of flying freedom, and the kindness of the hand on his elbow. The young man was amused by him, and he enjoyed that too, as he had been accustomed to provoke laughter.

When he came home he looked so innocent that Diana had the feeling that the barrier she was trying to maintain had dissolved, not through any deliberate action by either of them, but of its own accord. She had to continue for these three months a life of which the habits were not in accord with her intentions. There were moments like this when Wolfie, by some unconscious expression of his personality, so much more effective than his deliberate oglings, made the impulse of her habits irresistible. She had to stop herself laughing and ruffling his mousey hair. He did not notice how near she was to a reconciliation, as on the way home he had turned both his sorrows and his pleasures into music and they did not worry him any more. He went to his music-room where he stayed up late composing a little nocturne. He began in a minor key, in a melancholy reflective mood, which was interrupted by a succession of airy scherzos. He called it "Helter Skelter".

While he was composing this, Diana was trying to reason out and justify her own position. She told herself something like this: "I either have to stay or to go. If I stay, what happens? I shall be most of the time alone in this too large and shabby house, keeping it in order for no real purpose. I shan't have Josie. Wolfie will always go out for his amusements, respectable or otherwise. His behaviour has freed me from any duty to him. But I'm no longer angry. I can't use my anger as an excuse for leaving. That's weak and negative. But as I'm no longer angry with him, it makes the present situation more difficult. I may very easily behave in a way which he would afterwards be justified in thinking underhand. I'm walking on a razor's edge till I go, but I must go. Apart from my own wishes I must keep my promise to Russell. There can be no question of my not going—none at all. If I stay here what will my life be? Harry will come down from Queensland and disapprove of us for two or three weeks every year. Daisy will come to stay when she's tired of house-keeping, or is going to have a baby. Josie, the one who most cares for me, will be on the other side of the world. If I stayed it would be allowing sentimental feelings about the past to spoil the future.

"If I go what happens? I suppose some sort of scandal is unavoidable, but it may not leak out for a year, and it will only be talked of in Melbourne. The family may not like it, but I don't owe them much, and should I sacrifice the remainder of my life to them? No one will know what I am doing in Europe, and by the time a divorce becomes public, Josie will be well established with her in-laws, and it may even be possible to keep the details from them. Anyhow, surely I've come to the time when I may consider myself. My life with Russell will be wonderful, all that I used to long for. We understand each other perfectly. There is never a flat moment when we are together. I am very fond of him, and I'm sure that when once we are away and free from all these uncertainties and stratagems, I shall love him dearly."

She was determined to hold to her decision, but because of the danger of the habit of her life weakening her intention, she suggested to Wolfie that he should go and stay with Daisy for a while, as she and Josie were entirely occupied with preparations for the wedding, clothes, invitations and other details, which were of no interest to him.

In spite of this she found it more difficult to arrange meetings with Russell than before the engagement. If she went into Melbourne it was usually to go shopping with Josie, and if she went alone she attracted more attention as the mother of the girl who was to marry Captain Wyckham. People whom she only slightly knew, or who had let their acquaintance fade out when they found that she was not likely to be socially useful, now, as before Elsie's party, crossed the street to speak to her. Diana always responded to signs of friendship, but she felt the advances of these people to be more insolent than their former coldness, and they gave her a contempt for the society she was soon to leave, so that if it were not for Josie she would hardly have taken the trouble to conceal her meetings with Russell.

In those days it was impossible to go into Melbourne without meeting half a dozen or more people whom she knew, and it appeared quite natural that, when she was with Josie, they should run into Russell and have tea together. She wanted Josie to strengthen the liking she showed for him on the evening when they had dined at the French restaurant. One day she said to her:

"I think of coming to England soon after you're married. Would you like that?"

"Oh Mummy, that would be lovely!" exclaimed Josie, delighted.

"Do you think John would mind? I don't want him to think that he's to be saddled with his mother-in-law. I wouldn't stay with you."

"He'd love it. He admires you tremendously. He often says so. Would Daddy come too?"

"No. He wouldn't be able to leave the Conservatorium for so long. Daisy would look after him."

When Diana next saw John she told him of her intention, and he said with apparently genuine pleasure: "That will be splendid. You must stay at Wootton Speke. You'll like my father."

Although Wolfie was staying with Daisy and Bill Byngham at Frankston, it was not far away, and he sometimes looked in at Brighton to fetch a piece of music, or another pipe. He arrived one day at tea-time and as Josie was out, Diana took the opportunity of telling him that she was definitely going to Europe.

"Am I not to come?" asked Wolfie, looking offended but not seriously hurt.

"You can't leave the Conservatorium for so long," said Diana. "Daisy and Bill can come here to look after you."

"It is strange that my wife leaves me," said Wolfie. He made no further protest. After the bleak atmosphere of his home in recent weeks he was thoroughly enjoying the rollicking family affection in Daisy's house. The prospect of continuing this, with grandchildren clinging to his knee, continuous talk about art and music, students sleeping in all the spare beds and on the drawing-room sofa, wine and beer at any hour of the day or night, and no one to question his assignations, appeared more agreeable than trailing round Europe in Diana's exclusive and disapproving company. Also he was lazy, and his old ambition to gain a European reputation had died. He was rather frightened of the idea.

When she had told Wolfie, Diana booked her passage on a ship sailing on the eighth of August. John and Josie would have sailed a fortnight, and Russell a week earlier, the latter to await her and join the ship in Perth. A few days after this she met John, who told her, as if it were very good news:

"Miss Rockingham's going home by the same ship as you. She was very pleased when I told her that you would be on board."

Diana tried to show equal pleasure, and to conceal the dismay she felt. She rang up Russell in the evening and told him.

He sounded even more disturbed than herself, and suggested that they should postpone their departure for another week.

"I've told everyone I'm going on the eighth," said Diana. "I can't give any reason for changing."

They did not like to discuss it on the telephone, and they met next day in the Gallery to do so.

"Another thing," said Diana, "is that Miss Rockingham, who has been charming to Josie, and very friendly whenever I have met her, will think it extraordinarily rude if I change my ship for no apparent reason, as soon as I hear that she's going on it."

Russell admitted this, and suggested that Diana should also disembark at Perth and then they could sail together a week later. Or she could go to Colombo, pretending she had always wanted to see it, and wait there.

"But I hate those hot Asiatic places," said Diana. "I couldn't pretend with conviction. We can't really go dodging about the Indian Ocean like that."

They laughed a little at their predicament.

"I suppose I shall just have to appear surprised to find you on the ship," said Russell. "But people know we know each other—especially Miss Rockingham. She lunched with us."

"I wonder how well they know."

"It will make the voyage a bit difficult," said Russell thoughtfully.

A few days later, when she met him again, he was even more grave, and talked mostly about the effect of the assassination of the Archduke Ferdinand. This had shocked people in Melbourne but they regarded it as the sort of thing to be expected in the Balkans, and did not imagine that it could possibly affect their own lives, any more than Diana would have thought that the dismissal of a lift-boy in a block of Collins Street flats could decide her own future. Russell, probably more European-minded than anyone she knew, was anxious about its repercussions.

"But surely there couldn't be a European war nowadays?" she said, and added: "John is in the army."

"It couldn't last a month," said Russell. "It would be over before he got there."

"How would it affect us? One can't help thinking of that."

"I don't see that it need affect us. The war wouldn't be in England. We might get mixed up in a naval battle on the way."

262

"I'm prepared to risk that," said Diana. "Our affairs would become very unimportant."

The wedding was now only a fortnight ahead, and Diana was taken up with arrangements and could think of little else. The presents began to arrive. Although from the same people, they were far more expensive than those sent to Daisy, again on the principle "to him that hath". They had to be opened and a list made for Josie to write letters of thanks, and then re-packed and sent to Elsie's house where they were to be on view, guarded by plain clothes detectives in the billiard room. Arrangements had to be made to ship them to England after that. She had not only to arrange Josie's trousseau but to design the bridesmaids' dresses and to think about her own.

There were two rolls left of those beautiful stuffs which her mother had left her, one of blue silk, and one almost flame colour though soft in tone. She knew that she looked her best in red, that she could "carry it off", but she thought it would be too striking to wear at a wedding, especially her daughter's. Yet it was not only this consideration which made her choose the blue. She could not be certain that there would not be other acquaintances besides Miss Rockingham on the ship, when Russell joined her at Fremantle, people who knew her better, and that in far less than a year she might be the subject of scandal. Then, as was their habit, the scandalmongers would give a retrospective resumé of her character, and say: "What decent woman would wear red at her daughter's wedding?" All through the preparations, and at the wedding itself, she had this feeling that she was under the threat of hostile criticism.

Harry arrived from Queensland a week before the wedding day, and increased this feeling. He exuded disapproval. Diana had scraped some more butter from her bread to send him to the most expensive, and presumably the best "public school" in the state, from which he returned with reverence for the rich grandsons of Scottish crofters who were his schoolfellows, and contempt for his family and their characteristics, their lively wit, their spontaneous affections, their creative ability and above all for their indifference to public opinion when their sense of justice was affronted. When his schooling was finished he went off as a jackeroo on the sheep station of one of his school friends, obviously to escape from humiliating associations with his relatives. Diana was distressed at his attitude, and disgusted to have paid so much to turn her son from a real into a synthetic gentleman. He now talked about "good form" and called Wolfie "sir" though every intonation and gesture he used to his father was one of contempt.

She had hoped that a year on the station would have made him more sensible, but it had only made him a little coarser in appearance and defiantly "Australian". He saw, perhaps truly, that his relatives were simply the survivors of the early administrators of the colony, with the self-sufficiency they had inherited from those people, still half-English in their attitude and entirely so in their values, and that they had no future in the country. It may be of interest to note here that the 1914 war finished them. They no longer survived as a group of any importance, or at any rate of social importance, as their qualities could not survive amongst people whose only respect was for money. It was odd that Harry combined his talk of "good form" and his "sirs" with this attitude, but like most young people, he was slightly muddled. He was rather like a man who buys highly varnished imitation Georgian furniture, but thinks the genuine antique too shabby. So he was angry at Josie's marrying an Englishman, especially one with aristocratic associations, as he thought that it would perpetuate the malaise of his family. If, on the other hand, the daughter of one of his squatter friends had bought such a husband, as Clara Bumpus had done, he would not have objected, as that would have shown the power of their money, which he revered.

Wolfie came back from Frankston on the same day that Harry arrived. He was bursting with happy paternal affection and was about to embrace his son, but Harry shook hands and said offhandedly: "Hullo, sir." Wolfie looked very hurt and Diana was angry. A day or two later, when Harry again, beneath the formality of his address, showed his contempt for his father, she turned on him saying: "The slightest of Wolfie's preludes is of more value to the human race than anything you are likely to produce in the whole of your boorish life."

This sort of thing increased her feeling of being in a false position, of being in a way, treacherous. She hotly defended Wolfie when she was planning to leave him for another man, but she could not bear Harry's attitude. He must have inherited his pomposity from some ancestor of Wolfie's. On Wolfie it was an amusing gossamer film of manner which fell off at the slightest provocation. In Harry it appeared to be solid throughout.

Another incident, if it could be called that, which puzzled her, happened one afternoon when she went to tea with Maysie. Miss Bath was there and apparently found great difficulty in answering when Diana spoke to her. She seemed so offended that Diana thought that by some oversight she could not have been invited to the wedding, and when she got home she looked up the list, but found the tick against Miss Bath's name which showed that she had accepted.

At a brief meeting with Russell in the tea-room where they had gone on that first day, she said: "I am longing for it all to be over and to get away. I want things simplified."

She tried to escape her divided feelings by concentrating on the arrangements for the wedding, to make them as perfect as possible though this again was partly as a compensation to herself. Her own mother had been so bitterly disappointed at her marriage to Wolfie, that she had left all the arrangements to Cousin Sarah, her Calvinistc housekeeper, who had taken a sadistic delight in making them as drab as possible. She had made up for this by later generosities, trips to Europe and presents of good jewellery, and by leaving her more than her sisters, but Diana had never forgotten the humiliation of her wedding day. Through Josie she would wipe it out. All the same she could not rid herself of the feeling that the wedding was some kind of test which she herself had to pass through.

The wedding was at All Saints', East St Kilda, which was not as smart as St John's, Toorak, but it was the church where all the family had been married since the early days. The day turned out to be fine, full of the winter sunlight of Walter Wither's picture, but shining on a slightly different scene. In the morning Diana had to take Josie and her luggage to the Radcliffe's where she was to dress. Then she had to return to Brighton for a picnic lunch with Wolfie and Harry, dress herself, and supervise Wolfie's adornment in a new morning coat and white spats. He was more anxious about his appearance than the bride, and required nearly as much attention.

Harry had no morning clothes and he wore his best navy-blue suit, which was a year old, and too tight for him, as his muscles had developed on the sheep station. Diana had wanted him to have a morning coat made quickly in time for the wedding, but he had refused saying: "I'm not going to pretend to be an Englishman."

When they came out into the sunlight he looked at Diana and said: "You're too dolled up, Mum."

Diana had a black velvet toque, into which she had pinned with a diamond brooch, a tuft of blue feathers that matched her dress. She had long white kid gloves and she wore her pearls, and pearl and diamond earrings, but she did not think that she was over-dressed. When she was dressed for a party she always looked a little dramatic. She could not help it, and in fact she enjoyed it. It emphasized her natural distinction. When she had taken no trouble with her clothes, she attracted no attention, except from a connoisseur like Russell. Harry would not have objected to her appearance if she had looked like a rich Toorak lady, but she was not fat enough, and they did not have her kind of face. But she had a moment's qualm. Would they say afterwards that she had been showily dressed at her daughter's wedding?

Harry sat opposite her in the car, the contrast between his slightly gingery hair and his blue suit making him look like a Presbyterian empire builder on Sunday morning. Wolfie said: "Do I look nice?" When Diana, to make up for Harry's surly manner, told him with warmth that he looked very nice, he said: "I am the King of England," and he raised his top hat and bowed to the empty streets. Then she was annoyed that Harry had again forced her into this defensive attitude towards Wolfie, and when he showed so obviously that he did not find his father amusing, she said sharply:

"The wide open spaces seem to have made you exceedingly stuffy, Harry."

When they arrived at the Radcliffes', Jack Radcliffe said: "By Jove, Diana, you'll steal Josie's thunder," and she felt cheerful and confident again. She went up with a sudden access of happy excitement to see Josie, and to do the final arrangement of her dress, her wreath and the old lace veil which Lady Wendale had lent her.

At last she set out for the church with Harry and the Radcliffes, leaving with their butler the responsibility of sending Wolfie off with Josie at exactly twenty past two.

When she arrived at the church she went with Harry up to the front pew on the left. Daisy and Jimmy Byngham were already there, Jimmy looking arrogant and slightly mad. She had given Daisy a cheque to buy a new dress, but they had spent it on a week's holiday in Sydney, and Daisy, who had something of her own flair for clothes, had reconditioned a dress she had given her last year. Fortunately, though they looked odd, they had an air which prevented them from being entirely discreditable. If they had been in rags they would still have seated themselves in the most prominent position. Diana wondered if she and Wolfie had been quite as troublesome when they were young. But Harry's surliness, and Daisy's absolute selfishness in spending the cheque in that way, made her feel that it would not cause her such a great pang to leave them.

The test which she thought the wedding would be for her, was to behave towards these people, even to her closest relatives, with adequate and controlled friendliness, but with no open affection which she felt would make her vulnerable to their censure when she had left them. Combined with the need for this effort was the anxiety that everything should go perfectly.

The Governor-General, Lady Eileen, the Wendales, Lord Francis Blake and Miss Rockingham came and sat across the aisle. The State Governor and his suite followed and sat in the pew behind them. If the whole Royal family had been coming, Diana thought ironically, Daisy still would have spent her cheque on a trip to Sydney.

John, in dark green uniform, with Freddie in scarlet, came in from the vestry and stood at the right of the aisle. Diana, remembering what he had told her about Josie and the pot of daphne, with that instinct she had for making a simple decoration an allusion to something else, had pots of this plant, now in its waxy bloom, put at the chancel steps. He caught their scent and looked down. When he saw what it came from, he turned and gave Diana a quick shy smile of gratitude.

A few moments later Josie arrived at the west door, and came slowly up the aisle on Wolfie's arm, followed by six bridesmaids in peach-coloured dresses, carrying posies of coppery roses. Suddenly all Diana's intentions for herself and her demeanour were swamped in a wave of maternal pride and love. Josie had arrived safely, and her anxiety about the success of any arrangement which depended even in a partial degree on Wolfie, evaporated. She did not realize that this love which she sent like a blessing towards Josie, included Wolfie in the orbit of its kindness. When he had given his daughter away, obeying careful preliminary instructions, without which he might have followed her to the altar, he joined Diana in her pew. He had the blissful expression of a good boy, and continuing in this role he took up a prayer book, with some difficulty found the marriage service, and held the open book towards her, so that they might follow it together.

A little more than twenty years ago, where John and Josie were now standing, she had been married to Wolfie. Because of the way she had defended him against Harry, and because of her expression when he rejoined her in the pew, he thought that he was now quite forgiven for Mrs Montaubyn, and Diana realized that when he held the book out to her, he intended their sharing it to be a kind of re-marriage service. After a few minutes she turned away from it, as if she wanted to watch Josie at the altar.

She felt again a touch of the same kind of panic she had when she was waiting for Russell, before John and Josie arrived. In this church, the first she had ever attended, where she and her children had been christened, where most

270

of her relatives and friends had been married, from where her parents had been carried to the grave, she was the victim of more enduring and potent influences even than those of her own house at Brighton. She could not keep her reserved attitude towards her own flesh and blood, who were all around her. She did not want to become an outcast from them, and she wished that the service would soon end.

When it did, and they went with the Caves and the Wendales to sign the register, she looked down the church for a glimpse of Russell, to feel the reassurance which the sight of him might give her, but she could not see him.

At last they came out into the sunlight, and with all the liveliness and laughter she recovered her composure. Russell had not come to the wedding, and she believed that he had stayed away so that he would not embarrass her. She thought the only thing to do was to pigeon-hole him in her mind. She could no longer try to think of her intentions and her immediate situation at the same time.

Soon she was standing again where she had stood eight months earlier, at the end of the arcaded lobby leading to Elsie's drawing-room, but now with John and Josie and the Wendales, who were *in loco parentis* to John, as the Governors were not allowed to visit private houses since Lord Brassey had gone to the wrong people. Everyone was lively and charming and she could not help responding without reserve to the flattery and affection showered on herself as well as on Josie. The present was the only reality, and all her plans and problems were a half-forgotten dream. She was speaking to Arthur who was admiring the lace of Josie's veil, when suddenly she heard behind her the loud announcement of Russell's name. She turned with a start, and saw him standing before her, holding out his hand. She did not immediately offer her own.

"Oh," she said, almost with a note of accusation. "I thought you weren't coming."

"I couldn't get to the church," he explained. "The car didn't arrive." He passed on, leaving Diana dismayed by the sharp tone in which she had spoken. She thought that she had been like a child which repudiates a new friend when it meets its normal associates. She had acted from herd instinct. For the last hour she had been completely caught up in the atmosphere of the herd, and though it might be said that Russell was one of them, he was like that captive seagull which escaped and returned to its fellows, only to be destroyed by them because it bore the taint of humanity.

She was desperate now to speak to him and to have the opportunity to wipe out the effect of her involuntary rudeness. She sat by Lord Wendale at the wedding breakfast, and she hoped that he would put down her distracted manner to the natural feelings of a mother at her daughter's marriage. She could see Russell across the room, sitting at a table with Miss Rockingham and the Radcliffes. She found it hard not to look often in his direction.

There were speeches and John replied to the toast of the bride and bridegroom. "When I was young," he began, and everyone laughed, as in spite of his uniform he looked so very young. "Well, I am a married man," he protested, which made them laugh more. He went on: "When I was a small boy and wanted to do something and was prevented by the weather, our governess would say, it wasn't 'meant'. I first saw Josie in this house, and I am glad the wedding party is here, because it shows that it was 'meant', and I think the same about her today as I did then, or the other way round, and more so. I hope you see what I mean; thank you."

There was a great deal of laughter and clapping. After some more speeches Wolfie rose to reply to the toast of the bride's parents. He said:

"Today I am sad, because my daughter is taken from me across the ocean many miles. But I am happy because she is Eva who has found her Walther, and my smile is larger than my tears. Now all our little sparrows are flown away and my dear wife and I shall be alone in our empty nest, where there will be quiet and wistfulness. But today, in the same holy place where we were married together twenty-three years ago, my wife and I were, as it may seem, married again. Then we were married for our children. Today we are married for ourselves. Then we knew that before us were troubles, for man is a wayward horse which must sometimes kick the fence. Now we know that before us is calm and trust." He turned to John. "If you kick a hole in the fence, be careful you do not give your wife sorrow, for then you will be sad too. And you," he said to Josie, "if sometimes he gallops in another field, do not grieve, for he will come back to you who are beautiful and kind, like your mother, my dear wife."

If this speech had been delivered in plain English it would have horrified the listeners, but in Wolfie's idiom it merely struck them as quaintly sentimental and amusing.

Shortly after this John and Josie left the table to change into their travelling clothes. Diana went up to help Josie and to say good-bye to her alone. When she came down again Freddie was tying an old shoe to the back of their car. He had with great ingenuity smuggled it all the way from Government House without John seeing it. He was very proud of this, and it was his chief topic of conversation for some weeks ahead. Diana contrasted the picture of Josie whom she had just left, tremulous and happy, with this traditional oafishness, but she knew that it would be thought outrageous if she interfered.

Someone said: "Here they come!" and John and Josie, sheltering their faces, made a dash from the door to the car. Freddie thrust a handful of confetti down John's neck, and Clara Bumpus, shrieking: "Keep him in the home paddock!" flung another handful in Josie's face. The car door slammed and in a minute they were out of sight.

Diana murmured: "Bless them," and walked slowly into the house. Her responsibilities were over. She did not now mind much what happened and when she saw Russell in the hall she went up to him and said:

"It's over."

"Everything went perfectly."

"Yes, I think it did." They spoke a little about the details of the wedding, and went to the billiard room to look again at the presents. There was no one there except a detective eating *foie gras* sandwiches. They went to a seat at the far end of the room.

"It's been rather a strain," said Diana. "I hope I didn't show it."

274

"Not at all. You looked wonderful."

"When you arrived I wasn't expecting to see you." She was trying to apologize for her instinctive recoil, without admitting that it had happened.

"You looked a bit startled," he said.

"I was all strung up. Wolfie's speech was dreadful."

"He doesn't want to lose you, Diana."

"He goes into a cloud of emotion and rains down beautiful thought which evaporates in five minutes. He was using Josie to blackmail me. And to say that about kicking the fence! Thank Heaven no one understood clearly what he meant. Oh, I shall be glad when the next fortnight is over. How wonderful it will be. Did you notice what John said about this house, and it being 'meant'? Isn't he a dear?"

"It rather applies to us, too."

"Yes, the whole thing seems to be working out in a sort of pattern. I wish John hadn't been in uniform. He looked very nice, but it was a reminder of all the war in the air."

"Don't worry. It may not happen. The Kaiser has gone off on a yachting holiday, and he wouldn't do that if he were going to declare war."

"You say such sensible things, Russell. The other day I had to listen to Owen Dell, who, because he's a colonel in the Australian Army, thinks he must be accepted as an authority on European diplomacy. He's delighted at the prospect of war. He thinks he'd be made a general."

"I think one of the things that are tiresome here is that no one seems to know how much he doesn't know."

"Yes, I suppose so," said Diana. "I must go back to the hall. People will be looking for me to say good-bye."

Harry was in the hall, and Diana said: "That is my son. Shall I introduce him?"

Russell hesitated. He wanted to gain Josie's friendship so that it would be easier for Diana when they were in Europe, but he saw no point in making the acquaintance of a young man whom he would be unlikely to meet again, and who from his appearance, would almost certainly in the near future be going about saying that he would "like to shoot Lockwood".

Diana felt his hesitation and said: "Perhaps there's no point."

George and Baba passed through the hall. George stopped, congratulated Diana on everything, and said good-bye. Baba gave her a blank stare and walked on. Although Baba was consistently rude to her "in-laws", she had never before gone so far as to cut her hostess, and for a minute or two after this Diana had a curious feeling of puzzled anger.

Most of the people began to leave. They said the wedding had been "fun", "beautiful", "so nice, all our own sort", and one or two almost tearfully pressed her hand and said how sad she must feel at losing her daughter. While she thanked them she could not help wondering what they would be saying about her in a few months' time.

At last all had gone, except for a few relatives and old family friends who had lingered on to gossip, among them Steven and Laura. There was a Gilbert and Sullivan opera season opening in Melbourne, and as the sixth of August was Mildy's birthday, Steven thought that they might give her a theatre party on that day, partly in recognition of her kindness to me. They asked George and Baba, but Baba refused as she did not think it would be smart to be seen in public with Mildy, and as she was now a master of that underbred insolence, those tricks which any ill-natured person can pick up in a week, and which many people in society imagine are aristocratic, she gave as her excuse: "the plumber is coming in that day."

When Steven was leaving he also invited Diana and Wolfie. Diana hesitated and said: "That is only two days before I sail for England."

"Then it can also be a farewell party for you," said Laura.

She thought a moment and said: "Thank you. Very well, I'll come." She had an affection for Steven and Laura, and she did not think that they would blame her for leaving Wolfie. She was pleased at the idea of this friendly family meeting before she left.

Steven and Laura, with countrified simplicity, imagined that Cynthia might be "out of things" now that Anthea was away, though actually Cynthia, as well as her own, had Anthea's share of the "and Miss Langton" invitations. They invited her to the party—a birthday dinner at the Oriental Hotel, and then *Patience* at Her Majesty's.

Diana was going to find Elsie to thank her for lending the house, and also she hoped to secure from her, she didn't know how, some promise that nothing that happened should ever break their friendship, or at any rate convince her that whatever she did, it would not show any weakening

277

of her affection and gratitude to her. She felt more tranquil than at any time in recent weeks.

She was preoccupied with her thoughts of what she would say, when in the little arcaded gallery leading to the drawing-room, she was stopped by Mildy in a state of agitation.

"Diana, I must speak to you," she said.

"What about?"

"Everyone is talking about you. You mustn't be seen talking to Russell Lockwood. Baba saw you with him in a hansom going up Swanston Street, and Miss Bath said you had supper alone together. I know you would never do anything unbecoming, but you ought to be discreet."

"What impertinence!" exclaimed Diana.

"You don't want to be talked about."

"By Baba and Miss Bath? They'll talk about me whatever I do, so I may as well give them some reason."

"You wouldn't *do* anything!" said Mildy, round-eyed with admiration.

"I wouldn't allow Miss Bath to influence me. Where is she? I didn't see her."

"She didn't come."

"That's a good thing," said Diana, and she went on to look for Elsie. But Mildy had disturbed her mood of calm acceptance. Could it be true that people were talking about her, all those people who had been so flattering and affectionate this afternoon? Was that simply manner, and had they come with no friendliness towards her, but only because it was a grand wedding? She could not believe it, and yet she could not entirely put it from her mind. She remembered Baba, staring at her without saying good-bye. That, instead of disturbing her, reassured her a little. The others did not behave like that. But they were "ladies". Miss Bath, in spite of her repulsive magnetism, was also a lady. She did not approve so she stayed away. Only Baba would go to a party and cut her hostess, because although Elsie had lent the house, Diana had been responsible for everything else.

When she found Elsie she did not try to say what she had intended. Her mood was changed and was touched with bitterness. She felt that any attempt to retain the friendship of those whom she loved would be misunderstood. She thought that perhaps she ought not to go to Mildy's birthday party, but she did not see what excuse she could give.

CHAPTER FOURTEEN

Harry went back to Queensland three days after the wedding, and Diana was ashamed to feel relieved that he was gone. It was unpleasant to feel a faint dislike for one of her children, even if, perhaps, it was not much deeper than Harry's ridiculous "public school" manner which was partly responsible for it. Also, his presence had made her attitude to Wolfie more difficult. She continually felt the impulse to compensate him for Harry's rudeness.

She saw Harry off on the Sydney train and went to have tea with Russell.

"The situation is simplifying," she said. "You must think I'm rather like a potato that you've dug up with too much earth attached to it. But I'm gradually shedding it."

He laughed and said: "You're not like a potato at all. A rather graceful stick of celery, perhaps."

"Well, I'm not going to let the earth worry you any more. Perhaps it's been a good thing because it's shown me how I can rely on you. And it has eased me from my native soil. It's given me time to know what I'm doing. You've been so patient and understanding. No other condition might have shown me that. So often one finds vulgar people who are kind, and people with taste and culture who are insolent to harmless nonentities."

"Or vulgar people who are insolent to harmless nonentities."

"Like Baba," said Diana. She paused. "Russell, people have begun to talk about us. At least, Baba has."

"Oh." He looked serious. "How much does that matter, I wonder? For you, I mean. It doesn't matter for me at all."

"It doesn't matter for me, only for Josie. It may be nothing. Mildred told me, and she loves any excitement. I wish I hadn't mentioned it. Anyhow, there's really nothing she can say. Apparently she saw us that day when it was raining and we drove up to the Gallery in a hansom."

"It doesn't sound terribly vicious," said Russell.

"Baba cut me yesterday at the wedding."

"What! She couldn't!" he exclaimed.

"You've no idea what that type can do."

"It's inconceivable. You know I don't believe that you have the faintest conception of what you are. You talk about a potato with earth on it. You're a diamond or something better. If you could have seen yourself at the wedding, you couldn't imagine that that pathetic *arriviste* could 'cut' you. You looked superb, like someone who had stepped out of her place in history into our commonplace world. You had such a look of detachment and tolerance, and pride and kindness, and that with the bones of your face gave you a look of tremendous distinction, the look your mother had sometimes, especially when she was a little angry. I expect that every glance you give Baba unconsciously blots her off the earth, and she simply can't bear it."

"I was a little angry," said Diana.

"Not with me I hope."

"No, of course not. How could I be?" She hoped that this would wipe out her involuntary withdrawal when he was announced. "From what I've seen of you, I don't believe you could ever make me angry."

"I've tried to show you my best side."

"What's your worst side?"

"I don't forgive injuries."

"Oh! Not ever?"

"I wouldn't say that."

"You make me a little frightened. I might do you an involuntary injury—perhaps you might find that I'd done so by coming with you."

"That's absurd. You don't know how proud I shall be of you. And I don't mean accidental injuries. I mean those done deliberately—in cold blood. If I were Wolfie, I'm afraid I wouldn't forgive you."

"Are you blaming me?" asked Diana uneasily.

"Good Heavens, no. He did you the first injury, and I don't expect you to forgive that."

"But I have forgiven him," said Diana. "I wish him well. I'm very anxious about his future, but I don't want to share it."

282

"I'm not sure that's not a little immoral," said Russell, but he was smiling, and she tried to think that he had not meant what he said.

They talked about their arrangements. It was only a week till Josie and John returned, and a fortnight till Russell sailed. "It's easy for me now," said Diana. "There are only two things which I may find slightly upsetting. We're to dine at Government House on the night Josie returns, and there's a family birthday party only two nights before I sail. It's when I have to appear in public with Wolfie, as a dutiful wife, that I find it difficult, and feel a humbug."

"Think that in only a few weeks we'll be together and free."

"I do think of it. I'm thinking of it all the time. Although these past three months have been trying, they've been wonderful too."

They arranged when and how they should meet until he left.

"I'd like to see you on the day before you sail," said Diana. "Because after that I shan't see you for nearly two weeks."

"Shall we drive somewhere on that afternoon, if it's fine? I'll come to Brighton to collect you."

"Yes, that would be lovely. And it will be all right to call at the house, as Wolfie goes to the Conservatorium on Thursdays."

In the train on the way home she felt that everything was now clear ahead, and yet there was something at the back of her mind which prevented her from enjoying perfect tranquility of mind.

The dinner at Government House was a little trying, but not in the way that Diana had foreseen. She and Wolfie were invited to the big parties, but she had not dined there since before her marriage. If it had not been for Josie, they would not have been invited now. In her carefulness to be punctual they arrived early, and were shown into an empty drawing-room. Josie and John were the first to come down. Josie, in a pale yellow dress, looked blooming, and she embraced them affectionately. She seemed to fit with such natural grace into this setting that Diana was immensely proud of her. It was only a family party and when the others came down they stood about, talking with cheerful informal friendliness, but when they went into dinner the atmosphere changed.

Sir Roland began to talk about the probability of war. As a young man he had been in the Diplomatic, but had left it to go into Parliament. People in Melbourne, far from the scene of any wars, and at that time with scanty foreign news in their papers, did not take the rumours very seriously, but the people at Government House were English, and belonged to the class which regarded wars and diplomacy as their special province. Sir Roland was well-informed, and pretended to be even more so. Diana saw Josie looking puzzled and anxious, and she thought it not very well-mannered of them to keep the conversation on the likelihood of imminent war in the presence of a young bride, who was by way of being the guest of honour, whose husband was a soldier, and whose father incidentally was conspicuously German, and at the moment looking pompous, puffy round the eyes, and bewildered.

"But isn't the Kaiser on a yachting holiday?" asked Diana, remembering Russell's observation. "Would he go off if he expected war?"

Miss Rockingham looked gratefully at Diana across the table, and nodded her long head in approval of this intelligent remark. In the drawing-room she came up to her and said:

"I am so glad you said that about the German Emperor. It's obvious that he doesn't want a war. It's so foolish to talk of one as if it were a day's shoot. I have dear friends in every European country." She meant all the crowned heads, but left that to be assumed. "It would be the end of all of *us*." She waved her hand at Lady Eileen and Dolly Wendale.

"It *is* worrying," said Diana, "with John in the army, and Josie just off to Europe."

"You mustn't worry. It won't happen. As you pointed out, the Emperor has gone yachting. But you're going to Europe yourself. I am delighted to hear that we are to travel on the same ship. You know Mr Lockwood? But of course, you were at his luncheon."

"Yes," said Diana. "He's an old family friend. We played together as children."

"He will be on the ship with us."

"I think he's leaving a week earlier."

"Only to go to Perth. He joins our ship there. I thought you would know this."

Diana was puzzled by this conversation. She wondered how Miss Rockingham knew all this, and there seemed an odd hint of complicity in her remarks. Probably Russell had thought it wiser to tell her of his movements, than suddenly to appear on the ship. Perhaps she had been trying to find out how much Diana knew of his plans. But she appeared to be very friendly. She praised Josie highly, saying: "She will make all the young men come out to find Australian wives."

When the men came in from the dining-room, Wolfie did not look happy, and as they drove away he said:

"It was not good so to speak of my countrymen before my true face."

"English people can be hideously rude," said Diana carelessly, although they had been very polite to herself.

"But those are noble."

"That only makes them think it doesn't matter."

Wolfie was not soothed by this explanation, but Diana controlled a further impulse to comfort him.

Josie came alone to Brighton on the next day, her last in Australia for many years. Diana had thought that being alone with Wolfie and Josie might create awkward tensions, and disturb the delicate balance of her attitude to him, which, in spite of his speech at the wedding, he appeared to accept. And she thought that it might cause her some pangs, but on the contrary she had a sense of calm, that a phase of her life was over, and that this was its pleasant and peaceful ending. She did not repudiate this phase in her mind, but only regarded it as complete. It had been marked by anxieties and troubles, but also had its rewards, in the affection, if not the gratitude, of the children for the efforts she had made for them. They might feel gratitude in another thirty years, as she now felt a belated gratitude to her own mother. The children had chosen the lives, which, she thought, really suited them. Daisy was happy in her semi-squalor, describing every young man who came to the house carrying a violin or painting materials as "brilliant". Harry was happy to be away from the bright spirits of his blood, amongst the Presbyterian sheep-farmers, while Josie, the only one really fitted for it, was returning to civilization. She was saved from not exactly the wreckage, but from what, by the standards of Diana's youth, was a kind of disintegration of the family. Her own mother had been really cultivated, acquainted with people of note in Europe, and rich enough to express her taste, and also to sustain her family above the level of poverty. Diana thought that she was a rather dim reflection of her mother. When Daisy married the quite penniless but "brilliant" Jimmy Byngham, that was a further dimming of the same pattern. She hoped that Daisy's children would, in a violent reaction against artistic poverty, go into the city and make fortunes. As it turned out they sank even further into the creative midden. But she could not foresee this and she thought perhaps that everything was tidied up. The phase, the second movement as it were of her life had ended satisfactorily.

Josie stayed to tea, but she had to be back at Government House by six o'clock. Before she left she made a tour of the house and Diana felt that she was saying good-bye to it. But she did not seem to mind, as she said: "When you come back from England you ought to sell this house. It's too big for you and Daddy alone, and it's too far out. Miss Rockingham was praising you tremendously last night after you'd gone. She said that you had so much elegance. You waste it out here clipping hedges. You ought

287

to build a nice little house in South Yarra where you can see your friends."

Diana was amused at the new assurance in Josie's manner, but she only agreed that perhaps the house should be sold. There was plenty of time to think about it.

She called to Wolfie that Josie was leaving, and puffing at a meerschaum pipe he came out of his music-room. He might have been emotionally dramatic at this departure of his daughter from her childhood's home, but the slight melancholy that he had felt at luncheon, thinking that this was the last meal he would have with her for many years, had wakened a sad little cadence in his mind, and he was now preoccupied with working it into a prelude. He kissed her absently and said that he would see her on Friday on the ship.

When they went to Port Melbourne to see her off, and found her and John surrounded by the staff from Government House, Sophie, Cynthia, Aunt Maysie and all kinds of important people, he thought it a nice party, and became gay and pompous, and forgot to be sad.

Diana spoke to her for a few moments in her cabin.

"Well, darling," she said, "it's only about seven weeks till I see you again—no longer than when you went on that holiday to Queensland."

"But if there's a war, Mummy?" asked Josie, puckering her forehead.

"Don't worry. There won't be a war, and if there is it couldn't last more than a month—so Mr Lockwood says. People aren't as silly now as they used to be. They don't want to wreck their own countries."

288

"Still, I wish there wasn't all this talk," said Josie.

"You mustn't think of it. Everything before you is wonderful."

They kissed a little tearfully, and went back on deck, where Wolfie was entertaining a large circle.

Six days later Russell collected her, not at the house, as for some reason Wolfie had not gone to the Conservatorium, but at the Brighton Beach railway station. She felt that this kind of subterfuge was sordid, but as it was the last of their meetings she almost appreciated it as a reminder that it would never again be necessary. They drove on down the coast road to Mornington and sat under the ti-tree at the top of a cliff looking at the sands of the little bay below them, and across the placid waters of Port Phillip, which is practically an inland sea. On the horizon a ship was steaming towards the heads.

"I shall be out there tomorrow," said Russell, "and you in another week."

"Yes. The way's clear at last," said Diana, but there was not absolute conviction in her voice, He noticed it and said:

"You don't sound absolutely certain."

"Oh, I am." She was faintly surprised. "I suppose I was thinking about the possibility of war."

"But we've agreed that wouldn't change our plans. Even if the very worst happened, and we couldn't get to England, we could stay somewhere quietly in Western Australia, but I don't think that's likely."

"I don't mind what we do if we are together and free," she said.

They walked down the cliff path to the beach and picked up shells from the sand. Diana tied a few pretty ones in her handkerchief. After a while they climbed back and strolled round the little township, until they found a primitive tea-shop, where they sat on a veranda, drinking strong tea and eating dry, solid, yellow cake.

"I love doing this sort of thing," said Diana, "going to look at some pleasant place and having tea out of doors. I think my parents only felt at home in a coach or a train. I must have inherited the feeling. Perhaps all Australians have it or they wouldn't have come here in the first place, unless they were transported, and that may have given them the taste for travel."

"I'm really happiest travelling too," said Russell. "I can't imagine anything more perfect than travelling with you, and not having black tea under a tin veranda, but lunching under the vines at Frascati, and looking down across the Campagna to Rome."

"But it's nice here too," said Diana, "in the winter sunlight."

"Yes, but that will be heaven."

"Shall we have a house? We haven't thought anything about that? Or an apartment? Where shall we live d'you think?"

He thought the best thing would be to travel for a year, all the time looking out for some place where they might finally settle, which he felt would most likely be in Italy. He described places they might go to, a few of which she had seen, but only in brief glimpses, and twenty years ago.

"I'm just beginning to realize how wonderful it will be," she said. "Up till now, because of all the things I've had to deal with first, it has seemed a little unreal, like a dream. But now the dream is beginning to take colour and more definite shape. This afternoon is like a foretaste, but it's rather like a dream too. It's so peaceful here, and I don't mind the black tea and this sawdusty cake. Perhaps it will become a dream, and when we're at Frascati I shall say: Wherever was I sitting under a tin veranda, eating yellow cake and feeling blissfully happy?"

They sat talking until the sun was low across the bay, and the air became chilly. It was dark when they reached Brighton, and he pulled up by St Andrew's church, with its sandy, scrubby graveyard, from where she could easily walk home.

"This has been a wonderful afternoon, Russell," said Diana. "The first, when we could look straight ahead. Not only that, it was lovely to be with you down there by the sea. I felt as if we were in Italy already."

"There'll be thousands more like it."

"Thousands? Isn't that a great many?"

"There are three hundred and sixty-five days in a year. So only three years is about a thousand."

"When one afternoon has been so lovely, it sounds overwhelming. But I would have liked this afternoon to go on for ever."

"So would I. I don't want to leave you now."

"I don't want to leave you."

"Shall we just drive on?"

She smiled. "Not now—but quite soon."

It was nearly dark now and there was no one about. He took her in his arms and kissed her tenderly. He opened the door of the car for her, and stood watching her cross the road. They were not to meet again until Fremantle, as she could not very well go to see him off at the ship. When she reached the other side of the road, she waved her hand, and again before she turned down the side street which led to the sea.

CHAPTER FIFTEEN

Russell sailed the following afternoon and on the same day France declared war on Germany. On Monday England declared war on Germany. On Wednesday was Mildy's birthday party. On Friday Diana was to sail for Europe.

On the day England declared war Mildy rang up Westhill and said to Steven: "Of course my party's off?"

"No, why?" asked Steven peevishly.

"But the war!"

"I don't suppose the Germans will arrive in Melbourne before Wednesday," he said, and rang off.

In spite of this, during the next two days, Mildy talked more of the impropriety of her having a birthday party after war had been declared, than of the cataclysm itself.

We drove to the hotel through crowded streets, where newsboys were shouting special editions. People had streamed in from the suburbs to learn the last-minute news, and to enjoy the feeling of excitement. When we joined my parents in the hotel there was a slight feeling of apprehension, but no lack of cheerfulness. When the Flugels arrived Steven said: "We asked George and Baba but she couldn't come."

"That is nice," said Wolfie complacently. Cynthia arrived and we went in to dinner.

Steven said to Mildy: "What shall we drink? You're the birthday queen, so it's for you to choose."

Mildy did not answer, but opened her pale blue eyes with an expression of astonishment. This was meant to express gratitude at his magnificent generosity. He merely thought as usual that she was off her head, and asked irritably: "Well, what wine d'you want?"

"Is it right to drink wine in wartime?" answered Mildy pursing her lips.

"Good Lord! What wine d'you want?" he repeated.

"Any wine is a nice treat," said Mildy humbly.

"Champagne is nice," said Wolfie.

Steven laughed and ordered two bottles of champagne. Several people whom we knew were dining at the hotel. They were all talking about the war and some stopped at our table to ask Steven's opinion or to give their own. One with a red, jovial face said: "I bet it's over in three weeks." Another, more pessimistic, said he thought that it would last till Christmas.

Mr Hemstock came in with the Cambridge couple, who had just returned from three months' primitive sex observation in the Northern Territory. He stopped behind

294

our table and boomed: "Good evening, Miss Cynthia." Cynthia introduced him to Laura and Steven.

"Ah, the squire of Westhill," he said. Steven was not very agreeable, as he disliked being made part of the bogus eighteenth-century atmosphere which Mr Hemstock built up for his Johnsonian role, especially as he was still the authentic squire of Waterpark, which was not sold until after the war.

Mr Hemstock spoke with an air of immense gravity about the war, enjoying the feeling of moral grandeur this gave him. He had a sense of power, of inflicting a stern duty on mankind as he said: "I do not see how it can end before fifteen or twenty years. But we shall smite them. Be sure we shall smite them, and doubtless this young man will be of the first." He put a lecherous hand on my shoulder.

When he had passed on I muttered to Mildy: "The old fool! I'd like to stick a knife into his hot-water bottle."

Mildy giggled with pleasure at sharing a secret with me. She had now overcome her scruples and had drunk a fair amount of wine. About many things, in fact most things that did not affect herself, she was incapable of instinctive good feeling. She had to see what others were doing, and because she had the intelligence to know that her moral sense was, at it were, floating, she was always nervous of doing the wrong thing. Now that she saw that others besides ourselves were drinking wine in wartime, she was only too eager to have her full share.

The excitement which pervaded the streets was even more intense in the theatre. Just before the curtain went up the Governor-General and Lady Eileen with

Miss Rockingham, Lord Francis Blake, the Wendales, Freddie Thorpe and Clara Bumpus, came in and filled two boxes. The orchestra, with a tremendous roll of drums began: *God Save the King*. A fruity contralto voice from a few rows behind us began to sing the words, other people took it up, and soon the whole theatre was singing, inflaming every breast except perhaps Miss Rockingham's and Wolfie's, with patriotic ardour. I could not look round to find who had started this burst of song, until our own National Anthem was over, but when the orchestra began to plough through those of France, Serbia, Belgium and Russia, I thought it permissible to steal a glance. Four rows back I saw Mrs Montaubyn, and it was evident from her flushed and smug appearance, and from the way that others were looking at her, that she was the leader of the demonstration of loyalty.

Diana also turned and saw her. She had been very quiet at dinner, and this was attributed to Wolfie's being a German. It certainly was a complication she had not foreseen, but her gentleness of manner was due to her realization that this might be the last meal she would have taken in the company of her closest relatives. When she saw Mrs Montaubyn behind her, at first she had a sharp reminder of the scene in the ballroom at Government House, and a touch of her anger with Wolfie returned. She thought it must be "meant" that she should see her now, to justify herself on the very eve of her departure. But as the evening wore on this feeling disappeared, and she became rather worried lest they should encounter her as they went out. For this reason she did not move from her seat at the intervals, nor did

Wolfie, though Steven went out to talk in the foyer. Wolfie also was aware of Mrs Montaubyn's presence. He looked rather puffy and aloof, but neither guilty nor nervous, and Diana gathered that they must have parted.

We were seated in the front row of the dress circle, and at the first interval a Mr and Mrs Morris, people whom Diana knew quite well, but not intimately, made their way out across our feet. They apologized to Laura, Mildy and Cynthia, but their recognition of Diana and Wolfie was so slight as to amount to a "cut". Diana thought for a moment that it was because they must have heard some gossip about her through Baba and Miss Bath. Then in a flash of illumination she realized it was because of Wolfie's German name and birth. She was angry and felt that protective impulse towards him which was so difficult to reconcile with her intention to leave him. She thought she ought to be glad that Mrs Montaubyn was there as a reminder, to prevent her feeling too sharp regrets at the last moment.

I had been sitting next to Mildy, but at the second interval we all changed places and I was between Diana and Cynthia. It seemed as if the opera itself, the plaintive melodies and aesthetic absurdities of *Patience*, provided curious intervals of unreality in the excitement that possessed the audience, and though when the last curtain fell they clapped and cheered again and again for Bunthorne and his love-sick maidens, it was merely to release their patriotic excitement and enthusiasm for the war.

At last the audience began to move out. Diana said to me quietly: "Don't hurry. That woman who was tipsy at

Government House is behind us, and I don't want to run into her again."

I dropped my programme and held up the exit of our party by groping for it under the seat.

"What are you doing?" asked Steven. "You're blocking the gangway."

"I'm looking for my programme."

"It doesn't matter. If you want one you can have mine."

There was now no excuse for dawdling. I glanced apologetically at Diana and we moved out. Mrs Montaubyn had seen her and Wolfie, and she talked loudly in the intervals partly because she was elated at having started the whole theatre singing, and partly to let them know that she was there. She went out ahead of us and when we came into the foyer, she was half-way down the stairs. She was conspicuous enough with her brassy hyacinthine curls, but she wanted to draw attention to herself as a kind of goddess of patriotism, the splendid female embodiment of the spirit of the nation. She harangued any young men near her, inciting them to do various things to the Germans.

I was with Laura, and behind us Mildy, with one of those sudden sprouts of intelligence, which were so disconcerting to those who, like Cynthia, regarded her as mentally deficient, was saying: "Gilbert must have been attracted towards aestheticism, as we can only satirise those things which a part of us admires."

"Look, Mum," I said, taking Laura's arm. "Do you see that woman with yellow curls? She's the one I had to dance with, and who was so rude to Aunt Diana at Government House."

298

"She looks strikingly handsome," said Laura, "but excitable."

She turned to discuss how everyone was going home. She and Steven were walking back to the hotel where they were staying for the night. A car had been ordered for Cynthia, and Mildy and I were to walk down to the Toorak tram. Diana said that she did not want to walk to the station through the crowds in the streets, and asked if I would fetch her a cab from the rank. I ran down the stairs, and dodged past Mrs Montaubyn without her seeing me, to perform this errand.

The rest of our party went slowly down to the entrance lobby. Mrs Montaubyn, reluctant to leave the scene of her success, had stayed at the bottom of the stairs, where she was giving in lurid language her opinion of the Germans, and receiving good-natured chaff from some men standing near. When Wolfie saw her he was disturbed, because he did not want Diana to be reminded of her, but he did not imagine that she would embarrass him by actually speaking to him, as she had refused him admission to her flat, and their friendship was ended.

He moved to the far side of the stairs, away from the wall against which Mrs Montaubyn was standing. He attempted to walk past as if he were occupied with his own sublime thoughts. Mrs Montaubyn saw him, and she saw too the opportunity of wiping out, backed by the whole weight of public approval, the humiliations which she believed he had put upon her. With the fury of a woman scorned and the vigour of a great patriot, she crossed over to him, and shouting: "Here's a dirty German!" she slapped his face.

Our party, including Wolfie himself, stood frozen with dismay. Diana could not immediately take in what had happened, because for her it had infinitely greater implications than for the others.

Cynthia was the first to move. At that moment I arrived with a hansom, and through the open door she saw it draw up at the kerb. She took Wolfie's arm, and in her high-powered voice, vibrant with kindness and indignation, she said:

"There is your cab, Cousin Wolfie. Let me take you to it."

"He's a bloody German," jeered Mrs Montaubyn, "and the only good German's a dead one."

Some louts in the street looked in at them with curiosity, and one said: "There's a dirty German."

Cynthia, with the arrogance of the English gentle-woman in which she had been trained by Cousin Sophie, which is so atrocious when informed by self-importance, and so splendid when used as now, in the fearless service of humanity and justice, said, as if declaring a fact which her mere statement was sufficient to establish: "You wicked and horrible woman."

She led Wolfie to the cab, ignoring the menacing louts, who, quelled by the moral force of her personality, stood aside to let them pass. Diana came out of her trance and followed them. She touched Cynthia's hand in silent gratitude, and saying to me: "Thank Steven and Laura for us," she entered the cab and they drove away.

Cynthia's car drew up as they left. She thanked Laura and Steven for a delightful evening, and with no reference to the incident in which she had played such an eminent part, she went home.

Mrs Montaubyn looked almost as bewildered and injured as Wolfie when she had struck him. She had believed that she was behaving virtuously, fulfilling the role for which nature had intended her, that of a daughter of Britannia, the Spirit of Victory, for how could a war be conducted without women of her heroic mould, who encourage the boys with raucous shouts and fruity songs, and reward them with their bodies at a reasonable charge? She had thought that at last she had broken through the barrier excluding her from human society, into a rich companionship; but the men who had been chaffing her, not yet brutalized by propaganda, drifted away disgusted, and she felt as wounded as when none of the swells would talk to her at Government House. She went out into the street with her woman companion, for she was no more anxious to be seen in public with the hall porter than Wolfie had been with herself.

Mildy and I walked along with my parents to the hotel.

"That was nice of Cynthia," said Mildy, in a dreary, grudging voice.

I was glowing with love and admiration for Cynthia, and Mildy's half-intentional reduction of her action to the trivial, made me speechless with anger. My parents had something of the same feeling, as they ignored her remark beyond saying: "It was an unfortunate incident," and they talked about the opera until we arrived at the hotel. I asked if we could have some supper, but they said it was too late. They looked very tired, with a tiredness which was not merely physical. Steven might not want the war to interfere with the enjoyment of a party, but he and Laura saw clearly how it would affect our lives. They had three sons of military age, and the assault on Wolfie had horrified them, and they could not listen to Mildy's fatuous comments after it had happened.

They said good night, and Laura asked me, expressing a little more hope than usual, if I was coming to Westhill for the weekend.

"Good night," said Mildy. "Thank you for a lovely birthday party. But I'm not sure it wasn't a teeny bit naughty to have champagne."

When we were walking down Collins Street she said: "What a dreadful thing to happen! How could that woman know that Wolfie was a German?"

"She is the one who let fly at Government House," I said. "I think he knows her."

"He couldn't possibly know anyone like that," said Mildy. "She's not a nice woman. Some day you'll know what I mean."

She evidently wanted me to ask her to explain, which even if it had been necessary, was the last thing I would have done, as, apart from everything else, it was all I could do to be civil to her.

We waited by the Town Hall for the Toorak tram. Across the street I saw the oriflamme of Mrs Montaubyn's curls. She had recovered her self-confidence and was again the centre of a small chaffing crowd, to which she was apparently preaching a recruiting sermon.

"There she is," I said.

Mildy stared intently across at her. In her eyes was a strange expression, envious and evil.

When we arrived home, as usual after any outing, we sat down for our "cosy chat" over hot milk and biscuits. Mildy began to talk about the Germans in a way which would have made one expect her to approve Mrs Montaubyn's assault. I brought up the question of my going to the war.

"Oh no!" wailed Mildy angrily. "It's a ridiculous idea. Let those go who are fitted for it. You'd never make a soldier. You're much too used to comfort to sleep in a tent. You'd never stand it, the mud and the guns and everything."

This outburst, apart from the insult to my manhood and the reminder of the comforts she had lavished on me, destroyed the last traces of my respect for her, as it showed that her love for me, if it could be so called, had no moral basis of any kind. At the age I then was it is possible to have great affection for older people who increase our understanding and show themselves eager to help us forward in our lives, or who simply amuse us with the extravagancies of their generation, like Arthur. But Mildy all the time was trying to hold me back from any move which, however necessary or beneficial to myself, would, she thought, make me less her possession. She did not want me to have wider friendships or the ordinary associates of a young man, not to know anyone more worldly-wise or cultivated than herself, nor even to advance in taste or knowledge, or to fulfil the obligations of honour.

"It is you who make me ridiculous," I said brutally. "Everyone laughs about us."

303

This began dreadful recriminations, which, although I poured out my resentment at the innumerable silken threads, the subtle blackmails with which she tried to hold me, brought Mildy some satisfaction. It was an acknowledgement of the existence of her infatuation. From now on, until I went to the war, which was not for some months as the family decided I must go to England where relatives in the War Office would get me a commission, I accepted Mildy as a phenomenon, and when I acquiesced in her sentimental arrangements, it was without the exhausting effort to display appropriate feelings, which after the flare-up of this evening, she did not seem to demand.

But when I went to bed I forgot Mildy, and I thought of Cynthia's lovely head in its fearless beauty, the nymph's head restored.

CHAPTER SIXTEEN

Diana and Wolfie drove in silence down Collins Street. When the cab turned towards the railway station she put her hand through his arm.

"I am a German," he said, "and I love my country. But I do not love soldiers. It is sad." His voice trembled a little.

The trains were crowded. They found seats in the same carriage but not together. From time to time he gave her anxious glances, but they were no longer those reproachful oglings, which originally had been spontaneous, but which later he affected deliberately, as a child will repeat an originally unconscious gesture which has made its elders laugh. But she did not know whether Wolfie was different, or whether she was seeing him in a different light, seeing him as he was instead of through the film of a hallucination in which she had been living for the past six months. That loud slap, as Mrs Montaubyn struck his face, had awakened her to reality.

They drove home in the wagonette from the livery stables, ordered to meet them at the station. When they came into the hall, where the gas had been left burning, still they had hardly spoken. Wolfie, wondering if she was again going to blame him for his associations with Mrs Montaubyn, turned to go to his room, but she put her hand on his arm.

"Wolfie," she said, "I'm not going to England."

"You will not go?" he asked, not taking in at once what she had said. "It will not be safe?"

"That isn't the reason. Listen. Don't worry. Everything will be all right. Everything is all right."

He saw her looking at him with an expression he had not seen for a long time.

"My dear wife," he said, "my dear wife."

They kissed each other gently. Diana turned and went to her room, as the tears were streaming down her face.

She sat on her bed weeping for about five minutes, and then she tried to understand what had happened. She thought of her life further back than from the last few months. When she was young she had been more lively and therefore often more foolish than most people. Relatives like Arthur had been accustomed to refer to "Diana's idiocies". Her mother had brought her up to believe that she was something special, that she was destined for a more brilliant life than her sisters. When she married Wolfie, and so prevented any possibility of such a life, she was still reluctant to abandon the prospect. Her idiocies sometimes took the form of trying to make her life more decorative and exciting than her circumstances permitted. Not all her efforts had been idiotic. She had made a marionette theatre for the children, and done other things which likened her more to Pater's Duke Carl, who made "a heroic effort of mind at a disadvantage" from which perhaps all Australians suffered to some extent.

But for a long time she had thought that both the good and the foolish efforts to rescue her life from the commonplace were ended. They had consisted in not accepting the realities of her condition. Since her mother had died, and she was no longer able to pretend either that she would inherit a great fortune, or that she would be offered another two or three years in Europe, she had accepted those realities, and had found reasonable happiness in her home and doing what she could to give opportunities to her children.

Then Russell had suddenly appeared on the scene, just at the time when the children needed little from her but money. He had revived the dissatisfactions of her earlier years. Then she had learnt, in such a brutal fashion, of Wolfie's infidelity, and it seemed to her part of a design; and she told herself that it released her from the condition of her life, and so she had, at forty years of age, fallen into the greatest idiocy of all, and had believed that the fantasies of her youth had only delayed their fulfilment. With Russell she had been building up pictures of life in Italy, the sort of life which probably even Cynthia and Anthea would regard as an adolescent dream. Russell could live that rootless life of pleasure. He had been doing so for twenty years. But how could she begin now? She might perhaps adapt herself to it, but all the time she would be longing for stability, for the familiar things she had always known, and most of all for Wolfie.

She felt that she could not sleep until she had taken the first steps on the return to sanity. Also she must let Russell know immediately, and she went to the drawing-room, lighted the candles on the writing table, the same two she had put on the supper table on the night that they picnicked by the fire, and sat down to write to him.

She wrote two letters and tore them up. The one she finally decided to send was as follows:

"Tomorrow morning I shall send you a telegram to tell you that I cannot come with you. I shall take this letter to the ship, and give it to the purser to give to you when you come on board at Fremantle.

"This evening we went to a small family theatre party given by Steven and Laura. That woman who was Wolfie's mistress, and who was so offensive to me at the ball at Government House, was at the foot of the stairs as we came out. When she saw Wolfie she crossed over to him and struck his face, shouting: 'You dirty German.' I was too shocked to move, and Cynthia Langton, whom more than anyone I should have expected to walk by on the other side, with wonderful kindness and presence of mind, led him away. Russell, it is impossible to apologize for my failing you. Nothing can be adequate. But I cannot come with you. You have been so good and patient, and my behaviour must appear outrageous. It is not a thing that depends on my will, or rather I was putting my will against the natural circumstances of my life. I am tied here by all kinds of fibres. Whatever vegetable I may be, I am bedded in this earth.

"I expect you will be very angry and I cannot blame you. I have wasted months of your time. I have always thought that there was no one more despicable than a vacillating woman, and now I have been one. I wrote two letters before this, trying to give excuses for what I am doing. In one I said that it was because Wolfie was a German and that it would be unfair to leave him now. That may be true but it is not the reason. The real reason is that I am married to him, whatever he does. That woman was only an excuse I seized on, because you offered me such lovely prospects.

"I am worried because one day you said that you did not forgive injuries. If that is so you will never forgive me, as few people can have done you so great an injury. I shall hate to think that you do not forgive me, as I have loved every minute I have spent with you, and would like to be able to look back on those times, feeling that there is no bitterness between us. Perhaps this is too much to ask. It is curious to think that we imagined that our meetings were only a foretaste of pleasures to come, when they were the whole substance of those pleasures. But I always expected too much of life."

She had no reply to this letter. She thought that he might have written a short note before the ship left Fremantle, as he would have known from her telegram a week earlier that she was not coming. Then she thought that he might have waited until he had time to digest her letter, and have written from Colombo. When no letter came from there she thought that he had spoken the truth, and that he would not forgive her.

She did not tell Wolfie that she had intended to leave him. She thought this might be unfair. It was certainly more agreeable to herself, but her mind was not sufficiently afflicted by Puritanism to think that therefore it must be wrong. She came, on the contrary, to the conclusion that it would be wrong to tell him, as it would be gratuitous cruelty to let him know, at a time when he was being avoided by many of his former friends, that his wife also had intended to leave him.

Because of the tabu which attached to him as a German, they decided at last to sell the house at Brighton and move into the country. Steven offered them one of the farms at Westhill, which had become vacant owing to the two young men who rented it leaving for the war.

In addition to its isolation, it had the advantage that half the people in the neighbourhood had names as German as their own, and that they had known Diana since childhood.

A few months after they had moved in here, she had a letter from Russell. He said that he had not written before, not because he had vindictive feelings, but because he had not known what to say. He was writing now to tell her that he was engaged to Miss Rockingham, who, as Diana knew, had travelled home on the ship with him. They were to be married on the day after he was writing. He had a temporary commission in the Grenadier Guards. He would always remember the happy times he had spent with her in Melbourne, and particularly their last afternoon at Mornington.

Diana wrote to congratulate him on his marriage, and to tell him her own news:

"We came up here because it was difficult for Wolfie in Melbourne. It is twenty minutes walk from Westhill, and we only see Steven and Laura and people we know well. Harry has repudiated his parentage and changed his name to Fingal. This is much admired, but it was a shock to Wolfie. Cynthia on the other hand, is in disgrace for her kindness to him at the theatre, and is called a pro-German. So it is better to be away. Our little house is on a cleared hill-top, and on a fine day we can see far into Gippsland. It is something like the farmhouse in the picture "Winter Sunlight", which you said one day might be my spiritual home. I think you were right. I suppose one is always most at home in the places one has lived in as a child. I used to ride over here when I was ten, as Mrs Schmidt, who lived here then, used to give us a special sort of apple tart she made.

"I am so glad that you are marrying Miss Rockingham. I liked her very much. She was so graceful in every way, not only in her movements. As she is a friend of the Wyckhams, I expect you will see Josie sometimes. I hope you do."

He replied to her letter, and after that they corresponded regularly, writing four or five letters each a year. She wondered if Miss Rockingham (she found it hard to think of his wife by any other name) objected, but when she heard from Josie that her establishments in Belgrave Square and Derbyshire were on such a considerable scale, she doubted that they saw each other's correspondence. It all seemed very remote to her, as she sat with Wolfie at lunch on the veranda, while the winter sunlight gleamed on the hock bottle, and tinged with pale gold the far purple forests of Gippsland.

Text Classics

Dancing on Coral
Glenda Adams
Introduced by Susan Wyndham

The Commandant
Jessica Anderson
Introduced by Carmen Callil

Homesickness
Murray Bail
Introduced by Peter Conrad

Sydney Bridge Upside Down
David Ballantyne
Introduced by Kate De Goldi

Bush Studies
Barbara Baynton
Introduced by Helen Garner

The Cardboard Crown
Martin Boyd
Introduced by Brenda Niall

A Difficult Young Man
Martin Boyd
Introduced by Sonya Hartnett

Outbreak of Love
Martin Boyd
Introduced by Chris Womersley

The Australian Ugliness
Robin Boyd
Introduced by Christos Tsiolkas

All the Green Year
Don Charlwood
Introduced by Michael McGirr

They Found a Cave
Nan Chauncy
Introduced by John Marsden

The Even More Complete
Book of Australian Verse
John Clarke

Diary of a Bad Year
J. M. Coetzee
Introduced by Peter Goldsworthy

Wake in Fright
Kenneth Cook
Introduced by Peter Temple

The Dying Trade
Peter Corris
Introduced by Charles Waterstreet

They're a Weird Mob
Nino Culotta
Introduced by Jacinta Tynan

The Songs of a Sentimental Bloke
C. J. Dennis
Introduced by Jack Thompson

Careful, He Might Hear You
Sumner Locke Elliott
Introduced by Robyn Nevin

Fairyland
Sumner Locke Elliott
Introduced by Dennis Altman

Terra Australis
Matthew Flinders
Introduced by Tim Flannery

textclassics.com.au